Praise for Ladies' Day

"Four women. Four complicated lives where dreams just aren't coming true and insecurity, even danger dogs their days. Then, in an incredible twist of fate, their lives are changed forever. In Ladies' Day, Sarah Barton has written a moving, heartfelt exposure of contemporary life, which many readers will identify with and remember for a long, long time."
Sally Spedding, award winning Crime and Mystery Author

"What a fabulous read! Great humour and brilliant characters forged a story which has stayed with me. Kept me turning the pages until the wee small hours."
Glynis Peters, author of women's fiction

"Well-drawn three-dimensional characters interact superbly with a lovely underplayed humour threading through the drama. I look forward to more by Sarah Barton in future."
David Evans, author of the International Best-Selling Wakefield Series

"… an intriguing, heart-warming story, examining the lives of four women, written with warmth, humour and a finely honed subtle wit." Julie-Ann Corrigan, author of Falling Suns

"An endearing contemporary story of four women, told with an undercurrent of subtle wit." Jane Isaac, best-selling author of the DI Will Jackman series

LADIES' DAY

SARAH BARTON

ABOUT THE AUTHOR

Sarah Barton is a contemporary fiction writer from Manchester. A regular attendee of numerous Writers' Conferences, she has been writing for many years. Her style of writing has attracted many admirers who love the blend of subtle humour, strong storylines and compelling characters that populate her work.
Ladies' Day is her debut novel.

Find out more by checking out Sarah's website at:
https://www.sarahbartonauthor.com

on Facebook at:
https://www.facebook.com/SarahBartonAuthor

Instagram:
https://www.instagram.com/sarah.b.author/

and on Twitter:
@S_Barton_Author

ACKNOWLEDGMENTS

I have so many people to thank. I am very grateful to my wonderful friends and co-members of the 'Crayon Club' - Julie-Ann Corrigan, Jan Beresford, Glynis Smy and Manda Hughes. But a huge thank you to David Evans, who has read, and re-read my work, listened to my woes and self-doubts, and brought me through it whether I liked it or not. Thank you Dave for never losing faith in me.

A special thank you to Sally Spedding for her invaluable advice and encouragement. I owe an awful lot to my fantastic friends who have never wavered in their support, especially Naomi Lux, Denise Coe, Allison Cowan, Debbie Dawson and Marlene Starr. Thank you to Paula Simons for letting me test my writing out on you.

Eternal gratitude to my family – my mum and my sister Emma, for always being willing to read every word I write. To my amazing children – Sam, who has guided me through the maze of social media with his digital expertise, and Emily for always being by my side with her wise words and love no matter what. And to my lovely husband for believing in me from the beginning.

I wish I could say thank you in person to my beautiful friend Samantha Murru. Sam, it was you who inspired me to begin writing and your memory still inspires me. You are missed so very much.

To the memory of my father, Geoffrey Barton

LADIES' DAY

Sarah Barton

'God could not be everywhere, so he created mothers' –
Rudyard Kipling

1
May

Amanda looked in the mirror and adjusted the fascinator balanced precariously. I just don't have the right shaped head, she thought.

"You don't have the right shaped head," her mother said, "and the colour's all wrong – the fascinator, not your head."

"I know, I know. But I don't need this just now."

"So I try to be a good mother and this is the thanks I get. So what do I know?" Amanda's mother threw up her hands in despair. "I give you my advice but do you ever listen? You should have a hobby, a good Jewish hobby. Maybe you could take up dress making. Your Aunt Beatrice, God rest her soul... well, what can I say? She would rather rip your Uncle Max's heart out than put thread to a needle!"

Shaking her head, Amanda dismissed her mother's endless and mostly random pastime ideas and turned her attention back to the turquoise netting. She fiddled with the head-band once more before snatching it off her head and throwing it onto the bed.

From the few outfits she had, she had chosen the turquoise dress. Not for the colour, but for the coverage. It hid the bruises on her upper arms. The matching scarf shielded the fading yellow marks on her neck.

Her mother made no comment about Amanda's injuries, silenced years ago.

"I'll wear the black hat and shoes instead." Amanda dragged a chair over to the wardrobe and climbed onto it. Reaching into the depths of the top shelf, she pulled the hat-box towards her and carefully lifted it down.

"Good. At least you can return that head thing and get your money back. No point in spending when you can make do. Your Aunt Beatrice, God rest her soul, always her purse in her hand. She spent everything. That's why your Uncle Max died – he had a broken heart and an empty wallet!"

Amanda smiled. Her mother blamed everything on Aunt Beatrice. A moment later, she climbed up onto the chair and reached back into the cupboard, searching around the shelf until her fingers touched on the metal box. Just as she had the hat-box, she carefully lifted it down and placed it on the dressing table. The key to the box had been hidden in the toe of a pair of tights. She took a deep breath, turned the key, and opened the container.

It held every penny that she had been able to squirrel away. For the past two months she had been buying the cheapest brands of everything, carefully decanting them into the more expensive packaging. She had, she thought, covered her tracks well.

Two thousand, three hundred and thirty two pounds in total, including her small inheritance. She stuffed the pile of assorted notes into her handbag and snapped it shut. They would be here soon and she didn't want to keep them waiting. Slipping on her black shoes and dabbing a little more blusher onto her pale cheeks, she put the black hat on. Making sure the metal box was again safely stowed away she scanned the empty room. Checking that everything was in its place was a force of habit. Once satisfied, she scooped up her handbag and went downstairs. Pausing at the mirror in the hallway, she checked the angle of the hat and readjusted it. The last time she had worn it had been nine years ago, at her mother's funeral.

The doorbell chimed. Her stomach lurched with a combination of fear and excitement. Through the frosted glass she could see the bright colours of the outfits that her friends were wearing. She opened the door and was met with a chorus of hellos. Marianne was loudest. Her dark curly hair bounced round her heart shaped face as she jumped forward to embrace Amanda.

"Love the hat, Amanda! I could do with a hat like that." Marianne hugged her tightly then stepped aside to allow Jane to wrap her elegant arms around Amanda's slight frame. Hayley hovered behind the others, clutching an oversized handbag in both hands. After warmly kissing Jane's cheeks, Amanda released her and opened her arms to Hayley who stepped into them.

"Well, today's the day girls," Amanda said over the top of Hayley's wiry red hair. "Are we all ready for this?"

"Yes!" they said in unison.

"Has everyone got their money?"

"Yes." This united response held even more conviction than the last.

"Then let's go for it!"

Amanda slammed the door shut and began to follow the others down the path. This was going to be the biggest day of their lives. It could either save them or ruin them.

2
Two Months Earlier

Marianne

Box after box was being unloaded from the service lift. Marianne leant against the metal gate that guarded the shaft and willed the men to move faster. Old merchandise had been shunted to the corners of the large stockroom to make space for the new. The last box had hardly been dispatched before she began dragging the crates across the floor. For her small frame she was surprisingly strong and within minutes a mountain of cardboard was growing in the centre of the room. Satisfied that she had enough boxes within her reach to begin with, she carefully sliced open the first container and folded back the flaps to reveal their treasure.

She exhaled, long and slow. Lingerie – mounds of silk and lace lay underneath her fingers. Just touching the fine material made her tingle. She needed all of these things, she thought, as she reverently lifted one piece out after another. Yes, she definitely needed that one, and she couldn't possibly live without this one. And Jack, her husband, would love to see her in that. But, of course, she would have to have the matching robes, otherwise what would be the point?

It all made perfect sense to her. Whether her bank manager would see it in the same light she wasn't so confident. But perhaps if she was to drop in a photograph of the beautiful garments he would surely come to the same conclusion?

"Marianne, you're day-dreaming again, aren't you?" Amanda's voice pierced her enthralment with the swathes of soft lilacs and luscious pinks that now lay in puddles around her.

Marianne knew she should feel guilty, but it was hard to feel guilty when it was absolutely necessary to own these things. Looking at her supervisor, she casually lifted out a sheer satin dressing gown.

"Just checking that nothing's damaged." Marianne smiled innocently.

"Of course you are." Amanda didn't return the smile and shook her head.

"Anyway, you haven't seen the stuff they've sent this time." She held up a peacock blue and emerald green silk robe. "It's like wrapping the Mediterranean around your body," she said dreamily.

"Would you put it down, Marianne!" Amanda stepped forward and removed the precious material from Marianne's grip. "You can't possibly need any more night gowns, robes or anything else for that matter."

"But I do." Why didn't she understand that some girls could never have enough beautiful underwear – it was simple really. And why was she always criticising her and making her feel that she was somehow shallow and frivolous? Only that morning Amanda had scolded her for selecting a few items from the discount rail on her way in through the store – and they were in the sale which obviously doesn't count as a proper purchase, anyone knows that! Miss prim and proper Amanda with her doting husband who was always on the phone checking that his precious wife was surviving the day. Marianne slipped three camisoles and a silk chemise to one side and set about unpacking the remaining boxes.

"I'll help you otherwise you'll be here all day." Amanda crouched beside her and began to sort through the folds of chiffon and lace.

Marianne hummed to herself, she could wear her new acquisitions for Jack. He would love the way the material would cling to her body, emphasising her curves. She knew what his reaction would be. And she would delight in the power she had over him. Not that she wanted to control him. No, theirs was an equal relationship in every way, ever since she had fallen in love with him five years ago. She adored being Mrs Jack Drummond.

Everything was perfect in her world, apart from one tiny little speck of worry that flitted through her otherwise ideal life. She called it a speck because she wasn't prepared to see it as anything bigger than that. And for as long as she could, that speck would remain her secret.

3

Amanda

The balls of her feet were on fire. Amanda hadn't sat down for three hours and the thin, synthetic soles of her shoes were unforgiving. She should have taken a break earlier but instead she had to supervise Marianne unloading the new stock. Now her feet were at crisis point. 'Finally,' she thought, as a red haired woman, one of the temporary staff, came to relieve her from the lingerie counter she was currently responsible for.

She crossed the expanse of threadbare carpet that had once been a glorious homage to the Manchester department store's now faded grandeur. Hobbling towards the staff room, she tried not to look at the display of fluffy, well-padded slippers that hung from metal branches. Pushing open the door marked STAFF ONLY, she went straight to the cloakroom. Her coat was grey. It had no embellishments and certainly couldn't be described as tailored. Rummaging around in her pocket, she cursed. Where had she put those painkillers? She was usually so particular about keeping all her medication with her in a small felt pouch. She began to empty the pockets, her hands getting clammy. Shopping list, old receipt, hair clip, mobile phone... her mobile phone was flashing. Silently accusing her of wilful neglect. Six missed calls, it screamed.

She stared at the screen. Six missed calls! Her fingers seemed to swell to twice their normal size as she tried to push the right buttons that would reveal who had needed to speak to her so desperately. She already knew. There was only one person who would be so demanding – David. Her temples now began to pulsate in perfect time to the throbbing of her feet. She searched through her pockets again, feeling for a hole that the pouch could have fallen through –nothing.

Tiny, hot needles pricked her scalp. 'Speed dial David,' the screen said smugly. It could easily have followed with, 'and about time too lady!'

"Well hello, so nice of you to call me back." David's smooth voice floated through the ether into her ear. She wanted to clamp her hand over her ear to protect it, but she didn't

"Hi darling, so sorry I missed you, just one of those days." Her tone was overly bright to compensate for the fear that was weaving its way through her body.

"I'm sure it has been 'just one of those days'." Seemingly so re-assuring, calming, reasonable.

She slid down the wall and slumped onto the wooden bench below the coat rack.

"Don't worry," continued the silky voice, "I've got a meeting now, but we can talk later at home. That's probably best anyway. Don't be late, Amanda." The soft voice had hardened to cold steel.

"I'll see you later then. Bye David." Her hand trembled as she dropped the phone back into her coat pocket. Which monster would be waiting for her when she got home, and what had she done to antagonise it this time?

The minutes ticked steadily into hours and the hours marched on towards home time, and with every tick came the familiar certainty that she would have to wear her high polo neck jumper with long sleeves tomorrow.

When she finally finished her shift, the staff room was empty apart from the red haired woman who had taken over her till earlier. Amanda shrugged the oversized grey coat over her shoulders and wrapped the material protectively round her.

"N-n-night then," the red haired woman said quietly, as she picked up her own quilted anorak and made her way towards the staff door.

"Yes, good night." Biting her bottom lip to stop it from quivering, Amanda slowly gathered her belongings.

The woman stopped at the door and turned. "Are you alright?"

"Yes, yes, I'm fine... thanks." Amanda turned away. She didn't want a stranger, however kind, to see her fear.

The woman hesitated once more before eventually leaving the room. The door had hardly even swung shut before her mother's voice filled the silence.

"Now she seems like a nice lady – well for a redhead anyway." Amanda's mother stared impassively at the closed door. "You should take up knitting. Your Aunt Beatrice, God rest her soul, couldn't knit to save her life and look what happened to her. She practically drowned in synthetics!"

Amanda reached for the door. "Knitting wouldn't help Mum."

"So what do I know? I'm only your poor mother."

Amanda gently closed the doors – the one in the room and the one in her head – and braced herself to go home.

4

Hayley

The windows on the bus were steamed up. But as it travelled towards her, she could still see the jumble of shapes inside, meaning that getting a seat would be impossible yet again. The bus swept into the lay-by and its doors opened. The smell of musty clothes and damp hair beckoned Hayley aboard. She flashed her bus pass, thrust it back into the pocket of her quilted anorak and shuffled to the nearest free plastic loop to cling on to. On the seat to her right sat a young woman clutching a baby to her chest. She was gently rocking to and fro, murmuring into the child's soft cheek. Tiny fingers grasped strands of his mother's hair as she rocked. Hayley stared. She did try to look away but she found her eyes drawn back to the woman and her baby.

"What are you looking at, you bloody weirdo?" The woman glared at Hayley as she shifted the baby onto her hip and struggled to her feet. "Bloody ginger," she muttered, as she expertly lifted the collapsed pushchair out of the luggage hold and shook it open in one swift movement.

Hayley felt her face burning. She knew it would be the same colour as her hair. She hadn't meant to stare. To her relief the bus finally pulled up outside Peltham's Department Store. Tugging her collar up against the rain, she ran to the staff entrance and pushed open the door.

"Morning, Miss." Charlie the security guard tipped the peak of his cap and carefully placed his copy of The Racing Post on his wooden chair.

"M-m- morning, Charlie." She deliberately slowed her breathing down to control her stammer and smiled at the frail old man. She thought for the hundredth time that as far as security went he would probably crumble at the merest whiff of trouble. With a lot of huffing and puffing he managed to hold open the doors for her before sitting back down with a heavy sigh.

In the staff room she hung her quilted jacket on her peg, and smoothed down her sensible brown skirt, chosen to match her sensible brown shoes. Maybe today would be the day, she thought. She had been feeling a little bit queasy. She could hear voices in the corridor.

"You have no control, Marianne. You should curb this fixation of yours to spend money like it's going out of fashion. It's almost obscene!"

Two women burst through the staff room door. Hayley knew the one who was talking was a supervisor. She had noticed how thin and pale she looked. But the dark haired woman carrying several Peltham's carrier bags was unfamiliar.

"But I need these things." The dark haired woman turned away and was trying to shove the bags into her locker. Neither woman noticed Hayley. Sometimes she wondered if she was invisible, then she remembered the insult from the woman on the bus. Obviously not. The two women disappeared back onto the shop floor leaving her alone once more.

Before putting her handbag, which was almost the size of a holdall, into her own locker she unzipped the side pocket and took out a blue box. She stared at it, turning it over in her hand. Later, she thought. Then Hayley placed the pregnancy testing kit back into her handbag.

5

Jane

Ignoring the cool air on her naked body, Jane inched her way to the edge of the bed. She needed to get as far away from the sleeping mound of flesh beside her as she could. Stupid! Sliding off the mattress she grabbed her crumpled suit from the floor. Really stupid! She crept over to the bathroom and flicked on the light. Immediately the fan droned into action and she froze. Slowly, Jane looked over her shoulder. The mound hadn't moved other than the rhythmic rise and fall indicating life – unfortunately.

What had she done? She surveyed the bland array of uniform bottles containing shower gel and shampoo. Two tightly wrapped cakes of soap and a tiny box holding a shower cap. Who actually ever used a shower cap? she wondered as she sat on the toilet. The fire escape route was helpfully displayed on the bathroom door. Was there an escape route helpfully displayed somewhere to show her how to get out of this mess? She doubted it very much.

Why couldn't she say 'no' to him? She stepped into her skirt. God knows where her stockings were. She would have to collect a pair from work. Buttoning up her jacket to hide the creases in her blouse she pulled her blonde hair back into a ponytail and left the bathroom.

Taking one last look at his sleeping form, she picked up her briefcase and left the three star hotel in a taxi. Eighteen months ago it would have been a five star luxury establishment, or a quirky boutique residence renowned for its simple sophistication. Not anymore. Even the seduction of a four course Michelin standard meal had been reduced to a steak from the grill with a side order of fries. She was beginning to feel like a prostitute barely masked by a very fragile professional veneer.

Jane stepped out of the taxi and stared up at the Victorian facade of Peltham's Department Store. It had once been one of Manchester's finest emporiums. The splendour of its heyday still visible in the ornate mouldings either side of the grand entrance. Placing her briefcase at her feet she studied the window displays. Banners stretched across a brightly lit scene of mannequins in feathered bonnets sipping from tall cocktail glasses. 'It's Pimms o'clock at Peltham's!' In much smaller print an invitation for customers to attend a champagne launch of the store's summer stock, boasting 'an outfit for every occasion be it a wedding or Ascot'. Not exactly Harrods she thought. One of the mannequins looked as though she had had a few too many Pimms judging by the way her fascinator had slid over one eye. She would have to give the window dresser a strict talking to.

She could see the cleaners still buffing the marble floors of the perfume hall. It was one hour before opening. At least she had time to make herself look as though she hadn't spent the night drinking cheap champagne and having sex with a man who, these days, no longer stroked her thighs, or kissed her neck until she was desperate for him. The act was perfunctory and brief.

"Morning, Miss!" Charlie tottered to his feet before bowing slightly.

"Morning, Charlie!" She knew she looked shocking, and she also knew Charlie had seen her in a far worse state in the past.

Charlie nodded at his copy of The Racing Post which was neatly folded beneath his chair. "Three thirty at Musselburgh – 'Word of Warning' is the horse, eleven to one. That'll be the one Ma'am." He stared solemnly at her. Then he seemed to assess her appearance. "I'll just go and get you a coffee, Ma'am, and I'll pick you up some necessities."

He limped slowly towards the service lift. She watched him go. The 'necessities' is what Charlie called anything he felt you needed. Today he would return with a pair of tights, a brush, and probably a smashing blouse from 'Women's Wear'. He was her idea of an angel. He saw everything but said nothing.

An hour later, she was feeling a little more human. She resolved yet again to get a grip of her life. Sitting at her desk in her office on the top floor of the building, just down the corridor from Soft Furnishings, she checked the staff rota. The office door crashed open against the wall and he stood filling the door frame.

"You forgot these." He tossed a pair of stockings across the desk. Anthony Pickard, her boss, winked, turned on his heel and left.

6

Amanda

No sooner had she inserted her key into the lock than the door was flung open. David stood there his jaw moving from side to side as he ground his teeth. His cheeks were flushed. Whisky! That's what she could smell. He stood aside for her to pass, which she did hurriedly, flinching automatically whilst within arm's reach. Thoughts scurried round her head as she scurried to the kitchen. What had she done now? He didn't slam the door. He closed it with measured finality then she heard the chink of the safety chain being dropped into place.

She stood on the far side of the table, hoping that it would offer some sort of protection from the rage that was straining to be released. Floorboards creaked mapping his path from the front door to the kitchen. She knew each and every one. He stepped into the kitchen. Studying his fingernails, he seemed to be working invisible dirt from under each one. His nails were always immaculate, as was everything about him.

Finally he looked at her. "You see, Amanda, I just don't understand you."

His voice was calm and 'oh so rational'. It made her skin crawl. The calmer the voice the deadlier the punishment. He was shaking his head as if she had completely baffled him with her behaviour.

"Do you love me Amanda?" The colour deepened in his cheeks.

"You know I love you." Her throat felt dry, but she had no saliva to swallow.

"Then why?" He turned away from her and leant heavily on the worktop. Then his hands dropped. He reached for the drawer and opened it, still with his back to her.

"Why what? What's the matter?" Her voice shrill as her throat tightened. Taking a few steps back, she felt behind her for the handle to the back door.

"It's locked." He said without turning. Then he plucked something out of the drawer and gently closed the drawer to. She couldn't move, her eyes locked on his hand. Slowly he faced her and placed a small felt pouch onto the table. She looked from the pouch to his face and back again. A low groan escaped her lips.

"Why Amanda?"

She knew the contents of the pouch very well. Not only did it contain painkillers for the headaches that came all too frequently but it also contained her contraceptive pill. The very thought of bringing a child into such a relationship was unbearable and so she had taken the pill secretly for years whilst her husband lamented every barren month.

His knuckles were white as he leant across the table towards her. Spittle had formed at the side of his mouth and his lips twitched.

"David... it's not that simple... I know I should have talked to you about..." The speed he struck gave her no chance of protecting herself. He leapt at her grabbing a fist full of hair and slamming the back of her head against the door frame. Even in the height of fury he was careful not to mark her face. She felt her hair being ripped from their follicles and blood trickled down her back. He let go and her head fell forward onto her chest.

"Look at me!" He screamed.

As she lifted her face to his she could smell sour whisky on his breath. He held her wrists, squeezing them as though they were empty drinks cans.

"So you thought you could make a fool out of me?" His fist drove into the soft flesh of her stomach, twisting as it shot towards her spine. She felt searing pain then nothing as she was enfolded in darkness.

She wasn't sure how long she had been lying on the kitchen floor. She could hear the television in the front room and, quietly whimpering, she got to her feet. As silently as she could she hauled her body up the stairs and into the bathroom. Her hair was matted at the back and she could feel crisp flakes of dried blood on her skin. Holding her aching stomach she turned the shower on. Warm water mixed with her salty tears.

7

Marianne

"Just five more minutes?" Marianne stroked his broad shoulders, her fingers tracing his spine down to the rise of his buttocks. Making swirly patterns on his back with her finger nails "Please?" she whispered in his ear.

Jack turned over and smiled. "You are very naughty. You were even naughtier in that sexy outfit last night." He cupped her chin and lightly kissed her lips. "Tonight, I promise. I have to pick up the lads in ten minutes. I don't think they'll appreciate being kept waiting, no matter how sexy your underwear is." He rolled out of bed and went into the bathroom.

I did look good, she thought as she looked at the pool of blue and green silk now discarded on the floor. Jack went downstairs whilst she replayed the evening in her mind. With a sigh she sank deeper into the quilt. She wished she could stay in bed all day today, but she had her appraisal meeting with the 'Ice Queen' – Jane Farrell, and she couldn't afford to be late for it, let alone miss it. She had the distinct impression that the assistant manager didn't like her. She wasn't sure what she had done but she really didn't want to upset her any more.

"Three leaflets for frozen food, one take-away menu and a letter for you." Jack strode across the bedroom and dropped the post onto the bed. "Now you be a good girl and work hard today."

Kissing the top of her head he reached over for his 'high visibility' jacket. "See you later beautiful."

He left with a wave.

She picked up the leaflets for frozen food. No, she thought, the take away menu looks much more interesting and the prices aren't bad. Maybe we could go out for a meal tonight she thought, as she showered and dressed. Singing to herself she threw the covers back over the bed and left to go to work. The brown envelope slipped to the floor and landed softly on a cushion of blue and green silk.

8

Hayley

Perhaps she was a little too early for the pregnancy test and that's why it was negative yesterday. Yes, she felt sure that was it. She had just been too early. If she just waited a few more days and tried the test again maybe... Hayley closed the front door to the small terraced house that she shared with her husband Neil.

"It's not the end of the world," Neil had said last night when she told him about the test result. "We've got each other and if that's the way it's going to be then so be it." He patted her hand and returned to his newspaper.

It wasn't that he didn't care, she knew that. It was just that they had been trying for a child for so long she thought he had become resigned to being childless. She hadn't. Something deep inside her was screaming out for a baby. First the hope and then the desperation she felt each month gnawed away at her spirit, but still she couldn't give up.

When they had first decided to start a family, every month held butterflies of trepidation and excitement as she convinced herself that this was the month. Then, as the years passed, the butterflies had flown, replaced by a termite burrowing down and down. The ache buried so deep it was untouchable.

Today she didn't look at any of the passengers on the bus. Her eyes downcast, she dreamed of the pram she would push, and the lullabies she would sing. Just as the bus stopped outside the department store, she saw Jane slip into the staff entrance. Oh God, she thought, she was being appraised today. Absently, her hand slid over her flat stomach. She was only on a temporary contract and any mistakes she made meant that they could let her go – without any difficulty at all. She waited a few moments until she was sure Jane was safely on her way to her office then, she too slipped through the same door.

"Morning Miss." Charlie struggled to his feet.

"Good morning Charlie. Don't worry I'll get the door." She dashed past him before he was even upright. "You rest your legs." Hayley smiled at him as he gratefully sank back down onto his chair. Over and over she rehearsed her appraisal speech in her head. Highlight your strengths, minimise your weaknesses she chanted silently as she stepped into the staff room. A soft mewing sound filtered through her chants. She looked around the room and saw the pale woman huddled on the wooden bench, her slender arms wrapped around her body. Her eyes were closed but tears rested on her lashes.

"Are you... I mean is everything... alright?" Hayley halted midway between the coat pegs and the lockers. She realized that this was the second time she had asked this woman the same question.

Ragged breaths replaced the whimpers and slowly the woman's eyes opened. "Yes, yes I'm okay." And as if to confirm this she slowly stood up and smiled a smile that, to Hayley, seemed painfully strained.

"Oh, as long as you're sure?" The woman was obviously distressed. "If there's anything I can do." Hayley dropped her eyes from the frail figure and studied the scuff marks on her own brown shoes. "I-I-I'm Hayley by the way."

"Thanks Hayley. I'm Amanda, and everything is absolutely fine. I'd better be getting on," Amanda said, reaching out to open the staff room door. As she did so, her sleeve slid up a few millimetres – just enough for Hayley to see the black and purple skin beneath. Neither woman spoke as Amanda left the room.

9

Jane

She had managed to avoid him so far, managing to salvage some dignity. That hadn't been easy for Jane, working only a few feet away from him. Hopefully she wouldn't have to see him until their business meeting tomorrow. She glanced at the agenda: 1. Appraisals – actions required. 2. Staff Rota – time management. 3. Pimms at Peltham's. This item was highlighted. The event was to be held in a few weeks' time. At first Jane hadn't paid much attention to the initial preparations. But during a night of booze fuelled fumblings Tony had blamed his woefully inadequate performance on the pressure of work.

To hide her disappointment, Jane had teased him about his excuse.

"You see Janey, you don't know the whole picture," he'd said as he shrugged off her embrace. "Peltham's is in big trouble and this might be our only chance of survival."

Jane had looked at his clammy face in the half light of the bedside lamp. She could see deep lines that burrowed across his brow. "I don't understand. What kind of trouble?"

"An American buy-out – it's our last hope. The summer season launch will showcase Peltham's to our friends from across the pond. It's got to be good. No, more than good. It's got to be amazing." He had swung his legs off the bed and planted his feet firmly on the floor. He seemed to be talking more to himself. "The press will be there and as many celebrities as we can drag in. They want to own a little piece of England and, my God, we're going to sell it to them, Wimbledon, Ascot, the Chelsea flower show. Yes, we'll show them how we can dress Britain for anything."

Jane had half expected him to continue with "and we shall fight them on the beaches..." but he didn't. Instead, he appeared to be lost in his own thoughts forgetting she was even there.

"I didn't know things were so bad, I'm sorry." She had tentatively reached out and touched his shoulder. If she had prodded him with a red hot poker he wouldn't have leapt off the bed any faster.

"You mustn't say anything to anyone. Nothing, do you understand?" His eyes had flicked from her to the door and back again, as though he was expecting Peltham's managing director to burst in on his indiscretion.

She had nodded, still reeling from his reaction.

"And I mean nothing." He shook his head. "I shouldn't have told you." Regret had laced his voice as he went into the bathroom. She heard the drum of water on the plastic bath and knew that their night of passion, or more adroitly, their hour of sticky shoving and grinding had come to an end.

Who was she going to tell? She had no friends or confidants. Back in her office she looked at the photograph on her desk. A silver haired couple with their arms round each other beamed into the lens. She smiled at the image. She should see them more often. Make time for them. It wasn't as though she had a hectic social life. She had lost touch with the few friends she had made at university all those years ago. Putting studies and work before any relationships she had kept herself to herself, until Tony Pickard.

In the past at Peltham's, her duties had been mainly administrative and so she had little need to venture onto the sales floors and mingle with staff. But now as her role had widened she heard her nick name, 'Ice Queen', when she walked through the various departments. It was a sad reflection of a woman closer to forty than thirty.

There were three short knocks on the door. Jane checked her watch and leaned back in her chair. "Come in."

The door opened and a pretty, dark haired woman walked into the room. Jane noticed that she was wearing a suit from one of the store's most expensive labels.

"You are Marianne Drummond?" Jane eyed the girl from top to toe. She was also wearing Italian leather court shoes.

"Yes, that's me." Marianne smiled as she stopped in front of the desk.

Jane had seen her on several occasions and had been acutely aware of Tony's lingering glances in Marianne's direction. But the young woman seemed oblivious to the attention she attracted and remained engrossed in advising customers and assisting colleagues. However popular she was, Jane wasn't sure about this woman with her Latin looks and flirtatious manner.

"Sit down Mrs Drummond." She nodded at the chair Marianne was standing behind. She waited until Marianne had pulled the chair out and sat down before she addressed the appraisal form in front of her.

"I see you have been with us for seven years?"

"Yes that's right. I came straight from school when I was sixteen."

"Mmmm... and where do you see yourself in the next five years?"

"Well, here of course. Why would I want to go anywhere else? I love working here."

Lacking in ambition, she wrote on her notes.

"And would you say you are a good team player?" Jane waited with pen poised over the paper.

"Yes, yes I would. I've made lots of friends here and I always try to help colleagues." Marianne looked at her with wide eyes, the smile faltering on her lips.

Perhaps overly friendly and a little too confident, bordering on the cocky, Jane scrawled next to her other notes.

"How flexible are you? Would you be willing to work at different branches? Because here at Peltham's we are hoping to build a fluid staff base, you know staff transferring to branches nationally as and when required." Placing her pen down on the desk, she watched Marianne's face pale despite her olive complexion.

"I couldn't leave. I mean I couldn't leave Jack. I love working here and everything and I would do anything I was asked Miss Farrell, except be away from Jack."

She picked up her pen again. Totally inflexible, Peltham's certainly not a priority. Jane underlined 'Totally'.

Jane asked a few more standard questions. After recording her own interpretation of the answers, she stood indicating that the appraisal was now over. Marianne got to her feet too, thanked her and left the office. Not so confident now are you Mrs Drummond she thought as the door closed behind Marianne. She glanced once again at the photograph of her parents and guilt spread through her. Stupid! Being the jealous mistress has got to stop, she thought. What had happened to that focused university graduate who thrived on ambition? Anthony Pickard is what happened. Really stupid!

10

Amanda

She had seen the marks, Amanda knew it. She tried to think of a plausible excuse as to their presence without having to admit that yes, her husband did treat her like a human punch bag. She waited beyond the closed curtain of the changing room.

"Take your time Mrs Copburn. I have the other dresses in your size just here."

The curtain was pulled back and a portly lady wearing a lemon chiffon dress waddled out. "What do you think?" Mrs Copburn turned this way and that in front of the mirror.

Amanda pretended to consider it for a moment before sighing. "As beautiful as it is Mrs Copburn, I do think that the aquamarine two-piece would warm your lovely skin tone, and it would be a shame not to emphasise those fabulous blue eyes of yours." Amanda proffered her the outfit. Mrs Copburn nodded, smiling. Her small slate eyes took in the vibrant colour. She held the material up to her pallid complexion and, happily accepting Amanda's recommendation, she waddled back into the changing room.

"So you think that's going to work? Well if she's like your Aunt Beatrice, God rest her soul, then maybe you're right. She would see a compliment in anything, even if it was, 'My word Beatrice, I see you have a very good appetite.' She would nod that huge head of hers and say 'Yes it's marvellous isn't it?' and strut around like a peacock. Your poor Uncle Max."

Amanda looked at her mother. "It's called selling, Mum. That's what I do."

"You should take up flower arranging. Look at the flowers on your Aunt Beatrice's grave, God rest her soul. Wilted as soon as they touched the soil. Who can blame them I ask? Would you like to lie on top of your Aunt Beatrice, God rest her soul? Even your Uncle Max didn't."

Amanda's eyes filled with tears. She missed her mother so much. At times of extreme stress, and on the odd happy occasion, her mum would appear to her, extolling usually unwise words, involving the much criticised Aunt Beatrice. These were often followed by suggestions of hobbies Amanda should take up.

She remembered quite vividly when she had begun to 'see' her mother. She guessed it was about six months after she had passed away. David had been pressurising her to start a family. Every night he would plant his seed – it was as impersonal as that. One morning after he left for work Amanda sat on the end of the bed. The night had been exhausting. With clinical detachment he had lain on top of her, pumping away at her flesh until spent. Later the process was repeated again and again.

"Cake decorating, why not try that? It's inexpensive and can make a dog's dinner look like something you can eat. Your Aunt Beatrice, God rest her soul, was good at that. Your poor Uncle Max was fooled every time. What can I tell you?"

Her mother was in the corner of the bedroom. She could see her clearly. Arms folded neatly across her powder blue suit – the one she wore to the synagogue. Amanda's throat ached but her heart lifted and she knew at that moment that she could not bring a child into the house with that man as the father. She also knew that she had to get out and find a job before she went completely insane.

And here she was, still at Peltham's Department Store nine years later.

"Are you alright in there Mrs Copburn?"

The curtains rustled once more and Mrs Copburn stepped out. "This is definitely the one." Mrs Copburn smiled at her own image in the gilt edged mirror.

"It's perfect. All you need now are the shoes and bag." She nodded encouragingly at her client.

Mrs Copburn's bejewelled hand flew to her mouth. "Of course, I hadn't thought of that."

Amanda gently patted her arm. "Now don't you worry we'll sort it all out for you. You will certainly be the belle of the ball."

Mrs Copburn almost skipped back into the changing room just as Marianne turned the corner from the lifts. Amanda pulled her sleeves down over her wrists. "Your appraisal didn't last very long did it?"

Marianne shook her head. "No, she really doesn't like me."

"Well, maybe you need to show her a serious side and not be quite so flighty." Amanda didn't bother trying to hide the irritation in her voice. Everything this woman represented mocked her own frugal upbringing.

"I don't know what I've done but I think the 'Ice Queen' wants to get rid of me."

"I don't think she'll want to get rid of you. The store needs staff like you. I mean you buy most of its stock single-handedly!" She saw Marianne flinch. "Perhaps you could put your skills to good use and help Mrs Copburn spend her money on shoes and a bag."

Sometimes you had to be harsh, Amanda thought, to make sure people performed at their best. Wasn't that what David was always telling her?

11

Hayley

Hayley stared at the door long after it had closed. Amanda's wrist looked dreadful, she thought as she subconsciously rubbed her own. The moment Hayley saw the injury, a look passed between the two women. Hers was questioning, but Amanda's seemed to beg for silence. Hayley's natural concern and compassion would be difficult to gag, but she must try. Meanwhile her appraisal was looming and she needed to keep this job if she was going to be able to persuade Neil to agree to her plan. She had only been at the store for a few months, not very long to make an impression, but now was her chance. She was determined to show that she was confident and reliable.

"H..H..H..Hayley the j…j...jack hammer! H…H...Hayley the j…j...jack hammer!" Her older brother Adam's gleeful taunts stretched across time. Once again she was standing in the street whilst Adam circled her on his bike singing cruel jibes. Their mother insisted that he was only playing. Adam could do no wrong in her eyes.

Confidence did not come easily to Hayley. She had found ways, over the years, to suppress her stammer, but when she was stressed or anxious it took full rein of her speech and rode it like a bucking bronco. Her reliability was also not easy to prove. There had been a long gap since her previous employment in the estate agency, whilst she had nursed her father through an illness that finally killed him.

Snapping out of the past she patted her frizzy hair down as best she could and straightened her collar. She left the staff room for the soft furnishings department and ultimately Jane's office. This floor was the only one that didn't look tired and faded. Its walls were painted in rich creams and pistachio. A deep caramel carpet stretched from wall to wall below warm lighting.

As she walked towards the office she could hear voices beyond the half open door.

"I've told you Tony, no more. I'm not your play thing for you to pick up and put down whenever you feel like it." She recognised Jane's voice.

"You were definitely my play thing the other night." A man laughed.

"It was wrong and I was stupid." Jane sounded tired.

Hayley stopped. She didn't want to be caught eavesdropping, but on the other hand she could hardly resist.

"Now come on Janey, you know you don't mean that. Look, things will be different when we're together. You just have to give me time to tell her and then it will be you and me against the world."

She thought she heard a muffled protest from Jane, then silence. Hayley hadn't even realised she was holding her breath until she was forced to exhale, as quietly as she could.

"Friday then? I promise I will be a very good boy and lavish you with attention and anything else that gorgeous body desires." He laughed again.

"Okay. Friday. You will tell her soon though, won't you?" Any firmness had faded from Jane's voice, replaced by neediness.

"Of course I will."

In the brief silence that followed Hayley took several steps back and then resumed her walk towards the office as if it had never been interrupted. And Anthony Pickard strolled out of the door.

"Good morning Mr Pickard." So 'Tony' was Anthony, the store manager, she thought as she stepped aside to let him pass.

"Morning erm..." Anthony's face looked blank.

"Hayley." She knew he would never remember her name. She didn't fit into his model girlfriend portfolio, but Jane apparently did.

As she walked in Jane was hurriedly re-applying lipstick.

"Yes... er come in and sit down." Jane dropped the lipstick into her drawer and pulled her shoulders back, chin held high. "So you are... oh erm let me see..."

Hayley was convinced that her presence was diminishing by the day. "Hayley Townsend." Maybe she should wear a name badge and a luminous jacket.

"Yes, of course that's who you are. Now let me see." Jane went back to shuffling through the papers on her desk which seemed to be everywhere. Finally she found what she was looking for. "Temporary contract yes?"

"Yes, th-th-that's right." Hayley took a deep breath in readiness to deliver her prepared speech, without stumbling over her words. She was desperate to showcase her strong points.

"Well that all looks in order. Super, thanks for popping in." Jane went back to scooping up the stacks of paper that had clearly been disturbed moments before Hayley came in. Seeing that Jane was still flustered after her brief encounter with Anthony, Hayley tiptoed to the door and quietly left.

Although she felt relieved, she also felt cheated of her chance to sell herself, but at least she still had a salary and she was certainly going to need that.

12

Jane

All he had to do was look at her and flash that insanely white smile. God, she was stupid. What happened to, 'it's over, finished, I want nothing more to do with you,' mocked the voice in her head. Anthony Pickard, that's what happened – again.

A feeling of nausea swept over her as she picked up the final appraisal form. 'Amanda Freedman' was typed at the top. She took a deep breath and tried to ignore her mounting queasiness. She must be coming down with something she thought, as she scanned the rest of the form. Nothing extraordinary leapt out at her, she concluded just as there was a soft knock on the door.

"Come in." It was hard for her to hide the weariness that had crept into her voice. All day she had been appraising staff and not one had come up to the mark for the special role she had in mind. A tall, slim woman slipped through the door. Her dark hair fell over a face that was almost translucent it was so pale. Jane could see that she obviously was not dynamic judging by her body language, although she noted from her paperwork that she had recently been promoted to section supervisor.

"Take a seat Miss or Mrs Freedman? I'm sorry the form's not clear."

"It's Mrs." The words were spoken so quietly that Jane had to lean forward to catch them.

"Well Mrs Freedman, I'll just run through a few questions to see how you're getting on. And, of course, to see where you might like to go." She was surprised when Amanda's head jerked up at this last sentence. Suddenly there was a dim light in those dull eyes, not much of one, but one nonetheless. In a split second she decided to forge on with a line of questioning that a few moments ago she had no intention of touching upon.

"You see, Mrs Freedman we're not just interested in your current performance. We are also interested in what your own personal ambitions are. For example, would you consider leaving the area, travelling all over the country? It's a role that we're currently developing and, as such, we are looking out for possible candidates." When Jane looked up from her papers she could have been looking at an entirely different woman. Amanda's eyes were shining and colour had risen to her cheeks.

"You mean leaving here. Getting away?" There was something akin to desperation in Amanda's question.

"Yes, it would involve, initially, living from a suitcase. Moving from one branch to another as required. And I see that you've been with the company for some considerable time. Your attendance record is good, and I have noticed that you have just taken on a much more responsible position." She continued to watch Amanda bloom in front of her.

"I could do that. I could live out of a suitcase, I don't have much... I could get away." The last few words Amanda said were almost to herself as she seemed to drift off in contemplation.

"Well then, I'll make a note on your file and perhaps we can discuss it again when I have a more detailed job description to put forward?"

Amanda was nodding vigorously then she smiled a glorious, all-encompassing smile. "Thank you so much for considering me. I could do it, I know I could." And Jane believed her.

Suddenly Amanda leant across the table to shake Jane's hand but then, just as suddenly, she withdrew. Pulling her sleeves over her knuckles she thanked Jane and left.

I think I've found the person to fill that special role, she thought as she looked back over Amanda's profile.

Rubbing her forehead to relieve the tension that had built during the day, she decided that she should learn to relax more. Then, as if from nowhere, the hobby of flower arranging popped into her head.

13

Marianne

Marianne was in paradise. She had spent the last four days swamped in swathes of exotic fabrics, and the new stock kept coming. Gleefully she distributed the delicate garments between displays carefully setting aside a few items for herself.

It would be criminal not to offer an appreciative home to these exquisite creations. As for using her store credit card, well wasn't that just keeping the finance staff in employment? These were the thoughts that swirled round her head as she created luscious displays to entice the public to buy. She needed little enticement.

"Sorry to bother you." A tall dark haired man wearing an immaculate suit stepped into her line of vision. "I just wondered if you could tell me which department Amanda Freedman is working in?" His smile was charming, and Marianne found herself smiling back.

"Well today she's in Housewares."

"What about tomorrow?"

Marianne hesitated, should she be giving out information about a colleague?

"God I'm so sorry I haven't even explained myself. I'm David, Amanda's husband? I feel a bit of a fool actually. We had a few words the other day and I think she's still cross with me, so I thought I'd send her some flowers." He gave a deferential shrug. "You know, earn myself some brownie points? I hate it when she's not happy."

He looked so helpless Marianne felt a twinge of anger at Amanda. Who did she think she was, making this poor man suffer? She was obviously very lucky to have such a caring husband. "She'll be on Ladies' Wear tomorrow."

"Thank you so much. I just hope she likes them, and they do the trick. Thanks again for your help."

As she carried her shopping bags home, she thought about how some women didn't appreciate how fortunate they were. That would never happen to her. She would always be grateful for Jack's love.

"Cooee!" Joyce Mountford, Marianne's neighbour, was leaning over the fence with a parcel in her outstretched arms. "It came today, just after eleven, so I took it in for you."

"Thank you so much – again, Joyce." Shifting the bags from one hand to the other she took the parcel and turned to go in.

"Ordered anything nice?" Joyce was still looking at the package.

"Nothing exciting, just a few bits and pieces for the kitchen," she lied, as she juggled with the bags, keys and well wrapped box full of luxury toiletries. Finally, she was in the house and there was a brick wall between her nosey neighbour and the delights that she was just moments away from exposing. Dropping the bags, she feverishly cut open the cellophane. Discarding the delivery note and invoice, she pulled out hand crafted bottles of exotic perfume and body wash.

She had earlier booked a table at the new bistro round the corner – a treat for Jack. Now, before going out for a meal, she could indulge in a hot bath, immersing herself in the expensive bubbles and soft liquid silk - all for Jack of course. Scooping up the bags, empty box and packaging she passed the answering machine which blinked rhythmically on the hall table. She would dispose of any evidence of shopping tomorrow at the re-cycling depot.

An hour later, she heard keys in the front door, then the familiar sound of one concrete smattered boot being dropped onto the mat swiftly followed by the other.

"Hi baby, I'm back," Jack's voice floated up the stairs.

"Hi gorgeous, I'll be down in a second." She sprayed her body with orchid scented body mist and draped a cream cashmere robe over her shoulders. She fluffed up her newly washed hair and dabbed a few extra drops of perfume between her breasts.

Slowly she walked downstairs, pausing seductively halfway down just as Jack's finger pressed the 'play' button on the answering machine.

"Hello, Mrs Drummond, this is Scott Lawson from Finance International. I wonder if you could call us as soon as possible. The number is..."

She didn't hear the rest. Her mind jolted into action. "Of course, I must phone Scott. They're organising a savings scheme through work, and I thought it would be a sensible thing to get involved in." She felt sick. She couldn't remember who Finance International was and what she may have bought with their credit.

"Well aren't you the little financial wizard then?" Jack bounced up the stairs two at a time and kissed her firmly on the mouth.

"Aren't I just," she said through crushed lips.

14

Amanda

It had been several days since David had beaten her. Since then he had spoken to her coolly but politely. They exchanged only the barest minimum to get through day to day life. She knew she was still being punished, but whilst his fists were in his pockets she could cope. The lack of sexual attention was an added bonus.

Her father always used to refer to David as 'the nice Jewish boy'. Even when her father was explaining to her that he was leaving her mother to run away with a woman half his age from the synagogue, he re-assured Amanda that 'the nice Jewish boy' would look after her.

Her mother, even when she was ripping her father's shirts to shreds, swore that 'the nice Jewish boy' would never do that to Amanda. Now Amanda wished he would, although she didn't think she could allow another woman to suffer at his hands like she had, at least not without trying to warn her.

Again and again she mulled over her conversation with Jane during her appraisal. She just needed to save enough money to be able to pay for accommodation and food. The store would pay for her initial expenses but she did need a safety net to make sure she could escape for good.

Calling in at the supermarket on the way home she selected only the value products, comparing each and every price until there was nothing left to economise on. Once at home, she carefully decanted the food stuff into branded boxes and hid the value packets. She would dispose of them later at the re-cycling depot.

Five pounds and sixty three pence she had saved just on that one trip alone. In the bedroom, she climbed onto a chair and reached into the depths of the top shelf of her wardrobe and pulled out a metal box. The key was in the lock. It turned easily enough and she opened the lid and placed a five pound note and the change that she'd saved inside. She closed and locked it and shoved it as far back as she could.

"Your Aunt Beatrice couldn't save money to save her life, God rest her soul. She only had to wear a pair of tights once and then she bought new. And yet your Uncle Max had holes at both end of his socks – each as wide as the other – it was tragic but what can I say?"

Amanda silently thanked her mother, as she jumped down and buried the key in the toe of a pair of tights which she pressed to the back of her drawer.

"You should take up line dancing. It's good for the soul and the cost is so small. If it's good enough for Rabbi Silverman, who are we to disagree? Of course, at first they didn't like the spurs in the synagogue. Now, even Mrs Hyman won't take her cowboy boots off, so what can you do?"

Her mother watched from the corner of the room, next to the bedside table.

"I really don't think line dancing is for me, Mum." Amanda said as she carefully re-arranged the underwear in her drawer before closing it.

"So, I make a suggestion and you toss it aside. I'm your mother and I'm just trying to help."

"I know you are." But she was seriously beginning to question the 'help and advice' her imaginary mother was giving her, and what this said about her own state of mind. Without dwelling on her mental health for too long she began to think of ways she could cut even more costs to add to her savings. Escape she must and securing that new role at work was her way out.

On her way to work the next day she called at the recycling depot. Sidling up to the massive container she checked over each shoulder before hurling the value range boxes inside. Dusting off her hands she turned and walked straight into Marianne.

"Oh Marianne! Just dropping off some bits of rubbish I can't fit in the bin." Blushing, Amanda gestured towards the skip.

"Yeah, same here." Marianne hurriedly tossed a parcel wrapped in gold cellophane into the container. Amanda noted the elegant packaging and only just stopped herself from making a caustic remark about Marianne having money to burn. Instead she bit down on her bottom lip and the pair made the awkward and silent walk to work together.

15

Hayley

"I know it sounds like an awful lot of money Neil, but I'm sure we can raise it somehow." She stared at her husband as he continued to chew his muesli. Twenty times he had to chew food. That was the recommended number in order to digest it properly, he had told her once. Being an accountant he held a lot of store by numbers.

Eventually he swallowed. "That's not the point Hayley." He laid his spoon in the bowl and looked over his glasses at her. "When do we stop? Alright so it's four thousand five hundred pounds for the first attempt, and then what?"

She knew he was only trying to shield her from further disappointment. And although he was always careful with money, she couldn't believe that his reluctance was being financially driven. He knew how much she wanted, no, needed this. "We could be lucky f-f-first time." Her stomach knotted as she felt the chance to persuade him slipping away.

"And if we're not? Do we fork out another five grand?" He picked up his spoon, re-loaded it and began chewing once again. She pushed her chair away from the table and slowly stood. She studied the top of her husband's head. The hair that had disappeared from his pate over the years had been more than replaced with hair now sprouting out of his ears and nostrils. For one brief moment she hated him. In her mind he was standing between her and something that she wanted more than anything else in the world.

Without saying another word, she collected her bag from the hook on the back of the kitchen door. As she reached the front door she checked the inside pocket of her handbag. Safely tucked away was another pregnancy testing kit. Well it had been a few days since she last tested herself, and her breasts were feeling extremely tender. *This could be it*, her imagination whisked up thoughts of morning sickness and cravings.

16

Jane

He had hinted at spending more time with her, maybe even a weekend together. And he had been very attentive the last time they had gone out. Reservations had been made at a top class restaurant followed by a night in the executive suite of a four star hotel. And for the first time in a while she had felt as though she was more than just a body to lie on top of when the need was such.

That morning on her daily inspection of the store she had seen an exquisite raw silk tie in menswear and made the purchase. Hearing Anthony pass her door a few minutes earlier she quickly crept along the corridor and slipped into his office. She placed the gift box on his desk and was just about to leave when she noticed a brochure tucked under a stack of files. She tugged the glossy pages from under the pile. It was open at the section entitled 'Romantic weekends in Italy'. Feeling a flurry of excitement she hastily retraced her steps. This must be what he had in mind. Maybe she had been too harsh in her doubts about his commitment. The flurry had turned into a fizz as she wondered what she could possibly take with her.

Hearing him softly whistling as he returned to his office, Jane gathered her pens and notebook for their meeting and went to join him.

"Janey this is a great tie, really sweet of you thanks." He had opened the box and waved the strip of silk between forefinger and thumb.

"You're welcome. I'm sure you'll think of a way to repay me. Perhaps with something romantic?" She perched on the edge of his desk and slowly leant towards him. Her fingers almost touching the spine of the glossy brochure which poked out from the stack of papers.

"Yeah, something romantic, definitely." Without looking at her he scooped up the pile and dropped them into a drawer. "Now what about romance?" His hand brushed the inside of her thigh and his smile became a leer.

"I meant romance not just sex." She playfully swept his hand away. She didn't mind waiting for him to tell her about their weekend away. It made it all the more thrilling. She settled into a chair on the other side of the desk and smiled demurely at him. She would play along with him.

Their meeting covered the progress of the Summer Launch event. The local press had confirmed that they would attend, and invitations to local dignitaries had been sent out. But the visiting American contingency and their crucial role was to remain confidential.

Jane had scarcely listened to most of the conversation, her thoughts occupied by which seductive outfits she could take away with her. Once the meeting was over she waited until after the lunchtime rush hour before sauntering down to the lingerie department. A consignment from France had recently been delivered and she felt sure there would be something suitably sophisticated but sexy in that range. She made her way to the designer area, where plush chairs offered those tired of spending a short rest before continuing with their gruelling task. The lighting there changed to a gentle glow and the air was scented.

Jane honed in on a rich ivory negligee. She held the soft material up to the light. Was it too bridal she wondered?

"And I'll take the whole matching set in ivory. Size eight, don't forget... erm ..."

"Hayley, my name's Hayley."

"Yes well whatever." A statuesque woman with dark hair and sunglasses swept past Jane followed by a red haired assistant, tottering under a mountain of clothes.

Jane recognised her from the appraisals. She watched the duo make their way to the payment desk.

The woman flopped down onto a nearby chaise longue and flicked open her compact. "Pop it on my account there's a good girl, or better still put it on my husband's account. Yes that's right Anthony Pickard. Well if he will insist on whisking me away on a second honeymoon he'll just have to pay the price." Mrs Pickard laughed and snapped the compact shut. Rising to her feet she waved a well-manicured hand vaguely over the frothy heap now over-spilling the counter. "You can tell that Charlie to take all these things to the car, there's far too much for me to manage. Besides I think I might just call into the beauty salon. The Italians are red hot on grooming and it wouldn't do for me to look anything but perfect." She glided away leaving Hayley surrounded by tissue paper and scented beads to pack with the mounds of clothes.

Jane was still holding the ivory negligee. She hung it back on the rail. Her eyes stung as she turned and walked away.

She blindly managed to get back to her office. And she remained there until the end of the day with her door firmly locked. When she was sure the rest of the staff had left, she drifted through the empty floors down to the staff door. She didn't look at the reflection of her reddened face and smudged mascara in the mirrored panels that decorated the perfume hall.

"Ma'am?" The voice came from the shadows as Charlie stepped forward. He held a box of tissues out to her. "She's not a patch on you ma'am."

"Thank you Charlie, thank you so much." Jane impulsively hugged him before taking a handful of tissues and stumbling out of the door. The cool air hit her hot cheeks. So, so stupid Jane. She needed to get away. Get away from her stupid mistakes. Get away from the fool that she had been. Get away from Anthony Pickard.

Would there always be an Anthony Pickard? Yes, of course there would. As long as she was desperate for love and companionship there would always be an Anthony Pickard waiting for her. All that education. Years at university learning about business management, flow charts, evaluating retail statistics, for what? A quickie behind the staff canteen with an over ambitious, over sexed manager?

Her footsteps echoed as she walked towards her apartment block, mocking her solitude. No, she had to be worth more. At university she had been sharp, focused. She knew she was good. She was still good. The only thing that had changed was the unfortunate liaison with Anthony Pickard. She could start her own business, be her own boss. No Anthony Pickard. Charlie was right Mrs Pickard wasn't a patch on her.

She pushed open her flat door and went straight over to a stack of large boxes in the corner of the room. Each box was neatly labelled. The first read 'Growth and Exit Strategy', the next 'Finance'. Both appropriate she thought as she pulled one out and set it down on the floor. Before long she was surrounded by papers. She felt the thrill of being in control again, as if beginning to waken from a long slumber.

17

Marianne

As soon as Jack left for work Marianne replayed the answering machine. She scribbled the number down on the corner of a brown envelope she'd found on the bedroom floor and stuffed it into her pocket. Maybe the phone call was about an offer of interest free credit. Yes, that was it – he was probably just trying to sell her some financial deal. She collected the empty parcel and screwed up cellophane from inside the airing cupboard and pushed all thoughts of finances to the back of her mind. Heading out to work, she paused to pick up a brochure for 'Romantic Weekend Retreats' that had landed on the door mat. That's exactly what she could do with. Perhaps she should suggest it to Jack.

Approaching the recycling depot she realised that she had disposed of a lot of packaging recently. Although she was sure she hadn't bought that much really. It was just that they seemed to use a ridiculous amount of padding and wrapping. And it wasn't as though anyone needed the delivery note, invoice, returns label. It was a case of excessive administration she concluded. As she rounded the corner of the waste tip, she bumped straight into Amanda. As fast as she could she jettisoned the parcel hoping that Amanda wouldn't notice the expensive looking bundle.

The walk to the store was more than just uncomfortable as Marianne desperately searched for something to say. She opened her mouth to tell Amanda about the beautiful meal she and Jack had enjoyed at the bistro the night before, but quickly thought better of it. She didn't want to provoke any further disapproval. And anyway Amanda had probably already been there with her adoring husband. And after yesterday she was even more convinced that he must wrap her in cotton wool and pamper her to death. Marianne decided to say nothing and was more than relieved when they finally arrived.

Charlie hauled on the staff door with both hands and kept it propped open with his frail body. "Right you are ladies." He nodded as usual.

"Any tips for us today Charlie?" Marianne winked and tapped the side of her nose.

"Well, seeing as you ask, there's 'A Touch of Fashion' at Kempton Park. Odds are twenty to one." His rheumy eyes seemed to clear whenever he spoke of his precious horses. He shuffled back to his chair and picked up the newspaper. "That, my dears, is the best I can offer you today." He held the newspaper close to his eyes squinting at the print.

"Thanks Charlie." Marianne blew Charlie a kiss, which made his old cheeks glow. They left him studying the racing form.

"Are you coming up to lingerie Marianne?" Amanda had put her bag in her locker and was waiting by the staff room door.

"I'll be up in a second. You go and I'll catch up with you." Marianne's fingers closed round the folded envelope in her pocket. "Sorry I won't be long, just need to make a quick phone call."

"Okay, see you in a minute." Amanda pointedly looked at the clock on the wall before leaving the room.

Marianne studied the number she had written down and carefully keyed it into her phone. Pressing 'dial' she felt her stomach lurch. An interminable menu of options was delivered by an automated female voice, then she was placed on hold. Three minutes later she received an apology for being placed on hold before being put on hold again. After ten minutes of alternately being apologised to and being told how valuable her custom was she heard a ringing tone which was answered by a real person.

"I wonder if I could speak to Scott Lawson, he left a message for me yesterday?"

"Scott Lawson? Yes I'm afraid that's a different department. If I could just put you on hold..." Before she could object, the real person disappeared and the apologies began again. As she waited the staff room door opened and a red haired woman walked in. Marianne wondered if she was a new member of staff as she couldn't recall seeing her before. The woman smiled shyly at Marianne as she hung up a quilted anorak.

"Hello, this is Scott Lawson speaking. How may I help?" Marianne jumped at the sudden human voice on the other end of the phone. She turned her back on the red haired woman in a vague attempt at privacy.

"Hello , erm, yes this is Marianne Drummond. You left a message for me yesterday asking me to call you?" She spoke as quietly as she could into the mouthpiece

"If you could just speak up a bit – you're very faint."

She took a deep breath. "This is Marianne Drummond, you called me yesterday?"

"Ah, yes Mrs Drummond thanks for calling back. We really need to speak to you about your credit limit and the penalties for late payments. We have already written to you but unfortunately we haven't received any response."

She turned over the envelope in her hand and saw that the return address printed on it was Finance International. The voice at the other end of the phone continued. "Our terms and conditions are very clear Mrs Drummond. The minimum payments have to be made. Failure to do so will result in a charge on your account. You did agree to those terms and conditions, Mrs Drummond."

She remembered the suede boots she had seen. Eagerly she had signed papers which would mean she could leave the shop with the fabulous footwear that very day. Those had been the terms and conditions.

"... at this present time Mrs Drummond your debt is six hundred and fifty-nine pounds and ninety-nine pence with two additional late payments charges of twenty five pounds each and interest calculated at twenty-nine point nine five per cent."

She heard the numbers being spoken, but they meant little to her. She didn't have any spare money. "Can you give me some time to pay?" Her voice quivered.

"Now Mrs Drummond," his tone was placating, "we don't expect you to clear the whole debt but we must ask that you at least make the minimum payments. Interest will, of course, continue to be charged. The alternative is that we pass the debt on."

She didn't like the sound of that at all. "No, I understand I'll sort it out."

"Would you like to make a payment over the phone now Mrs Drummond, we accept most major credit and debit cards?"

She quelled a manic urge to laugh at this suggestion. All her other credit and debit cards were loaded to the hilt with debt. "No, I'll go to the post office and make a payment."

"Thank you for your co-operation, Mrs Drummond. Hopefully I won't have to call again. Have a nice day now."

She stared at the brown envelope still in her hand as she heard the staff room door softly close.

18

Amanda

The 'blue label' event was proving to be very popular and Amanda's till had hardly stopped ringing all day. In a brief lull she looked over at Marianne who was extolling the virtues of large knickers that not only covered the upper thigh but also most of the torso. On the face of it Marianne appeared to be her usual bubbly self, but Amanda sensed moments of slight reticence in her demeanour, perhaps she hadn't managed her daily quota of shopping today she thought.

"Excuse me, I'm looking for Amanda Freedman?" A voice spoke from behind the largest bouquet of flowers Amanda had ever seen.

"I'm Amanda," she said to the bouquet.

The flowers were thrust into her arms revealing a small man with weathered cheeks. He was clearly grateful to be rid of the burden.

"Thank you very much."

"You're welcome love. They weigh a ton. Hope you enjoy them." He disappeared into the crowd of ladies now forming a queue at her till. She hurriedly placed the arrangement down and turned her attention to the agitated group of women clutching their sales items. Eventually the store became quieter. The morning shoppers had drifted away leaving a gap before the lunch time snatch and grabbers would fleetingly make their appearance.

"Wow, these are divine." Marianne picked up the bouquet and was studying the envelope. "Mrs Freedman you are lucky." Marianne handed the envelope to her.

Amanda didn't want to open it. There was only one man in her life, and flowers did not necessarily mean good news.

To my wife, I forgive you. I think that you now understand what a mistake you made, and I'm willing to give you another chance to make it up to me. I'll see you later.

David x

She felt cold. His silent treatment had afforded her the luxury of distance and safety. Now that had gone. She would have to face the evil creature that smothered her until she stepped out of line. Instinctively she pulled her sleeves down over her knuckles.

19

Jane

She wasn't sure if she was strong enough to face him yet, not that she had much choice. It was probably nervous tension that was unsettling her stomach. So he had now got to her physically as well as emotionally. She was just going to put on a brave face and try not to let him get close. With her resolve not quite as steely as she would have liked, she gathered her notes from the night before and set out to work.

She pushed open the staff door almost toppling Charlie as he bent down to pick up his flask of tea.

"Morning Charlie." She strode past him and on into the store before he had chance to tip his cap or reply.

Her daily inspection was well under way. With fresh eyes she studied the shop layout, the window dressings and promotional displays. Perhaps she could make the Americans see that she was indispensable. By the time she returned to her office her head was brimming with ideas. Spreadsheet after spreadsheet filled the screen with projections and statistics. Recording previous years' figures and trends, she worked on. Lost, once again, in her old familiar world of academia.

Hours passed. Finally she leant back in her chair and surveyed the graphs and charts that summarised her findings and proposals. This was good. She knew it was. With a cocktail of nerves and pride, laced with a tiny drop of doubt about involving Tony she pressed send. 'Message sent to Anthony Pickard.' read the outbox display.

She drummed her fingers on the desk as she waited. She knew he wouldn't be able to absorb the whole report but he should be impressed with her attention to detail and grasp of figures. It was, at the very least, an attempt at putting their relationship on a more professional footing. She wasn't just an empty headed bimbo that he could just screw and leave. She had a brain – and yet she still allowed him to screw her and leave!

Who was she trying to kid? Suddenly an image of an unopened envelope flashed onto her screen announcing the arrival of a new message. 'To one of the sexiest assistant managers I know – You are an extremely clever girl and I have something very important to discuss with you. Tony x'

20

Hayley

She hadn't meant to listen, but she couldn't help herself. Even the pretty ones have their problems Hayley thought, as she considered the one side of the conversation she had heard. Unfortunately indulging in eavesdropping had made her late getting to her post in women's wear. The store would already be filling up with shoppers looking for a bargain in the 'blue label sale'. And she would have no time to use the pregnancy test.

"If you could just put these labels out erm..." A floor manager held out a stack of cardboard labels.

"Hayley, that's my name."

"Yes, right, well if you could just put these on the sale items... Hayley." The manager walked away leaving her to wonder why it was that no-one noticed her and when they did, no-one ever remembered her name. Even Anthony Pickard's wife the day before had asked her several times for her name, despite the fact that she had been wearing a name badge.

Hayley hadn't liked her at all, and then to expect poor old Charlie to carry all her bags for her was just beyond belief. Hayley had noticed Jane's hasty retreat from the department and wondered if she knew Mrs Pickard. Quite a tricky situation she surmised as she set about her task.

With tag gun in one hand and cardboard tags in the other she began labelling. As she moved from one display to another she noticed an old lady with a tartan shopping trolley. She was combing through the stock on a rail before systematically removing every other item and placing it inside the shopping trolley. She was completely absorbed in her mission and was oblivious to Hayley's attention. Having cleared half of one rack the old lady then moved onto the next.

Despite being fascinated by the woman's casual air and lack of discretion, Hayley decided that she really should call security. She edged past the knitwear, keeping one eye on the shoplifter and one eye searching for another member of staff. She finally reached the staff phone and dialled security.

"Hello Charlie, it's Hayley in women's wear. We have a code three situation here. Do you think you could assist?"

"Right oh, I'll be up in a flash," Charlie's frail voice quivered down the phone.

Hayley tried not to smile at Charlie's response. The woman had moved on to hosiery and was happily tucking glossy packs of stockings and tights into her already burgeoning bag. She had almost cleared that section by the time Charlie shuffled over to Hayley.

"Here we are then Miss, ready for action." Charlie looked nothing like ready for action. If anything he looked like he needed a lie down after the exertion of getting to women's wear.

"It's that lady there Charlie, the one with the tartan shopping bag." Hayley pointed at the elderly lady who was now examining the costume jewellery.

"Ah yes, of course, leave it to me. I'll have it sorted in a jiffy," he said, as he puffed his narrow chest out and hobbled at a snail's pace over to his target.

She watched him approach the thief and tap her on the shoulder before tipping the peak of his cap – he just couldn't help himself Hayley thought as she moved closer.

"Excuse me Madame." Charlie bowed slightly. "I do believe that you have items in your bag which haven't been paid for."

The lady nodded vigorously. "Yes, yes I have, and do you know what? I've over-filled it again." This time the lady looked sadly at the stuffed shopping trolley. Charlie followed her gaze, and the pair stood silently contemplating the problematic luggage. It was the police that interrupted the scene. Hayley stepped aside as two officers approached.

"Hello Ada." One officer removed his hat.

"Hello George." Ada smiled brightly at the young officer. "I haven't seen you in a long time."

"It was only last week Ada, remember? In Scottmill? When you had that set of pans that you couldn't carry out of the shop?"

A cloud of confusion crossed Ada's face. "Was that last week?"

"Yes Ada, now shall we let Charlie here put everything back and then we can get you home?" The officer gently held Ada's elbow.

"Ooh yes that would be nice. Will you come in for a cup of tea? Joe should be home now and you boys can have a chat." Her face had brightened as she turned to Hayley. "Joe's my son, and he always has a lovely chat with these young men when they bring me home."

Hayley smiled at Ada before helping Charlie to empty the bag. One officer carried the bag for Ada whilst the other led her to the exit.

"Bye Charlie," Ada called waving.

"Good bye ma'am." Charlie gave a small salute but continued to watch the would-be thief as she left the store. Had she seen a bit of a spark in Charlie's eyes, Hayley wondered?

With all the excitement of the almost shoplifter and the chaos of bargain hunters in their droves, her day disappeared without a chance to do the test. She would have to wait until tomorrow. Neil had banned her from using the kit at home. Still, she felt she was definitely feeling more exhausted than usual as she collected her anorak and left for home.

21

Marianne

Well she couldn't imagine why she had offered to make a payment at the post office. What could she pay it with? There was no way she could ask Jack. He had absolutely no idea how much she spent and, like her bank manager, she didn't think Jack would be very understanding, even though he did get some of the benefit – unlike her bank manager.

She sat alone at a table in the staff canteen. It was her last break of the day and she still wasn't any closer to finding a solution to her finances. Absently, she flicked through the local newspaper that had been left on the table along with a half-eaten blueberry muffin and the cocoa dregs of hot chocolate.

'Get Cash Fast – same day cash loans', the advert read. Marianne read it again, glanced over her shoulder then tore the article out of the paper. It wouldn't hurt to just give them a call she thought as she slipped the scrap into her purse. Ironically it was the only paper in her purse apart from receipts.

Moments after she returned home she heard the front door closing. She sincerely hoped that Jack's day had been better than hers. "How was your day darling?" She called from the kitchen doorway.

"Not too good actually, the work's just not out there." Jack's usually happy, handsome face looked drawn and tired. He was untying the laces of his work boots.

"It'll get busier though, won't it?" She hadn't seen Jack truly worried before and rushed to his side.

"Baby," he said, straightening up and taking hold of both her hands. "There's a recession on so who knows when the work will pick up again."

"But you still have a job?" She could feel panic beginning to bubble up from the pit of her stomach.

"For now yes, but we've had to lay two off this week. I don't know who'll be next."

She looked down at his hands holding hers. His were rough and ingrained with dirt. Hers beautifully manicured and enriched with expensive lavender oil.

"Don't worry too much sweetheart." He leant towards her and kissed her. "Anyway with my amazing building skills and your financial wizardry we'll be fine."

Oh God, she thought, as she watched him return to his boot laces.

That night her dreams were filled with counting money but, as she counted the notes, they disintegrated into tiny shreds that she couldn't piece together however hard she tried. By the morning she was exhausted. The one thing she knew was that she had to get money from somewhere. She discreetly checked that the scrap of paper holding the advert was still safely tucked away in her purse. She would call them on Monday. After all, what was the worst thing that could happen?

22

Amanda

She didn't want to take the flowers home. In fact she didn't want to touch them at all but she knew she had to. The sweet smell of lilies was giving her a headache, but of course her felt pouch had been disposed of along with everything it held including her pain killers. Forcing one foot in front of the other she made the journey home. She stood on the door step for a long time – until the neighbour's curtains started twitching. Finally she opened the door and stepped inside.

The radio was on and the aroma of Italian cooking wafted down the hallway. She could hear him humming as a pan clanked onto the hob. She turned the handle of the kitchen door and pushed it open.

"Amanda come in and sit down. Let me look after you." David pulled out a chair with a flourish and a mock bow. Beads of sweat glistened on his forehead and his lips were stained red with wine. She was still standing, flowers in her hand.

"Now, let me get you a drink." He pinched her cheek. She flinched. He didn't seem to notice as he turned away to re-fill his own glass before pouring a glass for her.

"I'll just put these in a vase." She went to the other side of the kitchen and filled a vase with water. Even putting a short distance between them helped her breathe more easily. By now she hated the flowers and everything they represented. Without any finesse she plonked them into the vase and placed it on the window sill.

"Now sit down." With his hands on her shoulders he pressed her down into the seat. She felt the heat of his palms through her blouse. Her whole body stiffened. She watched him as he moved around the kitchen. He was a big man with strong features. Strands of damp hair fell onto his forehead as he stood over the cooker, still humming.

He tasted the food. "Perfect." He smiled a merlot sodden smile. "It's almost ready then we can have a little chat." He busied himself with dishing the meal out and re-filling his glass, then sat down opposite her. Steam rose from the hot food between them. It reminded her of a horror film where the enemy looms out of the fog.

"Now Amanda, I've been thinking about our future and I've decided how things should change." He wound spaghetti round his fork, slowly, deliberately. He didn't look at her. It was as though the task in hand required all of his concentration. "When's your next period?" He raised his head and his eyes pierced hers.

"What do you mean?" Her fork dropped onto the plate.

"When do you next menstruate? It's quite a simple question Amanda." His eyes were narrow slits as he stared at her.

"I'm not sure. I would need to think about it." She looked down at her plate. She couldn't look at him anymore.

"Well I suggest that you do just that and then we can draw up a schedule. I intend to get you pregnant very, very soon."

In her head, she jumped to her feet, picked up the steaming dish of spaghetti and hurled it at him whilst screaming "Never! Never in a million years. I will not let you near me ever again. I'm leaving." Then she grabbed her coat and bag and swept out of the house leaving her husband sobbing at the kitchen table – a broken man.

In reality, she continued to stare at her food whilst the full horror of what he was determined to do sank in.

"Oh and one more thing Mandy," He reached over and covered her hand with his, "You will give up work. I want you at home." He patted her hand signalling that matters had now been concluded. The rest of the meal continued in silence. After clearing the table of his empty plate and hers, barely touched, he disappeared into the front room. She heard the television go on and she sank a little further into her seat.

"Maybe flower arranging isn't for you. It's a pity but what can you do? You can't be good at everything, who can?" Her mother examined the flowers in the vase and shrugged. "Your Aunt Beatrice, God rest her soul, wasn't any good at anything. Why did your poor Uncle Max marry her? How do I know? It wasn't for her looks – that, I can tell you." Her mother crossed the room to examine the contents of the pan. "Perhaps you should take up karate. It's good for the heart and the cost isn't great."

"You know what Mum perhaps I should. It might give me an outside chance of survival at least."

23

Jane

He couldn't even praise her without it feeling like a condescending slap on her back side. She didn't know what was so important that needed to be discussed but she wasn't going to jump this time. This time she would keep him waiting. With a strength of will she thought she had lost, she ignored the message from Tony and immersed herself in filing her finely detailed pie charts and stock proposals.

"Hello beautiful."

She hadn't heard him come in, and he clearly hadn't seen the need to knock.

"Yes Anthony, and what can I do for you?" She spun round to face him.

"Where would you like me to start?" He held a single red rose. He gently stroked her cheek with its petals before pulling her to him. Then his hand slid down tracing the curve of her shoulder before resting lightly on her breast.

"Not there." She brushed his hand away and stepped back. "In fact, let me re-phrase that. What do you want work-wise from me today?" She marched purposefully to her desk and stood behind her chair. She felt like a lion tamer with only a chair for protection. "Would you like to discuss the statistics that I provided or perhaps you would like to analyse the retail trend graphs?"

"Hey now, what's the matter Janey?" His bottom lip trembled in mock distress. "Is Janey cross with Tony today?"

"Jane doesn't give a toss about Tony today." She moved round the chair and sat down.

"I think she does." He put the rose between his teeth and struck up the pose of a Flamenco dancer.

"What are you doing?" Despite her earlier conviction to keep their partnership solely on a professional level she found herself wanting to smile.

"It's a clue." He reached into his pocket and took out an envelope. "For you, I mean us." He dropped the envelope onto the desk. "Open it."

She opened it and unfolded the piece of paper that had been inside. She slowly read the itinerary. It boasted a weekend for two in Barcelona, flights and five star hotel. What was he playing at? She was so confused.

"I promised you more time together didn't I? Well here it is, and this is only the beginning." He laid the rose gently down in front of her.

"But what about your wife?" Jane was lost in turmoil of hope and fear.

"She's not coming with us," he fenced, deliberately side-stepping the question. He sat on the edge of the desk next to her. "I've had to pacify her with a little trip to Rome. Nothing special, this is the real romantic getaway." He wound her blond hair round his fingers and smiled lazily at her. "How could I resist such an amazing and fantastically sexy woman as you?"

Her strength of will had merrily danced off hand in hand with her steely resolve.

24

Hayley

Once again last night he had been adamant. No IVF treatment. He had called it a slippery slope towards disappointment and debt. And once again she thought that the line between love and hate was a fragile one. Still, she was most certainly feeling sick this morning. She ignored the fact that she had hardly eaten and that she had cried herself to sleep following Neil's refusal to discuss the matter any further.

Having missed the opportunity to do the test the day before, she was determined to do it today. This could be it. This could be the month. Would her baby have red hair just like her or would its hair be mousy and thin like Neil's? She hoped it would be red like hers, although she could never understand why hair colour could provoke such negative feelings in people. She, herself had been a victim of name calling throughout her life. She had heard them all, ginger, copper knob, freckle face and many others she didn't want to think about.

Charlie must have seen her coming as he stood to attention at the staff entrance.

"Hello Charlie. That was a funny to do yesterday wasn't it with that little old lady Ada?"

"Ultimate Destiny," Charlie muttered as he closed the door.

"Well I thought you had taken a bit of a shine to her, but I'm not sure about her being your ultimate destiny," she said unzipping her anorak.

"No, the two thirty at Goodwood. Ultimate Destiny thirteen to two. It's a sure thing." Charlie scratched his head under his cap as he stood looking through the glass.

"Are you waiting for someone Charlie?" She thought he definitely seemed pre-occupied.

"No Miss, not me. I'm just watching the world go by, that's all."

He suddenly took a step towards the window. Scooping the cap off his head he bowed gallantly from the waist. Ada, pushing her tartan shopping trolley along on the other side of the road, stopped and waved in return. A young man wearing a trench coat walked by her side, he also returned Charlie's greeting.

'Ultimate destiny?' Hayley thought as she left him and went up to the staff room to get ready for the day ahead.

The morning dragged. She kept looking at her watch, willing the hands to move faster. Then, at last, it was time for her break. With damp palms she pawed through the contents of her bag and pulled out the test kit. She was convinced that it would be positive. She had been feeling lightheaded all morning. Hurrying to the Ladies room, she checked under the doors for feet. She was alone. In the cubicle she sat and waited. Two minutes the instructions said. She stared at the colour display window and waited. Two blue lines for positive and one blue line for negative. She waited.

She squeezed her eyes shut and prayed. She hadn't prayed in a long time, not since her father had become ill. She had prayed then. Prayed that he would get better, then prayed that he wouldn't suffer any more. She opened her eyes. A single blue line with no shadow of another was showing very clearly. No! She couldn't bear it. She looked at it again. Nothing had changed.

The tears began and so did the sobs. She couldn't control herself, even when she heard someone outside the cubicle. She couldn't stop. It was all so unfair. When the knocking began on the door she tried to calm herself, but her emotions would not be held back and she cried harder for the baby that simply wasn't there.

"I might be able to help," a voice said on the other side of the door. Hayley wanted to scream, "Can you give me a baby?" But that would make her sound as unhinged as she felt.

"Just open the door and we can talk." Coaxed the voice.

Leaning forward she slid the bolt back. Slowly the door swung open and Amanda's concerned face appeared in the gap.

Hayley looked down at her lap. In one hand she held a wad of tear soaked toilet paper and in the other the plastic tester. "I thought this time..." she swallowed a sob. "I really did think that this time..." She held out the test strip and looked up at her supervisor. Knowing that she must seem pathetic, but being unable to control the desperation in her voice, another tear dropped onto the tissue.

"Come on, I can't leave you in here." Amanda led Hayley out of the cubicle and pressed wet paper towels to Hayley's flushed cheeks. "Have you been trying for a baby for long?"

Hayley's mind drifted back to the day she had discovered that there was a serious problem.

The gel had been cold on her stomach. She had dreamt of this scene thousands of times. In her imagination her husband would be by her side, holding her hand as they stared in wonder at the grainy image on the screen.

The nurse gently moved the probe across her lower abdomen. The screen was not in Hayley's line of vision and her husband Neil was not by her side. Muffled echoes came in waves as the nurse continued the sweep across her pale flesh.

"I think we've gathered as much information as we need Mrs Townsend." The feel of coarse paper on her skin was almost brutal after the silky lubricant.

"I'll prepare the report and send it off to the doctor. He'll be in touch to discuss everything with you." The nurse's voice had been crisp and efficient and invited no further conversation.

They had already explained what they were looking for. Polycystic Ovary Syndrome – it sounded like something from a science fiction movie, rather than a hideous barrier between her and pregnancy. The door closed and she was left alone. It was all her fault. She was the defective one. She was the failure. It had been a conscious decision not to tell Neil about the possible diagnosis and subsequent scan. She couldn't bear the inevitable look of pity on his face followed by mock cheeriness as he reassured her that she alone was enough for him.

How could she be enough for him? She wasn't even a fully functioning woman for God's sake. Of course she would have to tell him. As dramatic as it sounded she would have to offer him an escape. Perhaps she should phrase it in terms that he would understand? Being an accountant he would probably accept it when she told him that he had entered into a contract that was based wholly on false representation which contravened the Sale of Goods Act and he would surely be entitled to a full refund and possibly compensation.

Within a week her fears had been confirmed.

"The problem, Mrs Townsend, is that you're just not ovulating regularly. It may be that you ovulate once or twice a year... or not at all. And without that Mrs Townsend..." The doctor lifted his palms skywards. It was a gesture of such futility that Hayley's stomach clenched involuntarily.

"I..i...is it treatable? I..I mean is there a cure?

"We have a few options open to us. None, of course, are guaranteed. There are fertility drugs that we can put you on that stimulate the ovaries to produce eggs. I won't deny, Mrs Townsend, it isn't instant, and with funding the way it is, well..." once again another silent supplication heavenwards.

That had been months ago. Neil had tried his best to reassure her that she was all woman to him, and insisted that she was all he needed. But the emptiness had continued, interrupted only once a month when she allowed hope to dance blithely into her heart. Swept along by her dreams she had become almost addicted to pregnancy testing kits. Sometimes the delicious optimism before the test followed by excruciating despair afterwards made her wonder whether it was another form of self-harming.

Amanda remained silent as Hayley described her experience. When she finished talking Hayley's eyes remained fixed on the floor. She didn't want or need any expressions of polite pity. She felt Amanda's hand gently rest on her shoulder. She looked from the slim fingers, pausing only briefly at the shadows on her wrist, up to Amanda's face. There was no pity in that face, no mock understanding, no superficial sympathy, just raw acceptance of the pain she was going through. There they were – two women each struggling with their very different demons and both a long journey away from the solution. Wordlessly a bond had been made.

25

Marianne

The weekend passed, to Marianne's mind, very frugally. The subject of Jack's precarious job situation was avoided. They went for long walks, and then stayed at home watching the television. Not an unpleasant weekend, she concluded, but one which would have definitely benefitted from a nice meal out.

Monday morning was dull and damp. She watched Jack pull on his work boots, and with them his worries as he trudged out of the door. She couldn't shake off the greyness that shrouded her. The walk to work didn't lift her spirits either. Rain bounced off the pavements, splashing her legs. She could really do with a holiday she thought, as another car sent a deluge of water over her coat.

Charlie was wearing a red carnation in his lapel. He held open the door whilst she shook water from her umbrella.

"Dubai Sunshine, twenty-five to one Miss, that's the winner today." Charlie nodded enthusiastically.

"Sounds excellent to me Charlie. I could do with a bit of Dubai sunshine right now." She looked down at her mud spattered legs. Charlie followed her gaze.

"Don't you worry Miss, I'll bring up some necessities for you in the blink of an eye." Charlie shuffled slowly away to collect her 'necessities'.

On her tea break she had chosen a table furthest away from the others. She slowly stirred the coffee in front of her. Glancing around the cafeteria she dropped the spoon and reached into her purse. She smoothed the crumpled advert out on the flat surface and re-read its offer of an injection of quick cash.

Not wanting to be overheard again she picked up her phone and started towards the Ladies toilets. She slowed her pace as she saw the red haired woman and Amanda leaving. That was all she needed – little Miss perfect in her perfect little world hearing her beg for cash.

Once inside she stopped to listen. Satisfied that she was alone, Marianne perched on a toilet seat and dialled the number.

"Good morning 'Cash today loans', how can I help?" sang a voice at the end of the line.

"Oh, erm hello, I need a loan really quite urgently." Marianne's voice trembled.

"Well, that's what we're here for. Cash today – the clue's in the name." A chuckle at his own joke and then, "So how much would you like?"

"I was hoping to borrow three hundred." She heard the door to the Ladies room open and close. She tucked her feet underneath her so that her shoes couldn't be recognised.

"Let me see now, we just have to run through a few questions..."

Someone was using the cubicle next to hers. Marianne whispered the answers as quietly as she could.

"There's an administration fee of twenty-five pounds and a charge of thirty pounds for every hundred that you borrow which has to be re-paid in two weeks. Is that all clear?"

"Yes, I understand, and the money will be in my account today?" She listened as he chuckled once more.

"That's right – the clue's in the name."

As she crouched on the toilet seat she felt the relief wash over her. Before long she heard the tap being turned on and then the hand dryer began its loud humming. At last the door opened and closed and she was alone once more. She stretched her legs and left the cubicle. Perhaps she deserved a little treat after all that effort she thought as she re-applied her lipstick. Maybe a lovely new perfume, Jack always liked her to smell nice.

26

Amanda

At six thirty in the morning the alarm rang into the still air of the bedroom. David, with military efficiency, rose, showered and was dressed by six fifty. He showed no signs of having a hangover despite the two bottles of wine he had consumed the night before. And she was grateful for his inebriation because that meant that sex was out of the question. She heard him clatter about downstairs as he prepared breakfast. Half a grapefruit, two slices of toast which had to be cut in two – each piece being exactly equal in size and a cup of Columbian coffee. The coffee was something she couldn't scrimp on. He would know immediately.

Finally she heard the front door shut and the tension in her muscles gradually seeped away. She looked up at the right hand corner of the room where the pieces of wallpaper were just slightly mismatched and her thoughts reluctantly rewound to the couple who had excitedly picked up the keys to their new home.

They had met at work. She was a travel consultant fresh from college and he was a business travel adviser for the corporate side of the company. He had made no secret that he was interested in her. In fact she found his growing attention flattering, if a little suffocating.

Everyone said what a fine catch he was. He was charming and good looking, and devoutly Jewish when it suited him or the situation. Her mother and father were delighted that their little girl had made such a match. Very soon after the wedding David told her that he wanted to look after her. He wanted her to give up work and start a family. That wasn't exactly the life she had envisaged for herself, so she tried to put off leaving her job for a short time but his constant cajoling became more and more intense. Eventually she gave in, and made her home her hobby.

Working hard to get the house how she wanted it she stripped walls and painted woodwork. David helped at the weekends but, during the week, she spent from morning until night decorating and dreaming of their rosy future together. After weeks of hard work she was decorating the bedroom – the last room in the house to be done. She was tired and the light was fading. With an aching back she hung the final piece of wallpaper on the top right hand corner of the wall.

She was in the bath when David got home, enjoying the luxury of deep water and bubbles. She heard him climb the stairs and go into the bedroom. Minutes later the bathroom door was flung open. Striding over to the bath he grabbed her arm, dragging her out of the water and into the bedroom.

"What do you see Amanda?" he snarled.

She was shivering with shock and cold. Her arms wrapped round her naked body she stood desperately looking around the room, and then back at him.

"Look, look. Do you see?" He was pointing to the top right hand corner of the room. His finger was trembling and his face was crimson.

"David, you're scaring me. What is it?" Water dripped onto the bare floorboards.

"Look at it, it's all wrong. Any fool can see that." He'd stepped towards the wall and was waving at the joint where the patterns didn't quite match.

"I..I..I'll do it again." She was shaking violently now.

"No, no you won't." He moved towards her, his face just centimetres from hers. "Leave it, but every time you look at it you will remember what a mess you made." He turned and marched out of the room, leaving her naked and, for the first time, terrified of her husband.

Now, as she looked at the flawed decoration which had been her focal point on many a night as her husband made love to her, she realised what a complete mess she had made.

27

Jane

So what if he was taking his wife away? As he said, his weekend with Jane was going to be the real romantic break. Anyway, she'd heard that Rome was so passé these days. Now Barcelona was definitely the place to be for lovers. All the doubts she'd had about him had been swept under the Persian rug in her office.

It was Saturday and the store was busy. She always worked on a Saturday even though she wasn't supposed to. It stopped her from thinking about what he might be doing with his wife in their smart semi-detached on the outskirts of town. She knew where they lived. She had driven past on a number of occasions. Part of her wanted to catch a glimpse of him on his home ground, and part of her felt terrified at the thought. She wasn't sure how she would react to seeing them together. Him casually linking his wife's arm, or his wife laughing up at him and kissing his cheek.

This weekend was different. He wouldn't be there this weekend. He would be in Rome with his wife. The whole idea of the two of them strolling hand in hand through Italian streets, perhaps throwing a coin in the Trevi Fountain made her feel physically sick. She pushed the thoughts away. It would be her turn soon enough.

Passing through the shop she made her way to the public restaurant. She didn't want to sit in the staff canteen amongst the cliques. She might as well feel an outsider here with strangers than in there with colleagues. Her position as assistant manager immediately alienated her from other employees, whilst at the same time not being quite elevated enough for senior management, unless, of course, you were sleeping with them.

From a table in the corner she studied the other diners as they queued for their lunch or a cup of tea and cake. She noticed a familiar figure. Wearing a dapper suit with a pink spotted cravat, Charlie carefully carried a tray with, what appeared to be, afternoon tea. Weaving his way through the tables he eventually stopped by an elderly lady with a tartan shopping trolley by her side. He gently set the tray down and with a flourish shook open a napkin before laying it on her lap.

Jane watched the pair, their heads close together, deep in conversation. Charlie looked twenty years younger, and his companion was giggling at something he had said. It was time for Jane to get back to her duties. Gathering her jacket and bag she couldn't avoid passing Charlie's table. She didn't really want to intrude but Charlie, it seemed, had a different idea.

"Ma'am may I introduce you to Ada?" Charlie stood up and presented his lady friend.

"Ada, I'm very pleased to meet you." Jane shook Ada's hand.

"Ada, this is my boss Jane Farrell, a very lovely lady." Charlie smiled at Jane whilst Ada continued to gently hold Jane's hand.

Jane blushed at the compliment and, after insisting that she wouldn't disturb them any longer, she waved them good bye. I wonder if that will be Tony and I one day she thought as she returned to the Saturday shoppers.

28

Hayley

Hayley's father had died after a long illness, and her mother, Sheila, resided in a care home. Dementia gradually taking over, she was just a shadow of the woman she once was. But Hayley went to see her three times a week. Each time Hayley would patiently explain to her mum who she was and why she was visiting her. She would always get one of two responses depending on what decade Sheila was currently in sync with. If she was in the earlier period the response would be: "Hayley? No I don't know a Hayley. Have you come to see Adam? He's not here I'm afraid. He's out playing football with his friends. He'll be a professional one day you know."

The later period would prompt a different response: "Are you a friend of Adam's? He's in Washington. He's a very important man is Adam. Very important and he's done so well for himself. Such a clever boy he is!"

After repeating who she was, Hayley would eventually see the vague glimmer of recognition. It was always at this point that her mother would tell her about a train journey she was about to embark upon. A journey that would never happen save from in her mother's imagination. And each time Hayley left knowing that the conversation would be exactly the same in a couple of days.

Neil sometimes came with her, but not today. Today he was working on their allotment. It was his dream to be self-sufficient one day. She had, at first, found his thriftiness quite endearing. She didn't any more. Sitting beside her mother, having just finished telling her who she was, a surge of weariness overwhelmed her. She blinked back a tear. Cry is all she had been doing in the last few days. Suddenly Sheila leaned forward, her eyes shining with clarity, and grasped Hayley's hand.

"Is it money you need love?" Her hand tightened over Hayley's.

She stared at her mother, and her heart seemed to miss a beat. "What makes you think that Mum?"

"I can feel your unhappiness dear, and if I can help I will."

The possibility that her mother had managed to put by some savings hadn't occurred to her, not that she would ever have asked.

"In the bottom drawer of the chest you'll find a building society book. Go and get it would you dear?" She released Hayley's hand.

She couldn't believe it. And hope which was never far below the surface leapt in her heart. Underneath thermal vests and bed socks lay a blue book in a transparent plastic wallet. "Do you mean this?" She held the book up.

"Yes love, bring it over."

She handed it to Sheila and resumed her seat. Sliding the book out of its cover and with hands stiff with arthritis Sheila opened it. She was squinting at the pages bringing it close to her eyes and then moving it to arms' length. "Yes, yes I thought so." The book was now being held upside down. "Mmm... yes that should do it." Hayley watched as her mother pretended to read the columns of figures.

"Twelve thousand pounds," she said, handing the book to Hayley.

Hayley looked down at the open pages. Five thousand and seventy-five pounds it read.

"There's actually only five thousand pounds in here, Mum." Hayley's heart was still pounding. Even savings of five thousand pounds would help tremendously.

"Oh, yes of course, well five thousand pounds then. You take it." Sheila lowered her voice, "It'll stop them from getting their thieving hands on it."

Hayley wasn't sure who she was referring to, but her mind quickly moved on to how she was going to persuade Neil to accept the gift and commit to IVF treatment.

She hugged her mother and kissed her soft cheeks. But as she said her goodbyes Hayley could already see the cloud of confusion descending over Sheila's eyes.

"Tell Adam not to come home late. His tea will get cold."

She gently closed the door and tried to dismiss the feeling of uneasiness that tapped away at her conscience. She would take the documentation showing power of attorney to the bank. Once the money was safely in her account then she would tackle Neil.

29

Marianne

She had searched the house for credit card statements. Some she found stuffed into old handbags. Others were marking her place in part read books, or nestled between copies of Harpers' Bazaar. How casually she had treated these documents in the past! Now she had to find them before Jack did and remove them. He was on a mission to 'tidy up' their finances. His favourite phrases were 'tightening their belts' and 'cutting their cloth to suit'. It had been belts and cloth that had got Marianne into so much trouble in the first place. She didn't know where else to look but already she had managed to fill a carrier bag with incriminating evidence of her extravagance.

At work she spread her credit and store cards out on the bench beneath the coat hooks. She had six in total which, judging by the hastily added up figures from the crumpled statements, held a hefty debt of six thousand pounds. That didn't include her overdraft which was always nudging its limit of three thousand pounds. This was serious. She had never really considered money an issue before. Her parents, whilst not being wealthy, always seemed to find the money to buy her the things that she wanted. Her older brothers had also spoilt her with gifts and treats. Looking at the pretty colours of the laminated plastic who would think that they were concealing a secret so damaging that it could wreck her marriage?

"Oh for heaven's sake Marianne, put them away!"

She hadn't heard Amanda come in.

"Is it not enough that you flaunt your purchases around the whole store without thrusting your credit cards in everyone's faces?"

Stung, Marianne opened her mouth to protest.

"You swan in here in your fancy clothes, and ridiculous high heels, throwing your money around. Well it's not funny and it's not clever. I suggest you put those things away and get back to the real world where some people have to work to earn a living!"

Marianne stared at Amanda's retreating back, and winced as the door was slammed shut. She looked down at the brightly coloured plastic scattered on the bench and suddenly she felt very small and very frightened.

30

Amanda

She knew she had been harsh with Marianne the day before. And she also knew that Marianne's spending habits weren't actually anything to do with her. It was just her reckless attitude to money that Amanda struggled to accept or understand. In contrast she had to try and claw back some money from somewhere – her escape fund would probably only get her to the end of the road at the moment. Sliding the hangers along the rail she examined the contents of her wardrobe. Over the years her light, floaty dresses had been swallowed up by more structured items with sleeves and collars. She had kept a few of her mother's clothes. Lifting an old fur coat out, she buried her face in the short, soft hair. She thought she could still smell traces of her mother's perfume on it.

"Your Father, he spent every penny of his wages on that coat. How it hurt him, let me tell you. The money he spent was written on his face every time I wore it. I wore it a lot." Amanda's mother sat on the edge of the bed looking at her.

"Your Aunt Beatrice, God rest her soul, she wanted it. I told her, 'Beatrice,' I said, 'you'd look like a hamster on steroids in this coat. It's not for you.' So she gave me the silent treatment. What a blessing! Your poor Uncle Max, he begged for the silent treatment until the day he died. Sad but true."

"I was thinking of selling some stuff on Ebay, Mum. Try to make a little money." Amanda put the coat back in the wardrobe and bent down to look at the pairs of shoes on the bottom shelf.

"Making a little money is never a bad thing. You're born, you eat soup and then you die. Money makes the soup more interesting."

She never knew where her mother got her sayings and dubious pearls of wisdom from, but they had a strange way of comforting her. Deciding that she definitely had enough clothes in her wardrobe to hide any that she sold, she closed the doors and got ready for work. She just needed to find someone who could tell her how to sell them on Ebay. Perhaps Marianne might know – she was certainly an expert in buying but whether she knew anything about selling was a different matter.

During her walk to work she considered her plan of action. She would try to keep David happy at home; be as compliant as she could and hope that he didn't bring up the subject of her leaving work. Meanwhile, she would continue to think of ways to save more money.

She found Marianne in the perfume hall behind a haze of eau de cologne. As Amanda walked towards her she heard a clatter. Marianne had dropped a crystal bottle onto the counter. She shot a glance in Amanda's direction before stepping away from the display of exotic scents. Was it just guilt Amanda saw in Marianne's expression or was there a fragment of fear? Amanda wasn't sure but she immediately hated herself for making someone feel frightened – she knew that feeling better than most. She gave Marianne what she hoped was a reassuring smile. "I need some advice. Maybe you can help me?"

Marianne frowned and laid her hand on her chest. "You want advice from me?"

"Well, yes, you see I need to sell some things on Ebay and I don't have a clue how to do it." Amanda chewed her nail. This was a new habit she had picked up.

Marianne frowned. "Selling things... mmm... I'm not sure about selling things. I can tell you all about buying things though."

"No, that's not terribly helpful Marianne. I know that you're an expert on buying...sorry that wasn't a dig."

Marianne looked away.

"It doesn't matter, I shouldn't have asked. Forget it." Amanda turned towards the bank of lifts.

"Hang on a minute, my brother can help you. He sells on Ebay all the time. I'll give him a call and ask him to come round to show you." Marianne's smile was short lived as Amanda said sharply, "No, he can't. I mean not to the house."

"Okay, okay, I'm sorry I didn't mean to upset you. I can easily ask him to pop into the store to have a chat."

Smothering her panic she smiled shakily. "Yes, thank you that would be fantastic - it's just that David doesn't like strangers calling." She knew that her answer sounded ridiculous, but she couldn't tell Marianne that she lived with a monster.

31

Jane

She hadn't seen Tony since his weekend away with his wife. Booking an extra day off, he had told the office staff that he needed a rest after his exhausting trip. 'An exhausting trip'. Jane had chewed this phrase over and over until she almost gagged on it. Stay calm and rational, she thought as she paced up and down. He probably meant that he was exhausted after the sight-seeing and all the shops his high maintenance wife dragged him to. Did he mean that, or did he mean he was exhausted after all the romantic dinners and passionate love making?

She felt very vulnerable and alone. She needed to find something else to occupy her mind. Picking up her clip board, she decided to check the shop floor for stock rotation. All the time images of Tony and his wife played like a slide show through her mind. His wife was feeding him ice cream from a long handled spoon and laughing when it dribbled down his chin. Then they were in each other's arms gently swaying to the sound of a violin being played, and so it went on. By the time she reached the sales floor her stomach was in knots and her mouth was dry.

"Good morning Miss Farrell." The red haired shop assistant popped up from behind the pay desk.

"Morning... erm..." Jane cursed silently to herself, trying to summon up the girl's name.

"Hayley, my name's Hayley."

"Of course, yes Hayley. How's everything going down here?" Jane looked over at the displays of sales items, with banners promising massive reductions before the sparkling Summer Launch.

"It's going quite well, we've been busy." Hayley pointed at the half empty racks that she was in the process of re-filling.

"Well that's good. I'm just going to check the stock levels and see what we can move around." She left Hayley hanging more clothes on the depleted racks and went into the stock room. Half an hour later she had assessed which lines to promote in the sale and which ones to hold back on. Studying the figures written on her clipboard she was satisfied that she had done a good job, and felt marginally better for the mental diversion it had afforded. She opened the door to walk back onto the sales floor then froze.

"I'm sure we don't have any more size eight in the pink." Hayley was checking the label of a rich ivory negligee.

"You see the thing is my husband adored it in the ivory – well actually he couldn't get it off me fast enough, but that's another story." The woman smothered a giggle with her well-manicured hand. "And I just thought if I could have the full set in the pink heaven knows what that would do to him. Would you be angel and have a look?" Jane watched as Hayley nodded at Tony's wife and turned to walk towards her. Jane stumbled back into the stock room still clutching her clipboard like it was a shield.

Hayley joined her, but instead of immediately searching for the pink lingerie set she had been asked for, she gently touched Jane's arm. "I'm really sorry you had to hear that."

Jane blindly shook her head. The imaginary slide show began all over again and tears soaked her cheeks. Hayley left and returned minutes later.

"I told her that the line had been discontinued in every colour and sent her away."

Jane saw concern written all over Hayley's face. Somehow Hayley knew about their affair, that much was obvious. "Thank you Hayley." Her tears had stopped but the ache in her heart had only just begun.

32

Hayley

"Thank you, Hayley." Hayley could see that Jane's tears had dried but her usual Ice-Queen facade was nowhere to be seen. She felt useless as she left her boss alone to reflect on all that she had heard. Even though Hayley believed that having an affair with a married man was wrong, she couldn't help but feel that Jane was a victim. It was so obvious that she was desperately in love with Tony, and no doubt he would have ruthlessly led her on, probably promising her the world.

Passing through the toy department she found herself in the baby and toddler section. She ran her hand over the solid pine headboard of a cot, marvelling at the intricate carving of Winnie the Pooh, Piglet and Tigger. She picked up a lilac baby blanket. It was incredibly soft with shiny satin edges. Before she could stop herself she was at the till and the blanket was being carefully wrapped.

"It is lovely isn't it? Is it a gift?" The shop assistant was poised with a silk ribbon in her hand.

"Erm... yes, it's a gift." Hayley watched the assistant expertly tie the ribbon and place the parcel into a gift box. Little blue and pink elephants danced in rows on the lid.

She had been to the bank that lunchtime to pay in her mother's cheque. The money was safely in Hayley's account, ready for her to spend. Now all she had to do was persuade Neil to accept the windfall and agree to begin the emotional journey that IVF is.

Once home she closed the front door quietly behind her and stuffed the gift box in the cupboard under the stairs. It joined several plastic teething rings, a teddy bear and six baby-grows in varying sizes.

"Hello love, is that you?" Neil's voice drifted into the hallway from the kitchen.

"Yes, won't be a second." She hung her coat and bag up and went to join him. He was reading his paper. She sometimes wondered if his paper was his protection from intimate conversation, or any conversation that may involve emotions of any kind.

"I need to talk to you." She pulled out the chair next to him. Slowly he lowered the newspaper and peered at her over his glasses. His expression was one of guarded apprehension. He seemed to always look like that these days.

"If we had five thousand pounds, not borrow it, but actually had it..."

Neil held up his hand. "Hayley I am not going to play the 'what if' scenario all over again."

"No, I mean, I have got it. I have got the five thousand pounds that we need." She held her breath as he absorbed this information.

He blinked several times. "Where have you got it from?"

"It was a gift, so we don't have to repay it or anything. It means we could start IVF straight away." She knew she was gabbling but she couldn't help herself.

"You didn't answer the question love. Where did you get it from?" He folded up his paper and waited.

She couldn't have felt less certain of her ability to persuade him than she did at that moment. "Mum gave it to me." She looked at the floor. She didn't want to meet his gaze. She could feel Neil staring at her. "She did give it to me. She said she wanted to help." Hayley nervously clasped and unclasped her hands. Tiny freckles covered her skin and she noticed a dry patch of eczema was developing between her thumb and forefinger.

"Hayley," Neil reached out to hold her hands. Whether it was a gesture of comfort, or whether it was to stop her from fidgeting she was uncertain. "You and I both know that your mother isn't capable of helping anyone. She just isn't..." He hesitated obviously searching for the correct way to describe her mother. "mentally able." He finished lamely.

"Yes she is. She is and she gave it to me. She definitely told me that she wanted to help if she could." She was on her feet. She could feel the heat from her cheeks and knew she was dangerously close to crying.

"Alright, alright." Neil was on his feet too. His arm wrapped around her shoulders. "I just think we should make sure that everything's above board and that your mother didn't mean for it to be a loan. You know I don't agree with emotional borrowing."

Although she didn't know what his next step would be, she did know that he hadn't completely closed the door on the subject.

33

Marianne

She let herself into the house, almost falling over Jack's boots.

"Hello?" she called as she looked at his high-viz jacket hanging up behind the door.

"Hello honey, I'm in the kitchen." There was nothing in Jack's voice that indicated a happy reason for him being home early. Little thorns of alarm pricked her head as she went into the kitchen. He was sitting at the end of the table, a can of lager opened in front of him.

"Well, cheers." He lifted the can to salute her. "Say hello to Mister Redundant." He tipped his head back and drained the can.

Suddenly she felt five years old. She wasn't grown up enough to deal with this. Her parents had always dealt with her problems and when they couldn't her older brothers had stepped in. And then there was Jack. She had never really had to worry about anything because someone else would always sort it out for her.

She crossed the room and knelt down beside him. He stroked her hair. "They have let five of us go. They're just keeping on a couple to finish off the jobs that we've got." His voice was flat as he continued to stroke her hair.

"Oh Jack, I'm so, so sorry. But you'll get something else won't you?" She looked at him, silently pleading for him to tell her everything would be alright, and he could walk into another job tomorrow. But he didn't. His silence was louder than any refute.

Slowly she stood and took off her designer coat. A purchase she had made only three weeks earlier. She twisted her wedding ring round and round her finger as she watched him. Eventually he rose and put his arms around her, holding her close.

"We'll be alright. We'll just have to sit down, and go through all our bank accounts. We can pool resources and anything we can't pay for with our savings, we can budget for. I'm sure we can get by. It's not as though we've got massive debts to repay."

The words which he meant to be re-assuring made her feel dizzy with fear. He couldn't find out that her credit cards held nothing but debt. Her savings account was, by definition, an anomaly and that was before she even considered her store cards. How was she going to get out of this terrible predicament before he checked her statements?

34

Amanda

She had been free of bruises for a couple of weeks now, and David seemed to appreciate the new compliant wife that greeted him at the door every evening. The new wife who succumbed to his advances with quiet dignity. Not that she had ever been rebellious or defiant, but she had always found it difficult to quell her natural spirit when it came to his constant and unreasonable demands for her attention. Now she had a plan. That was all she focused on to get her through her domestic life.

She swept her eyes over the late afternoon shoppers, looking for a tall blond man. According to Marianne her brother was a dead ringer for Daniel Craig. Marianne was very proud of her brothers, so whether this glowing compliment was slightly misguided, she wasn't sure. She smiled politely at the woman in front of her who was jabbing her pin number into the credit card machine.

"Is the receipt alright in the bag?" Amanda stood poised with the receipt in her hand hovering over the mouth of the bag. It was obviously a tricky decision for the woman to make as she stopped to consider the question. Amanda gazed over the woman's shoulder as she waited. Then she saw him. He did have a vague resemblance to Daniel Craig. It really was only vague. He was talking to another shop assistant who was pointing in Amanda's direction. He looked over and smiled. There was a flutter. It was tiny, almost inconsequential, but it was there. He was striding towards her, the woman in front of Amanda forgotten.

"Hello Amanda, I'm Sam, Marianne's brother." He held out his hand. Amanda realised that she still held the woman's receipt in her hand. She quickly dropped it into the bag, having not heard what the final decision had been on where it should be lodged. Thrusting the bag at the woman she took Sam's hand and warmly shook it, perhaps for a little longer than was necessary.

"Hi Sam." She studied his face as she held on to his hand. He didn't look at all like Marianne. He was fair as Marianne was dark. She finally released his hand.

"So you need expert advice on how to sell on Ebay do you?"

"Yes I'm absolutely clueless when it comes to technology. I just wouldn't know where to begin." The flutter was still there.

"Well I'm you're man." He smiled.

Yes you are she thought, before silently admonishing herself.

"We could meet up sometime this week if you like?"

"What about tomorrow lunchtime, say one o'clock? We could go for a coffee and I can try to explain what I want to do?... I mean with regards to selling on Ebay is what I mean." She tidied the already tidy pile of bags on the counter.

"That sounds great. I'll see you tomorrow. I'll be waiting for you in the store cafe."

She watched him walk away and was still watching even when he could no longer be seen. What was this? The flutter grew.

35

Jane

The room grew cold. Daylight had long since disappeared and yet Jane still didn't turn on the lights. She had stayed at home after calling in sick. She reasoned that in part, it was perfectly true. She was sick – mentally sick. There had been three messages on her answering machine, and five missed calls on her mobile. The messages all asked the same question, only the tone of voice changed.

"Hi Janey, I've missed you. I'll try you again later." Message one.

"Hi Janey, where are you? I've been trying to reach you all day. Are you avoiding me?" Message two.

"Hi Jane, obviously you're very busy. Maybe you can fit a chat in tomorrow if your schedule allows." Third and final message before Tony settled down with his wife for the evening she presumed.

She poured another glass of wine. Stupid, she thought to herself as she swallowed the ruby liquid. She stared at the blank television screen. She didn't need to turn it on. She was already a voyeur of a love triangle together with all the drama that that entailed. As though driven by an unknown entity she had, after leaving the stockroom, followed Tony's wife to the house wares department. Crouching behind scatter cushions and fur throws Jane had spied on her.

She watched her examining an exquisite set of crystal, before she ordered the staff to wrap it and charge it to her account. Perhaps, Jane guessed, they were going to celebrate the end of their second honeymoon with a glass of champagne from new flutes. How delightful, she thought as she ground her teeth. When

Jane saw her finally heading for the exit she was sorely tempted to follow once more but resisted. She still had some pride, not much, but some.

Now sitting alone in her small apartment, she tried desperately to harness the fighting spirit she had found the last time she had tried to escape her relationship with Tony. It was nowhere to be seen. Instead, self-pity whined in her ear. Why are you always alone Jane? Why do you always have to play second best? Is it because that's all you are and ever will be? Is she better than you? Is she? Is she? Is she? Jane clamped her hands over her ears to block out the whispering.

"No." She spoke into the empty room. "No she isn't better than me, and I'll prove it to him. I'll go to Barcelona and show him that I am the one for him. That's all I need, some time for just the two of us. We'll come home and he'll end it with his wife, because he will have realised that I am the one he wants. She knocked back the dregs of wine in her glass and rose unsteadily to her feet. I am not second best she told herself as she climbed into her cold lonely bed.

36

Hayley

By the side of the door was an intercom system. It guarded the entrance to the care home with a tinny voice and static crackling.

"It's Hayley Townsend to see my mum." She released the button and waited to be buzzed in.

"Have they not let you in yet?" Neil joined her, having parked the car round the rear of the building.

She shook her head and waited. Finally the locking mechanism clicked and she pushed open the door.

"Evening Mary." Hayley waved to a plump girl in a light blue uniform. Usually Mary would greet them enthusiastically before launching into an up-date about her fiancé and their wedding plans. Plans which she seemed to have been making for years. But not tonight. There was no trace of a smile on Mary's round face. Her eyes darted everywhere, never settling on Hayley or Neil. Alarm bells began to ring in her head.

"Is everything alright Mary? Is Mum alright?"

Mary marched on ahead. Her only response was a slight shrug of her wide shoulders. As they reached the door to Sheila's room Mary stopped.

"You'll find Mrs Westland is in with your mum. There's been an incident."

Before she could ask what she was talking about Mary had shoved open the door.

Mrs Westland, the care home manager, sat on the left of Sheila's chair. Sheila was staring ahead whilst plucking invisible bits of cotton from her dressing gown.

Hayley rushed to her mother's side. "W..w..what's the matter? Mum, are you alright?" Her heart was pounding as she watched Mrs Westland get to her feet.

"Mrs Townsend, something very serious has happened, and I'm afraid I've had no option but to call the police." No friendly 'Hayley', suddenly she was Mrs Townsend.

"The police? I don't understand." She looked from Mrs Westland to her mother and back again.

Neil, who had been standing silently by the door, stepped forward. "What's going on? What's this all about?"

Mrs Westland puffed her bony chest out and turned to look at Neil. "Money has gone missing, Mr Townsend. That is what this is all about. Sheila received her bank statement today and someone..." At this point Mrs Westland shifted her gaze to Hayley. "...has withdrawn money from her account."

"I don't know how it could have happened." Sheila's frail voice quivered. She was now pulling agitatedly at the blanket over her lap.

"Oh Mum!" Hayley knelt down by her mother's side and took her hand. "It was me, I took the money. You said you wanted to help, and you told me to take it."

Sheila looked down at Hayley's hand holding hers, and then slowly shook her head. "Why would you take my money? I need that money." Her voice steadier now, "I'm saving up, you know, for a train journey."

Hayley sat back on her haunches, unable to believe what she was hearing.

"So you admit taking it then?" Mrs Westland's eyes were bulging and her head was bobbing up and down. "It's been terrible. My girls have been worried to death over this. We have a reputation to maintain Mrs Townsend, and staff are hard to keep as it is."

She struggled to her feet as all eyes watched. "My mum did give it to me. I didn't just take it." She looked pleadingly at Neil who had not uttered a sound. She spun round. "You must remember Mum. You said you wanted to help." She could feel sweat on her upper lip and her scalp tingled as though tiny charges of electricity were being shot through it.

"I'm going on a train journey. I'm going to see Adam." Sheila nodded at no-one in particular.

She knew it was no good. Her mother either couldn't remember or refused to remember. Without realising she began scratching at the patch of eczema between her thumb and forefinger.

Neil took Hayley's elbow and turned to Mrs Westland. "I'm really sorry for the mix up Mrs Westland, and for all the worry. We'll put the money back immediately won't we Hayley?"

Hayley stared blankly at her husband. He was taking her chance away again.

"Well I'm not sure what the police will have to say, but I'll discuss it with Sheila when she's had some rest." After giving a meaningful look to Hayley she bustled out of the room.

"So how are you darling, you're looking a little tired?" Sheila was smiling brightly. She had stopped pulling at the blanket and Hayley had stopped hoping.

37

Marianne

Her salary would be going into her account in a few days, but already her overdraft would swallow that up and more. There was no way she could try and make her bank statements look healthy. As far as she was concerned they were terminally ill, and the last rites had been given. She had to think of a way of injecting a lump sum of cash into her finances to reflect a bottom line that wasn't too dire, whilst shoring the whole thing up by increasing her earning capacity. When it was said like that it all sounded quite simple she thought, as she quietly closed the front door. She had left Jack sleeping after a restless night.

Eric Mountford, Marianne's next door neighbour, was already out in his front garden, sweeping the path.

"Morning Eric." She waved as she passed him hunched over his sweeping brush.

"Good morning Marianne. How's you and your big man there." He straightened up and nodded towards the house. He had obviously noticed that Jack hadn't gone to work, but then that didn't surprise her because between him and his wife Joyce they noticed just about everything that happened on the street.

"Fine thanks, we're just fine." She smiled a tight smile. There was something unsettling about Eric. The string vest and three hair comb-over didn't help, but there was definitely something she didn't like. Not wanting to waste any more time on pleasantries that weren't pleasant, she hurried out of the gate and on down the road.

She had to think of a way to supplement her income. The first thing, she decided, was to arrange another pay-day loan, even though her payday was imminent. She might be able to convince Jack, temporarily, that she was actually in the black rather than the crimson her current status was draped in. By the time she reached the store she had made her mind up to approach Jane and ask her for some extra hours.

Charlie was almost spritely as he got to his feet when she stepped through the door. She thought his eyes seemed brighter, and he had taken to wearing a flower in his lapel. Today he was wearing a yellow rose.

"You're looking very smart Charlie." She smiled as colour infused his papery skin.

"Thank you Miss." He lifted the rose to his nostrils and took a deep breath. "The smell of fresh flowers costs so little but lasts as long as a memory."

She knew she shouldn't have bought that perfume. Perhaps he was trying to tell her something.

"Elegant Girl," he continued, still taking in the scent of the yellow bud.

It was her turn to blush. "Why thank you Charlie."

Charlie looked up, frowning. "No, Elegant Girl, nine to one at Kempton Park."

She really should be used to Charlie's cryptic racing tips by now. She left Charlie as he settled down on his wooden chair and went straight up to Jane's office.

Standing outside with her hand poised to knock, she remembered how Jane had looked at her the last time she had been here. To say she had been cool would be an understatement. Still, she had nothing to lose. She squared her shoulders and knocked firmly on the door.

"Yes?" The reply was a little muffled she thought as she pushed open the door.

"Hello Miss Farrell. I'm sorry to bother you." Marianne took a few cautious steps towards Jane's desk.

"What can I do for you?" Jane pressed her finger tips to her temple and looked at Marianne with blood shot eyes.

"Well, I was wondering if there was any chance of working more hours. I could really do with some extra cash you see." Her hands were clammy. Jane seemed to be staring straight through her. Marianne waited.

"Sorry what did you say?" Jane appeared to have re-focused.

This was clearly not a good time to be asking for anything. She pictured Jack sitting at the kitchen table studying her bank statements and pressed on.

"I was asking if there was any overtime available as I could really do with the extra money."

There was no hesitation, not even a breath had been taken when Jane replied. "No, I'm afraid not. I can't offer you any." No explanation was forthcoming and Jane went back to studying the paperwork on her desk. With the interview clearly over Marianne left the office without another word. She knew others had been given overtime. What had she done to upset the woman? She trudged back down to the staff room, her footsteps as heavy as her heart.

All morning she turned the problem over and over in her head. By lunch time she was still no nearer finding the solution. Amanda had almost skipped off to meet Sam and so she made her way to the staff canteen alone.

As she finished her lunch, she glanced through the morning's paper which, as usual, had been left on one of the tables gathering coffee rings and gritty with sugar.

'Adult Chat Line Operator Required. Applicants must be over 18 and open minded. Must have access to landline or mobile. Hours are flexible to suit. Up to eighteen pounds per hour.'

She stirred her coffee thoughtfully then re-read the advert. Could she really talk dirty to complete strangers? It was fun whispering her fantasies to Jack as they made love. That was one thing, but to pretend that she was turned on by another man on the other end of a telephone line was crazy. Eighteen pounds an hour wasn't crazy though. The canteen was almost empty. She rang the number.

A few seconds later she was listening to the instructions a cheery character on the end of the phone was giving her. "... so you see, the longer you keep them on the phone the better. You'll get the hang of it. Just remember an extra minute of pleasure for them is a few more quid in the pocket for you."

"And I just have to log on with my pin number and the calls will come through to my mobile?"

"Exactly, we will need you to email your application and photo I.D. and then we can get started."

It all seemed easy enough. It was only chatting to people after all. What harm could it do?

38

Amanda

He stood when she reached the table. It was a small but charming gesture and the flutter grew. He gently explained the ins and outs of selling on Ebay. She felt sure it was probably very easy, had she been listening to a word he said. But she just found herself watching the way his lips moved. The way his eyes crinkled at the corners when he smiled, which he did a lot.

"... and when you take the photographs, make sure the items are on a plain surface, or against a blank wall, okay?"

Amanda dragged her attention away from his face, hair and broad shoulders and tried to concentrate on what he was saying. "Photographs, which photographs are these then?"

"The photographs that you're going to take with your digital camera of the stuff you want to sell." He smiled encouragingly at her.

"Yes, well no, you see I don't have a digital camera, and even if I did I'm not very good at taking photos." She felt she had fallen at the very first hurdle, and he was going to think that she really was an idiot. He cocked his head on one side as if considering whether she was telling the truth. She could guess what he was thinking. Could she possibly be the only person in the world who didn't own a digital camera? And her phone was so old it was almost antique. As David always told her she only needed it to speak to him.

"Don't worry, I can lend you mine, or better still I'll take the photos for you."

Hope was immediately crushed by terror as this would mean Sam coming to the house. The risk of David suddenly coming home was too horrible to contemplate. She couldn't imagine what he would do to her if he found her with a man in the house.

She realised that she hadn't responded to his suggestion. "Thank you that's a very kind offer, but it's okay I'll sort something out. It's about time I caught up with technology anyway. I'll probably treat myself to a camera." She said this knowing that the last thing she would be spending her hard earned money on was a camera. Her plan to raise money had been dashed.

Of course she would have needed a camera. How foolish she was. How on earth did she expect to sell anything without having a picture of it? She chewed on her nail, as her mind's eye strayed to the top right hand corner of her bedroom wall.

"Amanda," he said softly. "We could always take the pictures here, and maybe we could make it truly professional and use some of the mannequins?"

Hope soared again and without thinking she reached out and touched his hand. "Thank you Sam."

"It's not a problem. Here's my number, give me a call when you're ready." He rose to his feet and held out his hand. She shook it once again, and reluctantly let it go. Just as she had before, she watched him leave, and continued to watch the space that he had filled long after he'd gone.

"He seems nice, but not Jewish." Her mother sat where he had been sitting moments earlier. "He's got good teeth and his nails are clean. That's always a good sign. Your Uncle Max's nails were always clean. We never knew about your Aunt Beatrice's, God rest her soul, they were always painted red like a common strumpet." Her Mother sat back in her chair nodding confirmation of the condition of Aunt Beatrice's outrageous nails. Amanda shook her head to clear it. She went back to the shop floor desperately trying not to think of the next time she would see Sam, but failing miserably. The flutter continued to grow.

39

Jane

Overtime! Who did she think she was? She minces in here batting her eye lashes, thinking she can get whatever she wants from whoever she asks. Jane fumed as her head pounded and her stomach echoed the complaint. She shouldn't have drunk the rest of the bottle. Wine was not the answer to her problems. Having said that, she had already decanted a bottle for tonight.

She could have given Marianne overtime, if she had wanted to. There was always some available. Perhaps she had been too hard on the girl. A hangover together with a large dose of insecurity may have influenced her decision. That really wasn't very professional of her she thought, as she popped another painkiller into her mouth – a necessity Charlie had provided.

She turned her attention back to the magazine she had hastily hidden beneath papers on her desk. 'The Hidden Gems of Barcelona', the headline curved over pictures of candlelit restaurants and bars that graced Las Ramblas. Historical museums jostled for position with ornate fountains. She leant back in her chair and closed her eyes. She could see them now. Tony, with his arm wrapped around her waist, strolling through the crowds, looking every inch the infatuated lovers that they were. Over the weekend he would fall deeper and deeper in love with her. He would stare into her eyes and confess his unwavering adoration. He would see what a sham his marriage had become and promise to make a clean break... she drifted off, deep in dreams of what her weekend with him would bring. The phone vibrating noisily against the wooden desk top jolted her out of her reverie.

"Hello?" She rubbed her eyes.

"Oh so you are alive then, and able to take calls?" Tony's voice was more than just a little sulky.

"I've been having signal problems that's all," she lied. "Anyway I didn't think you would have the time or the energy to miss me after the exhausting weekend with your wife." She hadn't planned to say anything about his 'second honeymoon' but, as so often happened these days, she couldn't help herself.

"Well yes it was exhausting actually. She dragged me round shop after over-priced shop. We waited for hours in restaurants to be served food that wouldn't feed a flea. Then to top it all we were delayed coming home which is why I had to book extra time off." He certainly did sound disgruntled, Jane thought as she digested this information. Then she remembered his wife giggling as she discussed Tony's passionate response to the provocative negligee.

"And there was me thinking that you might have fallen in love with your wife all over again, and completely forgotten me." She had wanted to sound playful. Instead she knew she sounded desperate. Stupid Jane, when would she ever learn to keep her mouth shut?

"Oh come on Janey, you know that's never going to happen." The sulkiness had disappeared from his voice. "Anyway how could I ever forget about you, when all I've thought about is our weekend away?" He laughed.

She sighed and for the first time in five days the taut muscles in her neck and shoulders relaxed.

"Listen I'm at head office this morning, but I'll catch up with you later and we can make plans." He blew a kiss and then hung up. She slowly put the phone back on the desk before it suddenly buzzed again. She snatched it up. He had forgotten to say 'I love you', she thought, as she huskily answered the call. "Hello, did you forget to tell me something, you naughty man?" "Hello darling, quite clearly you were expecting another caller."

Her smile froze. "Oh, Hi Mum, how are you? Sorry I thought you were someone else." Her mother always seemed to know when anything was happening in her life. She wasn't sure whether that was just instinct or an uncanny knack of tuning into Jane's emotions.

"Anyone interesting?" Her mother pressed on. Up to now Jane had avoided mentioning anything about Tony, knowing that it would be met with strong disapproval. With her parents living in the country and rarely visiting the city it had been easy to sidestep any awkward enquiries over the phone.

"No Mum, no-one interesting." She hated lying, but hopefully when Tony truly belonged to her she could introduce them and they too would love him, and forgive them both.

"Oh that's a pity. Anyway darling, I'm just ringing to let you know that we want to come over to see you at the weekend."

Her heart quickened. "This weekend? That could be difficult mum, I won't be here." Of all the weekends they chose, it was when she would be away with Tony. She silently cursed.

"Oh, where are you going?" She heard the disappointment in her mother's voice.

"The thing is Mum, I'm going away with erm... the girls, and it's been planned for ages. Could we re-arrange for the following weekend do you think?" It was ridiculous. She was a grown woman and having to lie to her parents about a romantic weekend away.

"That sounds lovely Jane. Fancy you going away with the girls, how exciting." Her mother seemed delighted that her daughter had finally got some sort of social agenda developing, and happily agreed to put their visit off for a week.

Relieved, Jane said goodbye. She looked at the photograph on her desk and her parents smiled proudly back at her. She felt ashamed and more than a little uneasy.

40

Hayley

The journey home had been a quiet one. Neil seemed determined to stay focused on the road ahead, whilst Hayley couldn't bear to look at him let alone speak to him. He had led her out of the care home like a naughty school girl, telling her they would talk about it when they got home. She didn't want to talk about it. What was there to say? You stole from your own mother to fund treatment to become a mother yourself. She could hear his words already.

The silence continued as they entered the house, each falling into their usual routines. Neil picked up the evening paper lying on the mat and flicked through it. She filled the kettle and put the breakfast dishes away. Both seemingly delaying the moment when they had to sit down and talk.

Neil was the first to sit. "Hayley, we need to discuss what happened today."

She felt exhausted and the last thing she wanted to do was discuss what had happened. If he was going to give her a lecture maybe she should just let him get on with it. She slowly sat down across the table and folded her hands in her lap, trying not to scratch at the tender skin between her forefinger and thumb.

"I love you Hayley. You are enough for me. Of course a family would be great, but I don't need a family. I know you think I'm being intentionally obstructive. But I just can't watch you go through all the heartache for, perhaps nothing." He held his hands out to her and his eyes were wet with tears. "I watch you squirrel baby things away and I hide behind my paper. I don't want you to see how it breaks my heart to know you want something so badly and I can't do anything about it. Don't hate me for that."

She looked at his thinning hair and the lines on his face. It was a face that she had loved for so long. They had met ten years earlier at the estate agents where she then worked. He was looking for a bachelor pad but ended up buying their little terraced house. Negotiations for both her and the house had been steady and methodical. The courtship had been comforting in its predictability. Perhaps she should try to concentrate on her relationship with Neil and bury her desire for a family once and for all. She took his hands in hers and tried very hard to suppress the feeling of despair that was threatening to suffocate her. There had to be another way.

The morning arrived with no comfort or solution and with eyes as red as her hair she left for work.

41

Marianne

Both her salary and another payday loan had gone into her account, and she had called at the cash point on her way home to get a print out – before the money all went out again. For a few hours her account looked as though it might have had a second lease of life. Tomorrow it would, once more, be in intensive care.

Sitting on the bed whilst Jack was downstairs, scouring the newspaper for jobs, she smoothed out the folded statement. Whether Jack would ask for any more information she didn't know. She would have to blame her abysmal filing system for not being able to find anything else to show her financial situation. She just needed to buy time, which was ironic since buying had been her downfall in the first place.

When she joined Jack in the kitchen she slipped her single bank statement in amongst his which were scattered over the table.

"I'll just leave my bank stuff here with yours." She pushed it deeper into the pile.

"Okay, thanks love. I'll go through them later." His attention hadn't strayed from circling potential employment opportunities.

She looked at his head bent over the newspaper. His tongue had crept out of his mouth as he concentrated on his task in hand. She felt a surge of love for him that almost overwhelmed her. Rushing round the table she hugged his neck fiercely.

"Hey, we'll be alright, don't worry." He stroked her arms as she held on to him. The chat line company had accepted her application and she had received her pin number. He might be Mister Redundant but say hello to Miss Whiplash she thought ruefully.

42

Amanda

Hayley had left work early, explaining to Amanda that she was going to visit her mum. Amanda was glad that she had Marianne to herself as they went down the stairs and out into the fresh air. The weather was getting warmer and the world just seemed a brighter place.

She waited as Marianne keyed in her pin number at the cash point and collected a print out, then they fell into step together. She was desperate to ask Marianne about Sam, but she didn't want it to look like anything other than general curiosity. That is, after all, exactly what it was – general curiosity.

"So Sam was very helpful today, you know with the Ebay thing?" Just saying his name made her blush so she pretended to be absorbed in the window display of the shop they were passing.

"Yes, he's a star isn't he?"

She knew how proud Marianne was of her brothers but the affection in her voice made Amanda's throat constrict. Being an only child she had never experienced the love and closeness of siblings, and she had never been more lonely than she was right now.

"He's one of those annoying people who's good at everything. He always knows what to say and when to say it. Everybody loves him," Marianne said wistfully.

Yes, Amanda thought, she could completely understand that. "I suppose his wife must count her lucky stars." She knew this was almost probing, but she had to know if he was married. A little voice popped into her head, 'but why do you need to know Amanda? After all it is only general curiosity isn't it?'

"His wife? No, our Sam's not married. He has a great social life mind you, but never settled down. I don't think he's ever met the right one."

Marianne's words stirred the fluttering in Amanda's stomach and she couldn't trust herself to ask any more. They walked on in silence before each going their separate ways.

Amanda began to roll out the pastry. A casserole of steak and kidney was bubbling away in the oven. At least David would be happy with her domestic efforts she thought as she flicked the radio on. A love song floated into the kitchen and she couldn't help singing along. The lyrics seemed to echo the 'general curiosity' she felt about Sam.

She wasn't sure how long he had been standing there. Stopping dead in her tracks she dropped the rolling pin onto the pastry causing a dent in the dough's smooth surface. She stared at it. It was as soft as flesh she thought as she tried to detach herself from the scene.

"You seem in a very good mood. Did something nice happen to you today Amanda?"

He had swallowed up the distance between them and was whispering in her ear. His hot breath made the hairs on her neck stand on end. His voice wasn't full of polite enquiry. It held menace in every syllable. His face was still next to hers, poised for her answer.

She had to say the right thing, with exactly the right tone, and in exactly the right casual manner. Without looking up she pressed the dough gently with her fingers, tracing the dent the rolling pin had made. "No, nothing particularly nice has happened today. I'm just happy to be home, making dinner for you."

His face moved even closer to hers. He inhaled the scent of her hair. Her nails sank into the flaccid pastry.

"Well isn't that just lovely." His fingers began to caress her shoulder then they slithered under her hair and began stroking the back of her neck. Her teeth clamped down on her bottom lip as she suppressed the urge to scream.

"You wouldn't be hiding anything from me would you, my sweet Amanda?" His lips pressed against her cheek, then his mouth opened and she could feel his teeth grazing her skin as though he was going to take a bite. She daren't speak for fear of the tremble in her voice giving her away.

David's hand slid over hers. His fingers pressed down until she thought her knuckles would shatter. Instinctively the fingers of her free hand curled around the rolling pin. Suddenly with a final nip to her cheek he moved away releasing her. She looked down at the deep imprint of her own palm in the pale dough and her hand dropped away from the rolling pin. Not yet, she thought.

She heard him leave the house. She didn't know where, and she didn't care. She was glad.

"I won't be late so make sure you're not asleep when I get back. Be ready for me Amanda," he had called over his shoulder as he left.

Her hand throbbed. Already the skin was changing colour. She picked up the pastry and threw it in the bin.

"So, baking's overrated. Everyone knows that. Your Aunt Beatrice, God rest her soul, she couldn't bake to save her life, but when you go into a marriage with that as your main asset..." With palms up to the heavens her mother sadly shook her head. "Your poor Uncle Max broke his heart on their wedding night, and his teeth on your Aunt Beatrice's Babka. A cook in the kitchen and a whore in the bedroom she was not, no matter what her wardrobe said. But what can I tell you?"

Amanda pressed cotton wool soaked in Witch Hazel against her tender skin. She had to stop the bruising somehow.

"Maybe you should take up potholing? It's inexpensive. You just need a torch and a hole, so what's so difficult?"

"Why potholing, Mum? You know I don't like feeling trapped."

"Trapped here. Trapped underground. What's the difference?"

Being trapped underground in cold damp caverns sounded infinitely better than being trapped here waiting for David to return. Her mother had a point.

She mounted the stairs as though they led to the gallows. After changing into pyjamas and brushing her hair, she climbed into bed. Her eyes drawn, as always, to the top right hand corner of the room. She waited, as she had been told to do, trying not to let her thoughts wander to Sam. David would know.

43

Jane

All week she had been feeling sick with excitement. She had barely slept. When she did finally drift off she seemed to be searching for Tony all the time. Just catching a glimpse of him as he turned a corner out of sight. She would run as fast as she could along marshmallow pavements to catch up with him but then, when she reached the corner, he had gone.

She had packed, unpacked and packed again. She wanted to show him that she could travel light with her capsule wardrobe. She felt sure that his wife, being extremely high maintenance, would have half a dozen suitcases brimming with expensive clothes, shoes and artificial enhancements. Not her, no, she was going to be carefree and frivolous with just a few well-chosen items which would endorse the natural beauty image that she was trying to convey. Well, perhaps a couple of killer heels, and that padded bra did look better with her new dress, and as for the false lash effect mascara, not to mention…

She only had two more days to wait. He had booked the sky bar at the airport so they could have complimentary drinks in luxury, away from the hustle and bustle of the crowds. She had never travelled as an executive passenger before, but she was determined to show that she was not intimidated by it. She would stride in as though she owned the place oozing confidence. After all it was the treatment that she both expected and deserved. Her stomach flipped again. She hadn't been able to shake off the bug that had been troubling her for the last couple of weeks. She would call at the chemists on the way to work. It wouldn't do any harm to buy some anti-travel sickness tablets, just in case.

The bell rang as she opened the door and she joined the queue of people waiting for the pharmacist. An elderly gentleman holding a Yorkshire terrier stood in front of her, and in front of him stood Ada with her tartan shopping trolley.

"Hello Ada." Jane waved from behind the Yorkshire terrier.

"Hello Jane, how lovely to see you. You look positively blooming my dear." Ada stepped out from her place in the queue to join Jane. "My Charlie's always talking about you."

So it's 'my Charlie' now she thought as she looked into Ada's blue eyes. "That's very sweet, I'm not sure if I deserve it mind you."

The queue shuffled forward as the man and his Yorkshire terrier were seen to.

"He's very fond of you. He's not sure about that Mr Pickle fellow though. Charlie's a very good judge of character." Ada smiled and patted Jane's arm. "He follows his hunches, and he's rarely wrong."

"Do you mean Mr Pickard?"

Ada nodded slowly. "He's rarely wrong I tell you." She winked and suddenly the years fell away and Jane felt as though she was looking at a teenager in the first throws of romance. It actually made her own romance with Tony look quite jaded in comparison.

The pharmacist called for the next customer.

"You go first, I've got all the time in the world." Ada gently pushed her forward.

"Thank you Ada." Stopping momentarily she turned and kissed Ada's cheek before moving to the counter.

Jane explained how she had picked up a bug and the symptoms it had caused. The chemist listened intently to every word. Finishing her list of complaints, she was surprised when she was asked to step into the private consulting room.

"So Miss Farrell, I have to ask this first just in order to rule it out, but when was your last period?"

44

Hayley

Her throat ached from hours of stifling tears. On her first break Hayley went to the bank as she had promised she would. She took one last look at the balance on her statement.

"Next." A bored looking girl leant towards the glass screen in front of her and waved Hayley forwards. She didn't want to move. She wanted to keep the money that her mother had given to her. It wasn't that she felt her mother owed her some sort of recompense for the care she had given both of her parents, but she knew that her mother, over the years, had sent large sums of money to her brother in America. Hayley however, had never asked for a penny.

"Next!" The girl was now standing with her face almost pressed against the glass.

Slowly Hayley went to the till and slid her card through to the cashier whose lips had tightened into a thin line. At least, Hayley thought, the girl didn't look bored any more. Just really cross. "I'd like to transfer five thousand pounds into my mother's account." Hayley's voice sounded course and low. She tried to swallow the pain away as she dropped her mother's bank details into the metal tray beneath the security screen.

The girl's fingers flew across the keyboard before she shoved the card and bank details back across the counter at Hayley.

"Anything else I can help you with today Mrs Townsend?" The sentiment of the words that were spoken did not match the tone which was used. The tone would be more suited to, 'Don't ever come to my till again you dozy mare!'

"No, I won't...I mean no thank you." Hayley left the bank five thousand pounds lighter but immeasurably heavier in her heart than when she went in.

She couldn't see any other opportunity of raising enough money for fertility treatment. She had just slid the last chance she had of having a baby under a glass screen to a disgruntled bank clerk.

45

Marianne

Sam had asked Marianne to leave a note in Amanda's locker. She didn't know why she felt uneasy about it. Perhaps it was the way Sam had smiled as he handed her the paper. It was a smile full of meaning, not just a casual 'thanks for doing me a run of the mill favour' kind of smile. She knew it was just about the Ebay thing, but even so the feeling of being a reluctant conspirator to something dubious persisted. And Amanda's cheerful willingness to allow her to take an early lunch break compounded her concern. Trying to dismiss her worries she worked through the morning.

By lunchtime she was once more perched on the toilet seat. The Ladies toilets were empty and she had carefully locked the cubicle door. The chat-line company had allocated her a prime-time telephone number which had been diverted to her mobile phone. It had all sounded very slick and professional as the woman explained how it worked. Once registered all she had to do was log onto her account, and her status would be shown as available for callers.

With hands shaking she logged onto her account and waited. She had no idea how she was even going to begin a conversation with her clients. Should she go straight in at the deep end with, "Hello big boy what can I do for you?", or should she play it cool and sophisticated. Perhaps she should put on a foreign accent, French always sounded sexy. Her phone rang at exactly the same time as the washroom door banged open and footsteps echoed round the tiled room. She had no choice but to answer the call – this was money.

"Ello, and ow are you?" She breathed down the phone in her best French accent.

"Are you Welsh?" a gruff voice enquired from the other end of the line.

"Er well no, I was doing a French accent actually."

"Blimey love, you need to practise that," the voice continued.

"I'm sorry, it's my first time you see, and I don't quite know what to expect." Her face was hot and she could tell that the silence outside the cubicle meant someone was listening.

"So, you're a chat line virgin are you? I like it!" A dirty laugh followed.

She felt sick. She couldn't do it, she just couldn't. She hung up.

"Excuse me." There was a hesitant knock on the door. "I've been asked to get all the floor staff together for a meeting about the Summer Launch. Could you come to women's wear as soon as you can?"

Marianne unlocked the door and stepped out to find the red haired assistant scratching the skin on her hand. "Right, yes thanks I'll be there in a minute... er ...?"

"Hayley."

"Yes Hayley, thanks." Marianne saw that Hayley's hand had started to bleed. She was just about to say something when her phone began to ring again. Both women looked at the vibrating handset.

"Aren't you going to answer that?"

46

Amanda

There was no hiding her bruised hand. She had applied enough witch hazel to fill a bath but still the purple hues stubbornly remained. She pulled her sleeves down over her knuckles before she pushed open the door. Charlie's chair was empty.

"Charlie? Charlie, are you there?" She had never known Charlie to take a day off. But then she heard his doddering footsteps.

"Sorry Miss, had to get a few necessities for myself." He began to cough. A cough that shook his whole body. He wiped his mouth before easing himself into his seat.

"On the way out." He nodded slowly.

"No, no I'm sure you're not." She ran over to him and knelt down beside him.

"No. On The Way Out, ten to one at Kempton." He pulled the Racing Post out of his inside pocket and jabbed his finger at the front page.

"Oh, I see." She got to her feet. He had seemed so jaunty over the last few days it was unsettling to see him looking frail once again. She left him studying columns of figures and went into the cosmetics hall. She needed industrial strength foundation to cover her skin. That was a necessity Charlie wouldn't think of providing. After smothering her hand in beige liquid that promised a 'flawless glow that would last as long as her partying,' she went to the staff room.

Jutting out of her pigeon hole was a neatly folded piece of paper. 'Hi, just wondered if you wanted to get together to discuss tactics for making a fortune on Ebay? Meet for coffee today at eleven? Sam x.' She read it and re-read it until beige fingerprints smothered the borders. Was it warm in here? Was her heart beating inordinately loudly? She sat down on the bench beneath the coat hooks and stroked the piece of paper which now bore no semblance to the crisp white sheet it had been only moments before.

The door opened and Marianne hurried in. "Is it okay if I take an early lunch break today?" She made no eye contact with Amanda just rummaged in her locker before pulling out her mobile phone.

"Did you put this note in my locker?" Amanda held out the grubby paper.

"Yes, Sam asked me to." There was a hint of wariness in Marianne's tone, and once again Amanda felt a sense of shame about the way she had treated Marianne.

"Thank you. I really appreciate your help."

Marianne looked up. "He must have reminded me to do it at least ten times!"

So, he had mentioned it ten times? Was there any chance he was feeling the same way she was? For heaven's sake what was she thinking? She was a married woman. As if on cue her hand began to throb and she felt that old familiar greyness drift over her, accompanied by the image of pale dough with her hand print ground into it.

"I know he'll do anything he can to help you. He's good like that." Marianne put her phone in her pocket and patted the bulge. "I need to make a few calls at lunch time. It's quite important. Is that alright with you?"

Amanda nodded and as the door swung shut she was left alone to contemplate her meeting with Sam.

At eleven precisely she pushed open the cafeteria's doors. She had been fifteen minutes early but had hidden behind a rack of towelling robes, hoping to spot him arriving. She hadn't seen him. Maybe he had changed his mind? But no, he was sitting directly in front of the doors. He must have got there even earlier than she had.

Once again he rose to greet her and kissed both cheeks before collecting a tray laden with coffee and cakes. With the formalities of distributing the contents of the tray over, Sam relaxed into an easy banter about the bidding wars on Ebay and stories of paying over the odds by getting caught up in the auction process.

She laughed at his tales of greed and competition, and was amazed at how comfortable she felt in his company. She was seventeen again without a care in the world. Before David. A first date with all the promise that a first date holds. She subconsciously twirled strands of hair round her fingers as she listened to his voice.

Suddenly he stopped mid-sentence and reached out for her hand. A pulse of pleasure ran through her as she willingly allowed her hand to fall into his. Then he very gently turned her palm downwards exposing her darkened knuckles. His eyes stared into hers. The unspoken question was frozen between them. She wanted to snatch back her hand and give him some excuse about getting it trapped in a door. But she couldn't.

47

Jane

The pharmacist had rushed out to get some paper towels and disinfectant to clear Jane's vomit from the side of the desk. Jane didn't think she had eaten very much, so she was surprised at how far the mess had spread. She wiped her eyes, blew her nose and waited.

"Don't worry it can easily be cleaned up." The pharmacist bustled back in with an assortment of cleaning materials and busily wiped around Jane's feet.

"I'm so sorry," Jane said, trying not to look at the spatters on her shoes.

"I'm sure it's nothing that can't be sorted out. We just need to find the cause."

But to Jane, the symptoms were now so blindingly obvious she couldn't believe she hadn't thought of it before.

"So I suggest you get a pregnancy testing kit and, when you're ready, do the test. Whether the results are negative or positive I would highly recommend that you make an appointment with your G.P."

"I'm going away this weekend to Barcelona. It was going to be lovely and romantic." She took a deep breath to quell yet another wave of nausea.

"Well maybe you'll have an extra special piece of news to take with you, to make your weekend even more romantic." The pharmacist smiled broadly as she helped her out of her seat.

Thankfully Ada had gone by the time Jane was leaving, so no explanation of her consultation was necessary. She somehow made her way into work, although she saw no cars on the roads she crossed and wasn't aware of any of the pedestrians she passed. Charlie seemed to sense her pre-occupation, as he made no reference to the 'Racing Post' that he held in his hand. He simply placed it down on his chair and shuffled over to the door which he hauled open. She smiled vaguely in his direction and continued on to her office.

First thing to establish, she thought as she sat behind her desk, was whether she was or wasn't. But deep down, she knew. She knew as soon as the words were aired. The test was a mere formality. She had to try to focus on the business of the day. She had only a couple of days before the weekend. She had already called a staff meeting to prepare for the Summer Launch. She needed to make sure that at least her professional life had all loose ends tied up, unlike her private life which was nothing but a writhing mass of ends which refused to be tamed. But before she could make her way to women's wear, yet another wave of nausea threatened to drown her and she dashed to the staff toilets.

48

Hayley

Hayley's eyes were red and swollen and too sore for contact lenses. "Amanda, would you mind if I just nipped to the Ladies and put some drops in my eyes?" Amanda didn't respond she seemed to be immersed in the crumpled piece of paper in her hand.

"Erm, excuse me Amanda?" Hayley stepped closer. Amanda hastily shoved the note into her pocket.

"Sorry Hayley I was... somewhere else."

"Would you mind if I just went to the Ladies and put some drops in my eyes?"

"No of course not. Could you tell any staff that you see to come to women's wear as soon as possible for the Summer Launch meeting?"

"Will do." Slinging her weighty bag over her shoulder and pushing her thick rimmed glasses back on her nose she went up to the staff toilets. She stood in front of the mirrors taking one last look at her dowdy image before the eye drop solution made it temporarily disappear. She had never felt less attractive, and less of woman than she did at this moment. And the way the bank clerk had spoken to her earlier hadn't helped her feeling of worthlessness.

A phone was ringing in the second cubicle along. She thought she heard a Welsh accent. Suddenly there was silence and Hayley remembered about the Summer Launch meeting.

"Excuse me." She knocked lightly on the door. "I've been asked to tell all the floor staff to come to the meeting about the Summer Launch. Could you come to women's wear as soon as you can?" The skin on her hand began to itch, deep below the surface, so deep that no matter how hard she scratched, it couldn't be reached.

Slowly the door opened and Marianne stepped out. "Right, yes thanks I'll be there in a minute... er...?"

"Hayley."

"Yes Hayley, thanks." Marianne looked as though she was going to say something else when her phone began to ring again.

"Aren't you going to answer that?"

Marianne began shaking her head and held the handset at arm's length. It was as though she was holding the head of a venomous snake instead of a Nokia. "I'm trying to be a chat line operator!" She burst into tears. "But I'm just no good at it!" The phone dangled between her fingers.

Without thinking Hayley took the mobile out of Marianne's hand and pressed answer. "Hello, can I help you?"

"That's not sexy. That's like talking to an estate agent." The man's voice at the other end sounded surprised and more than a little peeved.

Hayley took one more look at Marianne's distraught face. She tried to clear her sore throat. But the effect of her emotional night had given a rawness to her voice as she spoke softly into the handset. "You are absolutely right I am THE estate agent, and you are very, very late for your viewing you naughty boy. So I think I'm going to have to punish you." She listened intently to the man's sharp intake of breath. Was he going to buy it?

"Erm... yes I'm sorry I am late. What are you going to do to me Madame estate agent?"

She thought for a split second. "I'm going to bend you over the er... integrated appliances and spank you very hard with..." Her eyes darted round the washroom looking for inspiration. Marianne picked up the toilet brush and waved it in the air.

"... a toilet brush!" She held her breath as she waited for his response.

"Oh God that's really going to hurt!" Much to her relief he actually sounded delighted at the bizarre prospect of being beaten with a toilet brush whilst straddling a washer-dryer.

Marianne began to laugh and Hayley tried to signal her to stop.

"Who's that?" An edge had crept into the man's voice.

"That's the lady of the house returning home. Do you think she'll want to punish you too?"

"Yes. Yes I'm sure she will." She could hear his excitement. Suddenly the door to the Ladies room opened.

"Oh Christ..." Hayley groaned as she watched Jane stop halfway across the threshold. Marianne was still clutching the toilet brush and Hayley pressed the phone harder against her ear.

"What's going on now?" The caller sounded as though he could barely contain himself.

"My boss has just walked in." She had no idea what Jane would make of the scene before her. But she could tell, by the heavy breathing, that the caller was clearly delighted by this turn of events. That was all that was needed. He thanked her and rang off – a satisfied customer, just as Jane dashed into the nearest cubicle and threw up.

49

Marianne

She had gone from tears of frustration to tears of laughter and now her boss was throwing up in front of her. It wasn't how she'd anticipated this morning would go. And Hayley's performance had been amazing. She couldn't believe that she had never noticed her before. But then she looked closely at the woman in front of her. Shapeless clothes hung from her body so it was impossible to tell whether she had a figure or not. Her large glasses covered half of her face and apart from her head of red coils there was no other flash of colour to be seen. Marianne supposed it wasn't that difficult to understand her being overlooked.

Another retch.

"Miss Farrell, should I call a doctor?" Marianne felt as though she should be holding Jane's hair away from her face and rubbing her back. That's what girlfriends did for each other – but this wasn't a girlfriend, this was the 'Ice Queen'.

"No, please don't call anyone. I'll be okay." Her voice echoed in the pottery vessel.

"Do you think something disagreed with you? I'm sure Charlie would have a remedy." Marianne said leaning into the cubicle with a paper towel in her outstretched hand. It reminded her of a white flag.

Taking the towel Jane sat back on her haunches and wiped her mouth. "Unless Charlie's got a pregnancy testing kit, I don't think he'll be able to help." She pulled herself to her feet.

"Charlie might not have one, but I have." The words were spoken so softly Marianne thought she may have misheard. But after poking about in the bowels of her huge handbag Hayley finally lifted out a blue box. "You might as well find out for sure."

Marianne stood side by side with Hayley as Jane turned back into the cubicle. They waited. Eventually the door swung open.

"I'm going to have a baby." She sounded so forlorn, so far removed from the usual cool exterior.

Hayley turned away and noisily blew her nose.

"Can I get you some water Miss Farrell, you look really pale?"

"Jane, it's Jane and thanks Marianne but I should get back onto the sales floor. Everyone will be waiting for the meeting to start. This..." She waved the plastic stick "... I will have to deal with later." Jane's steps were unsteady as she left the room.

Just as the door closed Marianne's phone trilled into life, vibrating against Hayley's bag. "Would you Hayley, please?" Marianne didn't even want to touch keys that now somehow seemed contaminated.

Hayley took a deep breath and picked up the phone "Good afternoon Easy Estates here. Would you like me to value your assets or measure up your rear extension?..."

50

Amanda

Minutes had passed as they both stared at her swollen hand. 'Why do you let him do it Amanda? Does it make you feel like a Martyr? Is that all you're worth? Do you enjoy it Amanda?' These were her questions in her head not his.

"Talk to me." He had tenderly stroked her sore skin and looked into her soul.

Only once had she ever spoken to anyone about David's temper and growing violence and that was to her mother.

"So you don't wash now?" Amanda's mother had pointed to a dark smudge on Amanda's wrist. Amanda had yanked her sleeve over her hand. Immediately her mother's gentle teasing turned into concern. "What is it Mandy? You can tell me, that's what I'm here for." Her mother had reached for her hand and slowly rolled back the sleeve exposing a shadow of bruised fingerprints along the length of her arm. "What in God's name...?"

Amanda had pulled away. "I'll deal with it Mum."

"So you'll deal with it will you? What kind of mother would I be to let a daughter deal with this?" Her mother was shaking with anger.

"It was a one off. It won't happen again. He's promised."

"Promises are for nothing. Your father, he may be a man of few words but he will have something to say about this!"

"No!" She had stood her ground and made her mother give her word that it wouldn't be spoken of again.

It was a wedge that remained between them until the day she died.

"He was never like that in the beginning... " Amanda found herself telling Sam. David's odd outburst, followed by his shame-ridden apologies had then become more regular, but with fewer apologies. These had been replaced by accusations that she had driven him to it. Now it seemed that she managed to annoy her husband on an almost daily basis. As she talked, she saw Sam's gentle features harden. "I'm sure he doesn't mean to hurt me. He doesn't know his own strength. I must just frustrate him..." Her words dried up as she realised how pathetic she must sound.

"Amanda you have to leave."

It was final. It was a statement of fact. Not a request or a suggestion. She looked at him and she knew. That was indeed what she had to do.

There was something in the way he said goodbye to her that gave her strength. Sharing the burden of what happened at home made her feel that she wasn't alone anymore. It wasn't going to be easy, she knew that. She had nowhere to go for one thing. She didn't have her own bank account now that she had withdrawn the small inheritance her mother had left her to put in her metal box. And she had no other independent financial means. But Sam was right, she had to leave.

She left the staff room early and made her way up to Jane's office. A positive step. She would confirm her interest in the new role Jane had mentioned to her during her appraisal. Showing she was still interested and keen to know how it was developing, she felt sure, would stand her in good stead when it came to the selection process.

She knocked on the door and pushed it ajar. The room was in darkness. She exhaled and felt her spirit begin to sink. No, she had to keep the momentum going. Sam was right, she had to leave. When she at last saw Jane she was surrounded by workmen moving rails and racks like they were pieces of scenery for a stage play. She would have to bide her time.

With grim determination she walked home. Her pace was brisk, trying to distance herself from the fear that always accompanied her on the journey home. The end was in sight.

The house was quiet. She hung her coat over the banister and went straight upstairs. It had been a while since she had checked the contents of her metal box. Standing on the chair she felt for the box and pulled it out from within the cocoon of jumpers. Retrieving the key she unlocked it. Her eyes darting to the road outside every few seconds, she couldn't afford to get caught. Two thousand, three hundred and twelve pounds, it was only just enough for a deposit on a rented flat, and the first months' rent. She must secure the job Jane had talked about. That would help her get away from him and stay away from him if she kept moving. She didn't see his car pull up outside the house. But she heard his key turn in the door.

She stuffed the money back into the box. Her fingers shook as she tried to slot the key into the keyhole. She had no time. Hurling the tin back into the wardrobe, she pushed the chair to the corner of the room. There was a jangle as his keys dropped onto the glass table at the bottom of the stairs. Silence. She held her breath. Was he listening for her? Then the thud of his heavy footfall on the stairs. His steps weren't hurried. She quietly closed the wardrobe door and looked round the room. The drawer was open and tights hung over the side where she had dug out the key. She leaned her back against it, pushing it closed as he walked into the bedroom.

They looked at one another. Adversaries either side of a wrestling ring. Her hands gripped the edge of the dressing table. His gripped a worn piece of paper covered in smudged beige fingerprints.

51

Jane

The meeting went smoothly despite the turmoil in Jane's head. She struggled with the image of the two blue lines that confirmed her future, as she gave instructions about the location of the champagne bar and agreed the path that the catwalk would take. She had to find volunteers to model the new season's fashions.

"Now I know that it's a big ask, but is there anyone willing to show off our latest range of outfits on the catwalk?"

Immediately a fleshy arm shot up into the air accompanied by the rattling of cheap bangles.

"Yeah, I'll do it." Jane recognised Sharon's voice, one of the junior assistants.

"Erm thank you Sharon, anyone else?" She wasn't sure what the Americans would make of Sharon who was well endowed in every department. Jane desperately searched the room for any other willing candidates. Her eyes fell on Hayley and Marianne who had positioned themselves next to her. "Marianne, would you consider doing it? I would really appreciate it."

"If it helps, then why not?" Marianne's smile was warm, and Jane admonished herself for behaving so badly towards her. "And you Hayley, would you do it?"

The colour rose from the high buttoned neckline of Hayley's blouse right up to the roots of her hair.

"It'll be fun Hayley – nothing serious, please?"

Jane couldn't quite figure out if it was pleasure or fear in Hayley's expression when she dipped her head in acquiescence, but either way Jane was so grateful for the support. She couldn't tell anyone how important this event was. She might have lost control of her personal life but she was damned if she was going to lose control of her work life too. It had to be a success for the store's future and all those who worked in it.

52

Hayley

So Jane was pregnant. It was cruel. As much as Hayley had tried not to show her feelings they were there, just under the surface. Everything in her life was geared up for motherhood and yet she had been left barren. Jane jumps into bed with her married boss and hey presto she's pregnant. She didn't hate Jane. She hated the unfairness of it all. She only hoped that Jane wouldn't consider doing anything stupid like having an abortion. That would be too much for Hayley to bear.

She dragged her thoughts away from Jane and her condition. Hanging on to the plastic strap as she swayed to the movement of the bus on her way home, her mind drifted over the last few hours. It had been a surreal day. She had agreed to model clothes on a catwalk and from nowhere at all her alter ego, the dominatrix estate agent, had made her debut appearance. She casually glanced round the bus, wondering how many of these men with their briefcases and empty lunch boxes had spent a few minutes today being whipped, teased or played with in cyberspace.

What would Neil say if she told him about THE Estate Agent? He would never understand. He would probably be more horrified at the cost of a premium rate call than the actual content of the phone conversation. He wasn't what she would describe as adventurous in the bedroom. He was very fair. Every erogenous zone was allocated an equal length of time and attention. Foreplay took exactly twelve minutes and love making took eighteen. This made a total of thirty minutes which, Neil obviously felt, was conservatively sufficient. According to Neil, nothing should be done to excess, spending, eating, drinking or sex.

But her exploits on the phone today had made her feel strangely empowered. Being able to manipulate the caller's arousal, and ultimately bring pleasure, however short lived was oddly satisfying. Not only that, but the ease with which she had fallen into the role, was the last thing she had expected.

Ordinarily she was so self-conscious that she would even make sure that the lights were dimmed before getting undressed in front of her own husband. But during her last coffee break, when her caller insisted on being called Luke Skywalker as he searched for a property in a galaxy far, far away, she had, without hesitation, threatened to thrash him with his own light sabre if he didn't buy the imaginary apartment she had offered. Luke Skywalker seemed to enjoy that fantasy so much he had promised to bring Princess Leia with him next time.

Maybe she should introduce a little excitement into her own love life? She had spent so much time desperately wanting the potential product of the act of intercourse she had almost forgotten that it was also a meaningful part of a loving relationship.

She stepped off the bus, and all thoughts of ways to seduce her husband disappeared as she peered into the depths of a passing pram. She had been born to be a mother, but had she been born to be a dominatrix, and could she be both?

53

Marianne

So she was officially a failure at talking dirty. Something else she could add to her list of inadequacies. As Hayley had handled all the calls, Marianne didn't feel she could justify claiming any of the money that had been made so her financial situation remained as dire as it had before.

She opened the gate, its creak summoned Eric, her neighbour. He scuttled out from behind the compost heap at the side of the house. Licking his fingers he smoothed down the strands of hair that straddled his balding head.

"Evening Marianne, you're looking particularly lovely."

His shirt looked like it had been buttoned up by a three-year-old. Mismatched tail ends barely covered his open zip. She felt repulsed but nodded as she quickly turned away and fumbled for her front door key.

Jack stayed in the house most days writing and re-writing his C.V. She now didn't have the luxury of being able to get home first and sort through her mail in privacy, dealing with any incriminating correspondence there might be. Instead she was met by neat piles of letters arranged on the kitchen table in order of sender and importance. Jack would hover behind her as she casually flicked through the junk mail, giving each leaflet exaggerated scrutiny until he became bored and wandered off to do something else. Stuffing the rest of the post into her bag she would later carry it upstairs to open when she was safely alone.

That night, sitting on the edge of the bed she lifted first one corner of an envelope and then the other. She slid her finger under the flap prising the glued edges apart. She didn't want to know what was inside, but ignorance had got her into this situation in the first place. She had to face it. 'You have failed to make the minimum payment', the letters were red and uncompromising. She supposed there was no polite way of putting it, but she would have much preferred something like; 'It's probably slipped your mind but do you think, when you have a minute, you could just pop a few pounds in the post to us?'

She read on. 'In order to avoid legal action contact the following number immediately to make the minimum payment. DO NOT IGNORE THIS LETTER.' She couldn't make the minimum payment. The interest alone was devouring her salary as soon as it went into her account. She opened the second letter. 'You have not responded to our request for immediate payment. Our agent will call to collect the outstanding debt or seize goods to the value of the outstanding debt.'

Surely they wouldn't come here would they? She had to stop this somehow. She considered her options as she got ready for bed. Telling Jack was absolutely out of the question. Borrowing from her family was equally as impossible. Could she borrow from somewhere else she wondered?

As she explored the maze of blind alleys that presented themselves to her she heard her neighbour's voices in the adjacent bedroom floating through the dividing wall. She buried her head under the pillow. She really didn't want to hear them tonight. The bang of the headboard was rhythmic and almost hypnotic, until, in one last frenzy she could hear the usual climactic shriek of, "Don't stop now Princess Leia, Luke's coming!"

54

Amanda

David unfolded the piece of paper. He recited what it said although his eyes never left her face. "Coffee at eleven with Sam eh? Oh and let's not forget the kiss." His hand shook as he waited.

"Yes that's right." She deliberately turned her back on him and began to carefully tuck the stray tights into the drawer. Fury coursed through her. He had no right to even speak Sam's name. She pushed the drawer closed.

"Is that all you've got to say, 'yes that's right'?" He mimicked her voice as his fist clenched and unclenched around the note.

Sliding her fury beneath a blank mask she turned to face him.

"It's really very simple. I had a meeting about Ebay with Samantha from purchasing. Coffee at eleven – just as the note says. It's nothing to get excited about." With that she swept past him, her eyes fixed straight ahead. She left him standing in the doorway.

It was a gamble. The metal box was unlocked balanced on a pile of jumpers. She had to just hope that he would follow her and not investigate what she had been doing.

She heard his steps on the stairs behind her but she didn't hesitate. She marched into the kitchen. "Would you like a cup of tea or are you going to have something stronger." She didn't know if he had picked up on the disdain in her voice when she asked about 'something stronger' but she didn't care. Holding the kettle in her hand she raised her eyebrows.

"I...I'll have tea."

145

"Good." She wondered whether the kettle would make a decent weapon as she placed it on its base and snapped the switch on.

David had swapped one doorway for another and stood watching her. She felt, for the first time in her married life, that he was uncertain how to react to her. Victory, even though small, was hers for now.

He barely spoke for the rest of the evening. It was a sulky silence, full of uncertain reproach. She had done her best to ignore it and him. At the first opportunity she had she locked the metal box, buried it again beneath the pile of jumpers and returned the key to its twenty denier haven. Once satisfied that she had covered her tracks she lay down on the bed and stared at the top right hand corner of the room.

"So money, it isn't everything." Her mother sat on the chair that Amanda had earlier used to reach her savings. "I know it makes the soup richer, but in the end soup is soup."

"I need to get away mum." For the first time Amanda openly acknowledged her situation. "And I need money to do that."

"Maybe a little money, but strength is what you need. Money lasts only a short time. Strength is with you forever. Your Uncle Max, God rest his soul, he had no strength, then again he had no money either, but what can you do?"

"I'm working on the strength bit mum."

"You should take up skydiving. You leave your fears up there, and land, God willing, a stronger person." Her mother's pale blue suit seemed to shimmer in the half light of the evening.

"I don't think skydiving's for me." She was so used to her mother's eccentric suggestions, that she no longer felt exasperated.

"You should listen to your mother. I'm telling you, you should take that chance. The one that scares you to death, and when you do, strength will be waiting for you."

She thought about it. Did her mother mean take the chance of a life alone, or even a life with someone else – like Sam? That thought did both terrify and thrill her, probably similar to a sky-dive. "Are we talking about a leap of faith mum?"

"Amanda, a leap of faith is the only thing that will save you."

55

Jane

She was going to have Tony's baby. It clearly wasn't an ideal situation, but he had always told her that he saw his future with her, promising that he would leave his wife and they would marry. Well this was obviously going to have to happen a little sooner than anticipated. His marriage hadn't produced children. His wife apparently insisting that childbirth wasn't her cup of tea. Stretch marks and a weak pelvic floor were marginally better than small pox or rabies – but only marginally.

Being a father would be the makings of Tony. He would settle down to become the perfect family man. Dismissing any doubts she had about Tony's reaction to her news, she replaced them with visions of him weeping with happiness as she told him. Scooping her up in his arms and thanking her for giving him the most precious gift in the world. He would revere her, pander to her every whim. No pedestal would be high enough.

Excitement was twin tracked with a niggling fear as she re-packed her suitcase yet again for the coming weekend. When should she tell him? It was a question that reverberated round her head. Perhaps after a romantic day when they had both declared their endless love and adoration for each other? She could picture the scene now. A candle's flame flickers between them as they gaze into each other's eyes. After a perfect meal served under a perfect moonlit sky, he reaches out to hold her hand. An unspoken gesture of such sweet devotion. She smiles slowly at him, basking in his admiration before softly telling him that she is going to have his child. A wonderful affirmation to the world of their love and commitment to one another.

Lying on her bed she replayed the scene over and over in her head until eventually she drifted off into a deep dreamless sleep.

The morning wasn't quite as comforting, as she stared at the white porcelain toilet bowl for the third time in twenty minutes. She was going to have to drag herself into work and put on such a performance that only those who knew the truth would be aware that anything was amiss. When she felt sure that a fourth intimate reunion with the toilet bowl would not be necessary she re-applied her makeup. But to be on the safe side she tied her hair back into a tight chignon.

Feigning a bright and breezy air she did her best to glide into the staff reception area. She needn't have worried about Charlie's amazingly accurate sense of perception as his eyes were closed and deep breaths rattled in his chest. He looked more frail than ever. She tiptoed past him and on into the shop. She just had one more day before the momentous weekend that lay ahead.

56

Hayley

Although her newly acquired confidence as estate agent extraordinaire had given her a boost, she was still well aware that in the workplace she remained invisible. Other staff would gossip in front of her as though she didn't exist, swapping intimate snippets of their own personal lives and the lives of those around them in salacious detail. Overhearing conversations, it would appear, was a dubious consequence of being invisible.

"... I was only bending down to swap a till roll. Dirty bugger had a hard on!" The two young sales girls giggled.

Hayley quietly continued to re-arrange costume jewellery in the display case.

"Well he's always asking me out and we both know what that means. A quick leg over and not so much as a thank you." The girl's large chest heaved in indignation.

"He is nice looking though, and you could do a lot worse for a shag with no ties," the shorter girl said thoughtfully.

"Mmmm... I know what you mean. Maybe I will let him have a bit then. I haven't got much else going on at the minute, unless you count gormless Dave in catering." Both girls seemed to consider this sad state of affairs.

"Yeah I think I will give our Mr Pickard a little treat."

"Not so little Shaz!"

Their cackles sent shivers down Hayley's back as she realised that they had been talking about Tony Pickard all along. Poor Jane, did she have any idea what he was like? And now she was going to have his baby. It all seemed so wrong she thought as she carried on re-arranging the displays.

She checked that the jewellery had maximum passer-by appeal before locking the cabinet. Straightening up she tucked her sensible blouse into the waistband of her sensible skirt. How far removed she was in reality to the sexy woman she pretended to be on the phone. She had told one caller that she was wearing a black leather pencil skirt, see-through blouse and five inch, red stiletto heels. She smiled ruefully at her slightly scuffed brown brogues. Turning as she did, she caught sight of a flash of tartan disappearing behind the electrical appliances counter.

A tartan shopping trolley. That could mean only one thing – Ada. Sure enough, as Hayley rounded the pillar there she was. Ada was trying to fit a cylinder hoover from the display into her shopping trolley. She watched as Ada asked 'Shaz' the well upholstered shop assistant from earlier to help. Incredibly 'Shaz' appeared to be more than happy to aid and abet the shop lifter. Seemingly satisfied that most of the machine was in her bag she thanked the young girl and tried to manoeuvre the trolley.

"Hello Ada." Hayley couldn't help but like the old lady.

"Hello love, I do struggle these days." Ada nodded at the protruding plastic hose.

"I think we should put this back don't you? It will be too heavy for you to use anyway." She smiled encouragingly at Ada.

As if seeing the hoover for the first time, Ada's gloved hand touched the curve of the handle. "Yes I suppose you're right."

Hayley lifted the cleaner out of the bag and placed it back on the display stand.

"How's Jane?"

Hayley stopped. She turned to look at Ada's enquiring face. "Erm...she's...well she's alright. Why?"

"I saw her at the chemist yesterday. She said she had a bit of a bug. Maybe she's got what my Charlie's got, because he's not right you know."

"I don't think she's got what Charlie's got somehow, but I'm sure she'll be fine... eventually." She patted Ada's arm. "And I'm sure Charlie will be fine too." She was less certain about this last statement, as she had noticed only the other day that he wasn't his usual self.

Ada didn't look convinced either. "I'll just pop down to see him. I've got something that I think will make him feel much better." And she slowly pushed her trolley away.

57

Marianne

Jack hadn't come to bed until the early hours. She supposed he didn't have much to get up for these days. She pretended to be asleep when he did eventually climb into bed, not because she wanted to avoid him. Had he known she was still awake he probably would have held her close and stroked her hair until she fell asleep. She didn't deserve such comfort. Sheets stuck to her clammy skin and the silk nightie that she had convinced herself she needed wrapped around her like a tourniquet. Fear grew with each breath as she tussled with her financial nightmare throughout the night.

The redundancy alone had taken quite a toll on Jack without him even being aware of the mess she was in. He had barely smiled recently let alone laughed. She could hardly remember the carefree couple they had been only a short time ago.

Creeping out of the house she left her husband in his fitful sleep. Her stomach growled. But eating was the last thing she could think about. Damp air wafted around her. The early morning sun was still too shy to peek over the shops and offices. She didn't want to bump into Amanda, or anyone else. The fewer staff that were around the better. And after today both Jane and Anthony wouldn't be in the store for a few days, leaving the shop floors with little supervision. Bile rose to her mouth. She swallowed and marched on.

Charlie looked brighter than he had for some time as he held the door open for her.

"Morning Miss Marianne, and it's a fine morning isn't it?" He inhaled the scent from the purple freesia in his lapel before returning to his seat and unfolding The Racing Post.

"Good morning Charlie. Yes it's a lovely day." She felt like a traitor. She couldn't believe what she was considering doing.

Soon she was at her cash desk. The till figures had been tallied the night before, and just needed to be cross checked before start of business. How much she could siphon off each day would be the tricky thing. She looked at the tray of cash in front of her. Sweat trickled between her breasts and she felt sure she had a bright neon sign above her head flashing the word 'Thief'. Her fingers hovered over the notes. She slammed the drawer shut. She couldn't do it.

The morning drifted by and each note she received she placed into the appropriate section of the till, hesitating every time. Perhaps if she was to write an 'I owe you' whenever she 'borrowed' the money? She could put all the 'I owe you's' in a safe place and when she had enough money she would repay it all. She continued to battle with her conscience for the rest of the day whilst the money remained in the cash drawer and the bile remained in her throat.

58

Amanda

The next few days were filled with sideways glances and sighs. It was as though David was in unknown territory with his now not so compliant wife. It seemed to her that every ounce of confidence he lost, shifted the balance in her favour. Each time she looked up from what she was doing she caught him staring at her, then he would quickly look away.

Perhaps he was re-assessing her. Well he could re-assess her all he liked because she had a plan. Locked in her own world she baked and cooked. The kitchen was filled with the aroma of fresh herbs and warm cinnamon and the windows were misted with steam. She pretended that she was preparing a meal for Sam. It was her day dream and David couldn't reach into her head and snatch that from her.

After breakfast David had disappeared into the lounge. He only re-appeared later in the afternoon to pour himself a glass of red wine. Even his stride into the kitchen seemed less assertive than usual she thought. Picking up his glass of wine he suddenly stopped. He seemed about to say something but changed his mind.

"Something wrong David?" Her tone was brisk, almost business like.

"I'm not sure. I'm really not sure." He stared at her. His scrutiny was intense but apparently fruitless as he left the room without uttering another word.

She really had unnerved him and the scales tipped just a little further in her favour.

59

Jane

She sat at her desk. The photograph of her parents was face down. She stared blankly at the wall ahead. It was a collage of certificates and awards. 'Assistant Manager of The Year Award' three years running. 'Health and Safety Certificate of Completion', 'Certificate of Achievement in Effective Leadership and Management', 'Certificate of Achievement in Business Negotiating', 'Certificate of Achievement in Business Communications'. Stupid Jane. There wasn't one there saying 'Certificate of Achievement in Completely Ruining Your Life'. There should be.

The Jane that had sat at her desk the previous Thursday was not the Jane that sat there this Monday morning re-visiting the events of the last few days. She had managed to disguise the vomiting on the first day of her weekend away as travel sickness. But she could tell that the excuse was wearing thin by the second day. Their tour of Las Ramblas was constantly punctuated by dashes into the bars that they passed. She would avail herself of the toilet facilities whilst he would avail himself of the alcohol. He had hardly bothered to conceal his impatience. By three thirty in the afternoon he sat down in yet another bar, ordered three martinis and refused to continue the tour of the 'bogs and bars of Barcelona' as he put it.

She was exhausted. Anything she had managed to eat, she hadn't been able to keep down. Her hair was matted and stuck to her forehead. This was not the romantic image she had had of herself. The vision of her floating through winding streets in a cool linen dress that shimmered in the setting sun was shattered. Creases criss-crossed the dress like a road map, and dark rings under her eyes did nothing to enhance the look.

"Menu por favour," Tony slurred and clicked his fingers at a passing waiter. He had hardly even looked at her, let alone gazed adoringly into her eyes. This was definitely not going to plan she thought, as he knocked back another martini.

"Tony, I'm so sorry. I've ruined today for you haven't I?"

He placed his drink on the table, the glass half on and half off the coaster. He stared at her, denial wasn't apparently forthcoming.

"And I'm really sorry about last night. I know you wanted it to be romantic and everything, but with the travel sickness I just couldn't manage anything... intimate." She reached out and held his hand but it lay limply in hers.

"You didn't even try though, did you Jane?" He reminded her of a small boy who hadn't got what he had been promised, and was determined to sulk until he did.

She looked at his handsome face, and thought about the baby growing inside her. "I'll feel much better tomorrow darling. In fact I'm feeling much better already." Don't be sick, don't be sick, don't be sick was the mantra in her head.

He ate everything that was put in front of him, and most of what was put in front of her too. The combination of numerous martinis and a huge meal meant that he fell into bed in their bijou hotel room and snored loudly through the night, leaving Jane alone to retch as quietly as she could.

When the sun rose she did feel marginally better than she had. Probably because she was so tired that being physically sick was no longer a feasible option for her body. After showering she ordered room service whilst Tony slept on.

Finally he stirred.

"Hello sleepy head." She brushed the hair away from his face and tried to sound light hearted and sexy. She felt neither.

"Feeling better are you?" The question was more of a demand.

"Much better. Now what can I get you?" She waved in the direction of the breakfast trolley that had arrived.

The grin that appeared on his face would ordinarily have made her tummy flip, but today it just made it churn unsettlingly.

There was very little foreplay, for which, today she was grateful. Sex was performed without skill or finesse, just basic animal need and a lot of grunting. He seemed oblivious of the flesh he was crushing beneath him until his final jerking thrust. His eyes opened and he looked at Jane. Pushing aside self-pity and hurt she tried to smile into his soul, willing him to show her the love that she was desperate for. The blank expression remained as he pushed himself off her and strolled over to the breakfast selection. He seemed very pleased with himself as he shovelled eggs Florentine into his mouth, wiping his chin with the back of his hand. She found she couldn't watch him.

She got through the rest of the weekend in Barcelona by putting on a show of cheerfulness. She forced laughter at his jokes, and pretended to melt at his advances. These had increased since she had managed to keep the vomiting at bay. What had shocked her most was his total lack of concern at her ill health. He had shown only irritation at her inability to make love to him. There had been no re-assurance and no attempts to find ways of making her feel comfortable. The only time he had brightened was when sex was in the offing. She was not at all certain that this was what she wanted for her and her baby's future. Something had held her back from telling him the news, and so he had arrived home still unaware that he was going to be a father.

60

Hayley

As crazy as it sounded, over the weekend, she had missed her lunchtime flirts. And so today she was looking forward to her dinner break and donning the persona of Madame Estate Agent. She liked that Hayley. That Hayley could say what she wanted. That Hayley was always in control.

Marianne had agreed to give her the phone at lunch times and had explained to her how she should 'log on' for calls. Before Hayley had even reached the Ladies, which was the most private place in comparison to everywhere else to carry out her new business venture, Marianne's phone began to ring.

"Hello?" God they were keen she hadn't even logged on yet.

"Hello, this is Mister Spanker of Cloons and Dunnit debt solutions."

"Well hello Mister Spanker, I suppose you're going to tell me that you want to seize my assets are you?"

"Erm...yes, that's right. That's if you don't satisfy your contract."

"I can assure you that I can more than satisfy any contract Mr Spanker."

"I am very pleased to hear that because you don't want things to get out of hand I'm sure."

"Oh I never let anything get out of hand, Mr Spanker. In fact, I am extremely good with my hands you naughty man."

".Er... right then, well I'll call round and collect what's owed."

"Oh you saucy thing you...." The line went dead and Hayley found herself talking to a dialling tone. That's a new one on me she thought as she attempted to 'log on'. A debt collector, well whatever floats your boat, she shook her head as the phone rang once more.

"Hello, is that the estate agent? I want to view a property that has dungeons..."

Hayley settled into the twilight world of manacles, chains and conveyancing.

61

Marianne

For days she had battled with her conscience and up to now her conscience had won. She was relieved that yet another day was over and she had resisted temptation. When it came to going home Charlie was as usual the stalwart sentry to the building. He opened the door with almost a flourish had his gnarled hand not slipped off the door handle causing her to lurch forward to catch it before it closed again.

"Ada's got me something for the arthritis." He massaged the offending hand. "She says it's like magic."

"Oh I'm sure if anyone can make you better it will be Ada."

She could not fail to notice that since Ada had been around Charlie had been looked after very well. At the merest hint of an ailment Ada would scurry off to get a cure for him. She was his very own necessity finder.

He waved her through with a twinkle in his eye.

She was so fond of him. As she walked home she recalled the day she came for her interview, a terrified seventeen-year-old, desperate to please. He had treated her like a lady even then. Tipping his hat and holding the door open for her. He had even shaken her hand and wished her good luck when she asked him where the interviews were being held. On her first day at work he embraced her like she was one of the family, which, of course she was – one of the Peltham family. Over the years he had supplied her with so many 'necessities' she had lost count.

She could see Jack's shadow through the glass front door as she walked up the path. He seemed to be waiting for her.

"I think you had a gentleman caller today." Eric popped up from behind the hedge. He wasn't even pretending to be busy in the garden this time.

The front door opened and she felt a stab of apprehension as Jack beckoned her in.

"A man called for you today. He wouldn't give his name, said it was personal." Jack stared at her. She couldn't tell whether he was hurt or angry, or both.

"Who was he Marianne?"

If he felt so hurt and angry now, she couldn't imagine how upset he would be if she told him the truth. "He must have been from the private pension company. Before you were made redundant, I thought investing in a little pension would be a good idea. Of course since then I've tried to cancel it. I think they just don't like losing business and they've sent someone round to persuade me to stay in the pension scheme." She startled herself at how easily the lies fell from her lips. She watched Jack absorb this information.

Slowly a smile dimpled his cheeks. "You are so clever my angel, always thinking of the future. You're doing the right thing though. Cash it in and then at least we'll have a little more to boost our cash flow. How much do you think there'll be?"

"Next to nothing really." If you just omitted the 'next', she thought.

62

Amanda

She knew Jane had only just come back from a weekend away so she had left it a day. But she couldn't wait much longer. She didn't want her to think that she was pestering her just that she was keen and enthusiastic. The question was, could she keep the desperation escaping from her voice? She chewed the skin round her fingers whilst she waited for Jane to respond to her knock.

"Yes?"

Amanda put her head round the door. "Do you have a moment?"

Jane smiled, "Come in Mrs Freedman."

"Please call me Amanda." The step she took into the room was a bridge. A bridge to take her away from her marriage. And a bridge that almost allowed her to reach up and touch the right hand corner of her bedroom to rip the wallpaper of her life down. "I just wondered if you had an up-date on the new role you're developing. The one you mentioned at my appraisal? I'm very keen, you see, to put myself forward for it."

"Don't worry Amanda I haven't forgotten you, and yes we're very close to finalising the details. In fact I have a draft here of anticipated duties, proposed pay structure and the areas that the position will cover. You can take this away with you if you like. It'll give you the opportunity to consider all the elements of the job. I'm sure you will want to discuss it with your family or partner before putting in a formal application." Jane held out a folder. "Of course, I have to reiterate that this is only at the proposal stage and things still have to be firmed up."

Amanda stepped forward and took the folder. She could barely restrain herself from snatching it. She held it tightly against her chest. "Thank you Miss Farrell, you have no idea what this means to me. Nothing in here will change my mind about the job."

Jane seemed to study her for several seconds before saying, "You know Amanda, I don't believe there will be anything in there that will change your mind. I'll let you know as soon as I have a definite offer, meanwhile if you have any questions you know where I am."

"Thank you so much again Miss Farrell."

"Forget the Miss Farrell, it's Jane."

"Thank you Jane." She left the office still clutching the precious documents to her. Did she dare to hope that this was her chance for a new start? Was this the first step towards that leap of faith?

63

Jane

She was quite different from the timid woman she had appraised a few weeks earlier. In fact she would go so far as to say that Amanda had an air of gritty determination that had not been there before. She certainly seemed resolute about going for the new position that was being developed. But, there was something sad about her intense focus on this job. It was as though everything hinged on getting it. Although Jane felt some disquiet about whether the role would exist if the American takeover happened, she had been instructed to carry on as normal. She watched the slight woman leave, still clinging onto the folder she had given her. Even her posture exuded resolve. The round-shouldered creature that she had met previously was nowhere to be seen.

Her eyes drifted to the photograph on her desk. Her parents were due to visit in a few days. She had no idea how she was going to play this one. Would her mother sense that something was wrong?

She hadn't seen Tony since they had arrived back. He had meetings scheduled for most of the week. Jane was glad of the space and time it gave her to think. She wished there was somebody she could talk to. Never being one to set much store by friendships. Always driven by focusing on professional goals, she really didn't have anyone to turn to except her mother. But she wasn't ready for that conversation yet.

She wandered down to the staff canteen. Sitting alone, as usual, she studied the other groups. Laughter and conversation flowed around her. But she was in her own bubble. She could be seen but no-one could reach her. More than anything she wanted to burst out of that bubble.

Hayley and Marianne bustled into the canteen. Hayley was telling Marianne a story. Wild hand gestures accompanied the tale and they were both laughing. She could see there was something different about Hayley, something vibrant and confident. Jane looked away. She didn't fit in with anyone.

"Do you mind if we join you?" Hayley and Marianne stood side by side with their lunch trays poised over the table.

Jane couldn't explain the rush she felt as she looked up. "I'd love it. Thank you."

64

Hayley

It had been a while since Hayley had spent her coffee break in the nursery section of the store. And she had refrained from buying any infant clothes recently. Instead, today, she found herself in ladies' fashion.

The mannequin didn't do it justice, she thought as she circled the black leather pencil skirt. It had been teamed with a sheer, animal print blouse. She stepped closer. Not too close. This was something that she would never have looked at in the past, and she was definitely out of her comfort zone. The leather looked like exceptional quality, even to her. The skirt moulded itself round the cold plastic figure, drawing the eye to hips and buttocks. It skimmed the knees, tapering so tightly at the shins she doubted that she would ever be able to get on or off a bus wearing it. She blushed. Already, in her head, she had purchased it and was now trying to clamber onto a bus in it. Where was she going to, a high class knocking shop? Or was she just going to go swinging her handbag on a street corner?

But the more she looked at it, the more she wanted it. Estate agent Hayley would look great in it, and not in a cheap way. That Hayley would wear it with confidence. That Hayley would challenge anyone who questioned her choice of clothes. She wouldn't play safe and choose only brown and beige to hide in. That Hayley would revel in the attention she commanded, flirting with the limelight.

She reached out and stroked the supple leather. It felt smooth and sensuous under her finger tips as she traced the ebony hide down to the hem line. Her hand dropped away. She wasn't ready for this yet. But it won't be long, whispered estate agent Hayley in her ear.

"We can't have staff drooling over the merchandise now can we?"

She jumped. She had been caught, and estate agent Hayley was nowhere to be seen. Willing her cheeks not to burn bright red she slowly turned and looked into the pale blue eyes of Anthony Pickard.

"I don't think that's quite you, do you?" He smiled as though sharing an intimate joke.

She stared at him through narrowed eyes, she really didn't like this man. "Quite the reverse, it's very much me. In fact I have one similar at home." She glanced back over her shoulder. "No, actually you're right, now I look at it. The one at home is much shorter." Mentally she chalked up a point before swiftly walking away.

"Lesbian," she heard him mutter. She really, really didn't like him, and everything he stood for. She hoped Jane would see him for exactly what he was before it was too late.

Catching up with Marianne later that afternoon Hayley told her about the man who had wanted her to take him on a fantasy tour of a three bedroom semi-detached with dungeons. She demonstrated to Marianne how she had whipped the cubicle wall with the strap of her handbag as she counted out the lashes in the well-appointed but compact dungeon – well she had very little to work with in such a confined space. Hayley didn't have chance to tell her about Luke Skywalker and the debt collector before she spotted Jane sitting alone in the canteen. And having heard the shop girls gossiping about Anthony Pickard's antics, she knew Jane was going to need all the support she could get. "Do you mind if we join you?" Hayley was rewarded with the biggest smile she had ever seen.

65

Marianne

The debt collector's visit to Marianne's home had been the last straw. She was cornered. She had no option but to go back to her plan. All morning she had been working up the nerve to do it.

"I'll just pop the receipt in the bag okay?" Her palms were sweating and she felt sure that everyone could see her guilt. She had made a big fuss of removing the security tag, whilst sliding the customer's cash underneath the till drawer rather than in it. Finally she slipped a blank portion of till roll into the woman's bag. "There you are, now you have a lovely day." She held the handles tightly together as she passed the bag over the counter. The customer smiled in return and wandered away.

She exhaled slowly. She couldn't understand how people could steal for a thrill. This was not her idea of thrilling at all.

"Interesting technique."

Marianne spun round and just caught the pop of pink bubble gum before it was noisily sucked back into the mouth of Sharon, one of the junior assistants. Sharon continued to chew. Her jaws grinding the rubbery pulp and her lips parted to show a sliver of it wrapped around her tongue before it was once more inflated into a small sugary bulb.

"I....I....don't know what you mean." Fire shot up through her stomach until the heat reached her scalp.

"I saw what you did." Sharon leant back against the pillar that had shielded her seconds earlier. Her large breasts lay heavily on her folded arms as she studied Marianne.

"I didn't do anything."   She attempted a haughty glare.

"Course you didn't." Sharon smiled widely fully exposing the gobbet of gum lodged between her teeth. Her mascara laden eye lid closed in a slow wink. "Your secret's safe with me."

The two women stared at each other.

"Eh Shaz give us a hand will yer."   A young girl appeared dragging a box full of coat hangers.

"Yeah be along in a sec." Sharon leaned in towards Marianne and blew another bubble. "Catch you later." She turned and walked towards her friend.

Fear and desperation filled Marianne's heart as she watched the swagger of Sharon's sizeable hips as they swayed in time to the jangle of her Creole earrings.

She must tell someone about the mess she was in. She had added the real possibility of a criminal record to the growing list of reasons Jack should divorce her. As soon as she saw Hayley go for a break she closed her till and followed her to the canteen. They collected their coffee. Marianne took a deep breath and was about to launch into her confession when Hayley turned and made a beeline for Jane who was sitting by herself. The opportunity had gone and she was another step closer to the edge.

66

Amanda

She waited for him to leave the house before she opened the wardrobe and dragged out a selection of clothes. Bundling them into plastic bags she wondered how she was going to carry them all to work. Today Sam was going to take photographs of the clothes to put on Ebay. She surveyed the half a dozen bags that lay on the floor. She could call a taxi, but then that would eat into her precious savings and every penny counted. Bin bags, she would use bin bags. And so, laden with three bin bags, she hauled the load to work.

Charlie helped her through the doors insisting on taking a bin bag from her before almost toppling over with the weight of it.

"Don't worry Charlie, I can manage, I don't want you to put your back out."

"No One's Perfect." Charlie stooped as he walked back to his chair.

"Oh no I'm not criticising Charlie, it's my fault I've overloaded them."

Charlie frowned, "No, 'No One's Perfect', nine to two at Dundalk."

"Right, yes I see... horse racing of course." She gathered the bags and went up to the staff room. The familiar flutter began as she thought about meeting Sam.

"Good heavens, what have you got in there?" Marianne was applying lipstick when Amanda shoved open the door to the staff room.

"Just some clothes that your Sam is going to photograph for Ebay." She couldn't help smiling.

"It's really not a bad idea to get some extra cash. I think I might dig out a few things to sell myself."

"Just so that you can make room to buy some more?" The words were out before she could stop them.

"Oh I know exactly what you think of me. You stand there judging me from the security of your perfect little marriage in your perfect little world. What are you going to do with the money you make from Ebay? Give it to one of your cosy charities to make you feel even more righteous?" Marianne's eyes were blazing. "It's not enough that you have your doting husband pandering to your every whim, now you want my Sam to do the same, well it's a good job he's leaving, that's all I can say!" Marianne hurled her lipstick into her bag and rammed it in her locker.

He's leaving. That was all Amanda could grasp from the string of words. The absurdity of the rest of Marianne's tirade had slithered onto the floor. "Sam's leaving?" Her stomach twisted. The flutter had turned into a dull pain.

Marianne still had her back to Amanda. Her shoulders rose and fell and eventually her voice was calmer. "He leaves in a few weeks." She turned and looked directly into Amanda's eyes. "We'll all miss him. But don't worry I'm sure you'll find someone else to do your little jobs."

Amanda reached out to stop Marianne from walking away. "How long..." she swallowed. "How long is he going for?"

"He's got a two year contract with a huge technology corporation. He'll be heading major international projects. It's the chance of a lifetime. He's wasted enough time here."

Marianne shrugged off Amanda's hand.

The blow that Amanda felt was far worse than any David had inflicted upon her.

67

Jane

Sitting in the waiting room she tried to focus on the posters splashed all over the walls – 'Contraceptive Advice Clinic', 'Pregnancy Testing Service', 'Meet Your Midwife', 'Post Natal Depression?', 'Incontinence Advice Line'. That summed up life and it didn't give you much to look forward to.

"Miss Farrell? We're ready for you now, if you'd just like to come through." As quickly as the nurse had appeared she disappeared and Jane hurried after her.

The doctor's office was a much less cluttered affair than the waiting room. The walls were white and unadorned and the bed was covered with a crisp white paper strip.

"So Miss Farrell, we're expecting a baby?" The doctor stared at her over his half-moon glasses.

"Yes, well I am."

"Quite so, quite so." He began scribbling some notes on a pad. "I'm going to refer you to the antenatal clinic. Now then, they will write to you with an appointment for a scan, which you can attend with, or without your partner." He placed his pen down on the desk. "I do need to ask you a few questions about your family medical history, and of course that of baby's father."

She hadn't thought about that. "What kind of information do you need?"

"You know any family history of... let's say diabetes, or heart disease. Things like that."

"Oh." She was going to have to tell her mother an awful lot sooner than she had expected. Then there was the tiny matter of telling Tony.

"Are there any questions you would like to ask me Miss Farrell?" The doctor leant towards her as he waited. The legions of questions that had previously queued up in her mind abruptly marched out of her head just as the prospect of telling Tony marched in. She had nothing.

She looked helplessly at the doctor, her hands twisting in her lap.

"If anything does spring to mind, you can always call the surgery. Meanwhile if you could gather as much medical information from relatives as you can, that would be wonderful." He sat back in his chair. The appointment was clearly over.

She thanked him and left the clinic. She was feeling nauseous once more, but this time it wasn't morning sickness.

68

Hayley

"You're doing really well!" Marianne waved a piece of paper in Hayley's face. It was a printout showing the commission made on the adult phone calls. Hayley's lunch breaks certainly had been busy. She had no idea what the other visitors to the Ladies room thought as she fulfilled strangers' fantasies between bites of a sandwich. It wasn't the most hygienic or practical arrangement, but then if she had her own office and more time she probably wouldn't need to do this kind of work anyway.

As she looked at the statement in Marianne's hand an idea began to form. Would Jane object to her using her office when she didn't need it? It may be worth sounding her out. Only the other day she had heard 'Shaz' the buxom shop assistant and her friend giggling away outside her cubicle door. An audience was extremely distracting. It was difficult enough to sound like a highly sexed dominatrix whilst perched on a toilet seat clutching a cheese and pickle barm cake. Of course 'that Hayley' wouldn't be eating cheese and pickle barm cakes. Her image of 'that Hayley' was one of a sultry siren reclining on white silk sheets. Her long red mane tumbling over her shoulders in sharp contrast to the black lace bra and black leather skirt that she wore. She really couldn't get that leather skirt out of her head. Marianne's voice interrupted her musings.

"Has anyone been asking for me?" Marianne scanned the shop floor.

"Like who?" Hayley looked around too.

"Just anyone?"

"No, no-one's spoken to me. Is everything alright?"

Marianne nodded and looked away.

Hayley sensed that everything wasn't at all alright but perhaps now wasn't the time to pursue it.

"Listen I'm going to see Jane to ask if I can borrow her office. Having somewhere more private for the telephone business might be easier for you to have another go don't you think?"

"Maybe." Marianne didn't sound filled with confidence. "Is it okay if I come with you, I want to ask about overtime?"

"Yes of course, I'll let you know when I'm going to see her." She left Marianne with her troubles and made her way to the fashion department.

Ten minutes later she stood in the changing room. A leather pencil skirt hung next to the mirror. Beside it was a black gossamer blouse. Just the act of taking the items into the changing room had seemed wanton and dangerous. Try them on whispered the voice. It can't do any harm.

She unbuttoned her beige cardigan and lifted her cream polo neck over her head. Her fingers trembled as she undid the tiny buttons on the blouse before slipping it on. Her grey bra which had once been white was clear to be seen through the material, but even taking that into account the effect was remarkable. She stepped out of her own skirt and carefully removed the leather garment from the hanger. Holding her breath she pulled the skirt over her hips. The zip glided up its runner, firmly embracing her waist.

'That Hayley' stared out from the mirror and a smile slowly spread across her face. 'I told you,' she said. She was amazed at her own figure, usually hidden under layers of sensible clothes. Here was the slim silhouette of a sophisticated woman. She ignored the American tan tights which bunched around her ankles. Clothes had never bothered her before. They were merely a way of keeping her flesh covered and warm. But this she loved.

Reluctantly she peeled off the skirt and placed the blouse back on its hanger. These clothes weren't for her

– were they? Her fingers lingered over the rail that she had returned them to. She walked away closing her ears to that Hayley's cries of 'No, no, no.' And started back towards the staffroom.

"Excuse me Madame?" A tall man in a trench coat was standing by the door to the stairwell. "I wonder if you could help me?"

She looked around to see who he was talking to. She realised, for once, she wasn't invisible and he was talking to her. "What can I do for you?" She noticed he had a warm smile.

"I'm looking for someone and hoped you could point me in the right direction?"

"Who are you looking for?"

"Marianne Drummond. Do you know where she'll be?"

Hayley hesitated, torn between the desire to be helpful and a wariness to protect Marianne.

"I'm Mister Spanker, she is expecting my visit."

Her mouth dropped open. She quickly shut it and pointed back to the department she had just come from. "Women's wear, just through there."

He thanked her as he held open the door to the stairwell for her.

With eyes downcast she raced down the stairs to the cloakroom.

She sat panting on the wooden bench below the coats. So Mister Spanker from the debt solutions company wasn't another chat-line client. Obviously Marianne hadn't been able to sort out her financial problems. She had to help her. At least she was going to see Jane about office space. She just needed to decide how she could get Marianne to overcome her sex chat fears. This was a dilemma she never thought she would have to face.

She took a notebook from her bag. Perhaps she could make up some cue cards that Marianne could use as a prompt, rather than stick to a whole script. She knew Marianne became painfully shy when it came to the chat line business. Maybe she could play on that, make it work for her rather than against her. She clicked her pen on and off thoughtfully before she began to write:

'*I'm new to all of this, but I'm a very willing student.*'

'*Would you like to guide me through your fantasy? I know I would be in safe hands.*'

'*Be gentle with me big man, I am a chat line virgin after all.*'

She closed the notebook. Suddenly she felt very tired and as far removed from a dominatrix as she could imagine.

The day over, once more she found herself in an empty house. It looked as though Neil had been home and gone out again. His office shoes were placed neatly by the back door. She could still smell the shoe polish which he applied every three days to 'extend the life of the leather' he often told her as he buffed and buffed.

The wellington boots were gone from the folded newspaper that he usually parked them on. A few clumps of dried mud remained. He must be at the allotment. He was spending more and more time there recently. She wondered if she should be worried about this. She decided not. He enjoyed gardening. It wasn't as though he was having a mad passionate affair in his potting shed.

Halfway through clearing the draining board of breakfast dishes she stopped. When was the last time they had made love? She couldn't honestly remember. A fact that Mister Luke Skywalker would be very surprised at. He had phoned that lunchtime to tell her that he was looking for somewhere with a granny flat for R2D2. Now that man was seriously strange.

The evenings were longer and she supposed it was only logical that Neil would want to take advantage of the daylight. Even more so than spending time with her? An hour later she saw the top of his head as he passed the kitchen window.

"Your tea's still warm, it's in the oven." She pulled out a chair for him, whilst he removed his boots carefully making sure the mud was confined to the newspaper.

"Sorry but I've already eaten." His back was to her as he washed his hands in the sink.

"Did you take a sandwich?" She didn't know why this bothered her so much, but she needed to ask.

"No, I picked up something on the way to the allotment."

To anyone else this wouldn't mean a great deal, but to her this was huge. Neil would never spend money on a sandwich as long as there was bread in the bread bin and breath in his body. Was there something going on? Had she neglected him so much that he was seeking affection elsewhere?

He smiled in her direction, "Just going to get a shower." Then he left the room.

She sank onto the chair she had pulled out for him and stared at the closed door. What should she do? What would that Hayley do? Immediately she thought of the leather skirt hanging on its rail in the shop. 'You could wear that. That would make him think,' the voice said. She shook her head. That wasn't the answer. She wasn't sure what the answer was but introducing him to that Hayley certainly wasn't.

SARAH BARTON

69

Marianne

She shouldn't have exploded at Amanda like that. The stress of her situation oozed out of every pore and it was getting more and more difficult to present a rational facade. But she really shouldn't have snapped. Her disquiet about Amanda's casual treatment of her adoring husband and her interest in Sam still rankled but even so her reaction was wrong. Did she expect that lashing out at Amanda would ease her own torment? It didn't. And seeing the look of utter horror on Amanda's face gave her no satisfaction at all. Throughout the day her thoughts had swung from Amanda to her own problems and the imminent visit from the debt collector.

Even though Hayley had confirmed that no-one had been asking about her yet, her nerves still jangled and her eyes were constantly drawn to the flow of shoppers shuffling on and off the escalators. Hayley's suggestion that she could try again with the chat-line experiment had done nothing to calm her. And she couldn't believe that she had made the situation worse by telling Jack that she had invested in a pension scheme. The edge was getting closer and closer.

The money that she had 'borrowed' from Peltham's store now amounted to the grand sum of thirty-eight pounds. It wouldn't even cover one interest payment to the loan company. In fact, she thought, the interest probably grew by that amount each hour. She had decided to approach Jane again about overtime. She would ask when she went with Hayley to see her. Even if she had to work every weekend and every night to make headway into her debts, that's what she would have to do.

"Hello beautiful." She felt a hand slip round her waist.

"Excuse me?" She turned and stepped sharply away from Anthony Pickard's grip.

She noticed the sheen on his slicked back hair. Its shine was in direct competition with his overly white teeth. She shrank further away.

"Have you been working hard? Marianne isn't it?" If possible his smile broadened threatening to split his face in two at any moment she felt sure.

"I always work hard." She tried not to sound too defensive. She just wanted him to go away.

"I'm sure you do. You certainly seem to have been very busy."

Was there an edge to his voice? What did he mean? She stared into his tanned face, but couldn't see anything other than polite, if over friendly, interest. She tried to smile back, but she was certain it came across more like a nervous grimace.

"Well I'd better let you carry on." He winked at her and nodded in the direction of a waiting customer before retreating.

She sighed deeply, planted a professional smile on her face and turned to greet her waiting shopper.

As soon as she saw him she knew. He was wearing a trench coat. It was open at the neck and revealed the collar of a grey suit, which had acquired a shine that only age and relentless ironing could achieve. His hand burrowed into his inner breast pocket and he produced a white business card. She couldn't move, she just stared at him. The card remained suspended between them. He didn't look like an ogre. In fact he actually looked rather pleasant she thought.

"Joseph Spanker, Cloons and Dunnit Debt Solutions. I believe you've been expecting me?"

Over his shoulder she could see Sharon watching her through narrowed eyes.

She wasn't sure how long she had stood there staring at him. He'd coughed and repeated his introduction before she was jolted into responding. She took his business card without looking at it. She didn't need to.

"Yes, I suppose I have been expecting you." All the doors of escape were slamming shut. Banging closed one after the other in her corridor of debt. She knew about the reputation of debt collectors and loan sharks. He looked like neither.

"Shall we go somewhere quieter?" By his tone he could quite easily have been offering her a cup of tea.

"I can't leave my till for long." She realised she was clinging onto the edge of the counter as though it was a life raft.

"I won't take up too much of your time," he said gently.

Sharon had edged closer and closer during their exchange. "I'll take over here for a bit. You know, keep a close eye on things whilst you sort out your... business."

Marianne wanted to slap her sly face but instead she reluctantly let go of the life raft and plunged once more into the murky depths of panic. She led him over to the seating area where bored husbands waited for their wives to try on endless garments before settling on the first.

Twisting her wedding ring round and round her finger she sat down and waited for the threats and blackmail to begin.

"Now Mrs Drummond, we have a bit of a situation here, don't we?"

"Yes and I'm really sorry. I didn't mean for it to come to this. It wouldn't have been so bad if my husband hadn't been made redundant." She dropped her voice. "But I haven't helped, I know I haven't. I've been so stupid, and selfish." She nodded as tears coursed down her face. "If Jack finds out, that will be the end. He trusted me you see? He's always trusted me, and I've let him down badly. He works so hard too, and then there's me just frittering it away. I wouldn't be surprised if he divorced me, and I wouldn't blame him. No I wouldn't."

"Please Mrs Drummond, calm down. Oh dear." He handed her a neatly folded hanky.

"I am trying, really I am. I'm applying for overtime, and I'm having a go at a second job... I'm not very good at it, but I'm going to give it another go. It really isn't my kind of thing you see, but I know I've got no choice. So you see I am trying." She looked desperately into his eyes, silently begging him to understand. She watched his shoulders slump.

"No, well this isn't my kind of thing either."

She felt sure that the lecture would begin any moment, dismissing her excuses, and demanding payment in kind, or worse seizing her and Jack's home. It was hopeless. The sheer magnitude of what she was facing made her feel weak and her head began to spin. Her sobs were quieter now as she waited for her fate.

"Listen Mrs Drummond, I hate seeing you so upset. It's clear to me that you're doing everything you can to pay and the interest rate is scandalous I have to admit." He paused as though reaching an important decision. "I'll tell you what, how about you try to sort out a payment in the next few days – for as much as you can manage. I'll try to put together a realistic repayment plan. Meanwhile I'll stall the company?"

She blinked. "Really? Do you mean that?"

"Yes I do. As I said this really isn't my kind of thing either. You can see I'm no good at it, but like you, I have no choice. I will try to help."

She leant forward and kissed his cheek. "Thank you, thank you so much. I won't let you down." She stood and made to walk away. Suddenly she went back and kissed his cheek again. "You don't know how much this chance means." And she turned once more to go back to her till.

"Now that's what I call customer service!" Tony was lounging on a velvet upholstered armchair a few feet from where she had been sitting. He slowly stretched before sauntering away. The hairs on her arms stood on end and the feeling of revulsion swept through her body. She just wanted to be at home with Jack. The job she had once loved was becoming more and more of a nightmare from which she couldn't escape.

70

Amanda

She felt numb. Marianne's news about Sam had snuffed out the tiny flame of hope that flickered inside her. She had come on to the sales floor and logged onto her till. She remembered doing neither. It was the sound of someone humming that drifted into her thoughts.

Ada was happily folding up bath towels and filling her trolley with them. She seemed oblivious to the ones which kept toppling out as she tried to drag the trolley across the floor.

"Oh dear, it's such a struggle these days."

Amanda scooped up the stray towels as she followed her. "Ada, I don't think you need all these do you?"

Ada looked from Amanda to the wad of towels hanging out of her tartan shopper. As though surprised that they were there, she slowly shook her head. "Now I come to think of it I probably don't."

"Let me help you put them back." Amanda guided the overloaded trolley back to the bathroom display and began to empty it, re-folding each towel as Ada looked on.

"Can I help?" She hadn't seen Sam arrive. He reached into the bag to take more towels out and his hand brushed hers. She jumped and stumbled back.

"Sorry I didn't mean to startle you." He cupped her elbow with a steadying hand and grinned.

He had no idea of the effect he had on her as she tried to slow her breathing.

"You ladies, nervous creatures aren't you?" He winked at Ada and Ada giggled behind her gloved hand. He pulled out the remaining towels and stacked them neatly on the shelves.

"Coffee now I think." He offered Amanda his arm to link and made a cheeky salute to Ada. Ada giggled again before pushing away her empty cart.

"I... I can't just leave my till." How dare he be going away.

"Yes you can, I've asked one of the other assistants to cover. I told her I had a sales issue that needed personal attention."

He steered her through the mid-morning shoppers and into the cafe`.

"So are you ready for the photo shoot?" He pretended to click an imaginary camera.

"When do you leave?" The question leapt out of her mouth.

He looked down at the cup in front of him and began to stir its contents. When he looked up, all remnants of light hearted flirtation had vanished. "In three weeks."

She nodded. "Well, as Marianne said, it's the chance of a life time." Please don't go she screamed in her head. "It'll be a fantastic experience for you, and will look terrific on you C.V." Stay here with me, she begged as she mentally clung onto him.

"Yes, it's an amazing opportunity. I'm very lucky." He continued to stare at the coffee.

"Brilliant. Well I'm ready when you are for the photo shoot." Her voice was overly chirpy, but she just needed to get through this. She had only known this man for such a short time, and yet she felt a connection with him that she had never felt with any man before. And now she was going to lose him. She looked at his bent head and without being able to stop herself she reached out and touched the soft waves of hair. His head jerked up and she saw an expression of surprise on his face. Was that all, or was there also a hint of pity there too? She sharply withdrew her hand and looked away. She had mistaken his courteous attention for something else. Of course he was just helping out his sister's colleague. They finished their coffees and with all the bravado she could muster she laughed at his jokes and played photographer's assistant until all the photographs had been taken.

"Thank you for your help. I really appreciate your time and effort." She bundled the clothes back into bags.

"It was no problem at all. I'll put the pictures on Ebay and let's see what happens."

"Great, you could just let Marianne know and I'll sort it out with her." There was nothing left to put into bags so she concentrated on repositioning the mannequins.

"Do you mind?" He held the camera in front of his face and pointed the lens at her.

"Why, what are you doing?" Blood rushed to her cheeks.

"Just one for me, please?" He clicked the shutter. "Beautiful," he murmured.

No-one had ever called her beautiful. Not even David when they were courting.

"I'll bring my laptop next time and show you how the clothes look." He placed the camera in a leather bag.

"Next time?"

"Yes, next time I see you. You didn't think I was going to let you go that easily did you?" He smiled his cheeky smile and blew a kiss as he left.

'Please don't ever let me go' her heart whispered.

71

Jane

Her parents were coming over to see her. How was she going to tell them her news? Of course if circumstances were different they would be delighted. Thrilled at the prospect of welcoming their grandchild into a perfect world where mummy and daddy would treasure the baby in their little cottage with roses around the door. Sadly the reality was that she lived in a one bedroom apartment on the fourth floor with no roses around the door and quite possibly no daddy either.

As always, when she was pre-occupied, she found inspecting the store's sales floors therapeutic. The store was busy. Early summer stock filled window displays and there was an air of optimism. A promise of a glorious summer, and long lazy days in fragrant gardens. It reminded her that the Summer Launch was now only a week away, and final preparations had to be made before the American contingent arrived.

Tony had been conspicuous by his absence and apart from a few short phone calls she had hardly spoken to him. He had been spending a lot of time at head office, and when he was at the store he managed to avoid her very successfully. She hadn't tried too hard to seek him out either.

Suddenly, as though she had conjured him up, he appeared behind Marianne at her cash desk. She could see the flash of his smile. She had been the recipient of that smile so many times, but not so much now. His arm was casually placed round Marianne's waist, although

Marianne didn't look very happy about it. A few weeks ago a gesture like that would have sent her into a paroxysm of jealousy. Today she felt only mild curiosity. Their conversation seemed to be cut short by a man in a trench coat who was waiting by the till.

She watched Tony move to the other side of the pay desks but his attention still seemed to be fixed on Marianne. This suited her as she continued her survey of the store, although she kept checking over her shoulder to make sure that Tony wasn't anywhere near.

Today the bright colours of the clothes and exotic smells of the perfume had done little to distract her. Wandering through the various sections of merchandise she felt thwarted by the emotional mess she was wading through. She just wanted to see a friendly face, someone who never judged her. Charlie, she would go and see Charlie. Waiting by the antiquated lifts she thought about her parents' looming visit in the morning. "What a complete and utter mess. I can't get anything right."

"Pardon?"

She hadn't realised that she'd actually spoken out loud. The man in the trench coat was standing next to her, with a polite look of enquiry on his face.

"Sorry, just talking to myself. Life can be rubbish sometimes can't it?" She didn't know why she felt the need to talk, especially to a stranger.

"It can be rubbish you're right. Do you sometimes think 'what am I doing with my life?' I know I do all the time." He had a kind face, one that you might look for in a crowd and feel at home when you found it.

"Me too, I know exactly how you feel. I wish at the moment I wasn't me. I wish I was someone else, somewhere completely different." Alarmingly, she could feel the all too common prick of tears.

"Oh dear, please don't get upset. I'm always making people upset. Unfortunately it's a hazard of the job, and I hate it. I'm so sorry, I certainly didn't mean to upset you."

The lift door pinged open and he stood aside to allow her through first.

"Thank you," she acknowledged his gallantry. "I'm sorry it's just me. I'm an emotional wreck at the moment. Please don't take it personally."

He nodded. He seemed relieved that she had exonerated him. As they stepped out of the lift he stopped and looked round, "Could you tell me which way is the exit to Bower Street? I really should know, my mum comes here all the time, but since I let my own shop go, I try not to make a habit of frequenting other people's. Sometimes it's easier not to be reminded of what could have been."

She nodded sympathetically, "I understand completely. Come on I'll show you, I'm going that way myself. The staff exit is closest."

They walked together through the perfume hall and into the foyer where Charlie was on duty.

"Here we are, Bower Street." She led him into the staff reception. She was surprised when Charlie got to his feet and warmly hugged the man before hoisting open the double doors. "Good to see you son."

"You too Charlie." He squeezed the old man's shoulder as he passed then turning, he said to her, "I'm Joe by the way. It was really nice meeting you. I hope everything turns out alright for you. Perhaps next time I see you I won't make you cry, although I can't guarantee it." With a wave he left the store and Charlie closed the door behind him.

"He's a good one that one, a fine man." Charlie nodded at Joe's retreating back.

"He did seem very nice actually." She smiled, Charlie seemed to know everyone. "But anyway let's talk about you. How are you feeling? I thought I'd just come down and ask."

"I'm much better now. Ada's looking after me very well." He sniffed the flower in his lapel, a white rose bud then his watery eyes fixed on her. "But it's you who needs to be looked after though Miss Jane, it's you. You know that if you need me for anything I'm here for you."

"I know that Charlie and thank you." She dropped her eyes from his. She couldn't start blubbing again. She smiled weakly and left Charlie with his paper. What a strange afternoon. For a brief moment in the lift she felt as though she had met a kindred spirit and she'd probably never meet him again.

72

Hayley

"... yes I know you're here to rescue me... you want me to do what with your light sabre? ... Luke Skywalker get on your knees and beg for mercy!"

The phone call didn't last long. She was worried that perhaps she was getting too good at it. She needed to slow the pace down a little. The more time they were on the line, the more money she made. Hayley sighed as she stretched her legs out in front of her. Her sensible brown brogues had been replaced by sensible black lace-ups. She didn't own anything that even vaguely resembled stilettos. That was going to have to be addressed she decided, just as she heard the door to the Ladies room swing open.

"Hayley, are you in here?"

She stooped and could see Marianne's beautiful black patent shoes under the door. "Where else would I be?"

"True. Listen Hayley, there's been a call from the care home. They want you to call them back as soon as you can."

Hayley fumbled with the lock and yanked the bolt back. "What's wrong, what's happened?"

"I don't know, they just said to call them back."

She dashed past Marianne and ran down to the cloakroom where her own phone was. Her fingers trembled as she found the care home's number and dialled.

"Hi, this is Hayley. Someone called about my mother Sheila?"

"Hello Hayley, we don't want you to worry but Sheila's picked up a bit of a chest infection and we've taken her to hospital for some checks. We haven't had any results yet but we wanted to keep you informed."

"Is she at St Mary's?"

"Yes that's right, ward A2."

"Thank you." She ended the call just as Marianne caught up with her.

"Mum's got a chest infection, so I'm going to finish early to go and see her. Would you let the office know, and cover for me?" Hayley thrust her arms into her coat.

"Yes of course I will."

Her rush to the hospital was unnecessary she soon discovered.

"... so you see, my son, Adam, he's in Washington you know? He's a very important man, and I'm going to take a trip to see him." Her mother nodded emphatically at the young nurse. "He lives in a huge house, with two garages, two! Can you imagine?"

The nurse had a glazed expression on her face so Hayley guessed she had probably been her mother's captive audience for some time. "Hi mum, how are you feeling?" Hayley took a seat next to the bed.

"Do I know you? Are you a friend of Adam's?" Her mother frowned and tapped her cheek with a bony finger.

"It's Hayley mum, your daughter?" Suddenly she had a flash of inspiration. "Adam's sister?"

"Of course, Hayley, how lovely to see you." The frown was replaced with a smile. "What are you doing here? Have you come to see Adam?"

Hayley exchanged looks with the nurse. "No, mum I'm just here to see you." She stroked her mother's hand relieved that she wasn't wired up to several machines. On the way over her imagination had presented her with a scene of bleeping screens and an oxygen mask strapped to her mother's face.

"We've given her antibiotics and she's responding extremely well." The nurse hurried over to the door. "I'll give you five minutes then you must rest Sheila." And with a rustle of her blue scrubs she was gone.

"He's such a good boy, Adam. He's always checking how I am. Such a good boy."

Hayley was used to the constant adulation that her mother bestowed upon Adam. It had always been the same. The irony was that he had left for America at the very first opportunity and had only ever been back once. Contact was rare and brief. He never remembered birthdays even though her mother insisted that he had called. The nursing home had never spoken to him. He had, Hayley felt, discarded his family, not even returning for his father's funeral. And yet he was the one her mother would remember, the apple of her eye.

Hayley watched her mother drift off to sleep. She kissed her forehead and crept out of the room.   The bus route home took her past the allotments and, in a split second decision she jumped off at that stop and picked her way through the narrow dirt paths to Neil's patch. The vegetables were no longer surrounded by rich dark soil. In fact the rows of carrots and potatoes could hardly be recognised beneath the tangle of weeds that now covered the plot. In the potting shed cobwebs lay undisturbed over the spade and fork. She looked no further. Her heart felt like lead, and she only had herself to blame.

Abandoning any idea of climbing back on the bus she began the long walk home. She had to think. She didn't know how she was going to tackle Neil's blatant lies about his frequent absences from home.

73

Marianne

Jack had an interview – the first one since being laid off. Hayley had left early to see her mother so Marianne's hope of also finishing early were dashed. Racing home she hoped to catch Jack before he went out. He was already dressed in a crisp white shirt and a pair of chinos. His attention focused on fastening a cuff link. As she watched him from across the room her heart ached. He was the love of her life and she adored him. She went over and fastened his cuff links. She could smell the musk of his aftershave. Leaning in towards him she kissed his neck. Her eyes closed as she savoured his scent.

His arms went round her and he held her to him. She didn't want to move. She wanted to stay in the circle of his arms forever. She was safe and loved and everything else seemed very far away. But all too soon he released her. Smoothing down his shirt he stepped away and put his hands on his hips. "So, how do I look? Would you employ me?"

"Employ you, eat you, whatever." She smiled at him.

"Wish me luck." He picked up his jacket and checked the pocket for his keys.

"Good luck my darling. They would be mad not to want you to start straight away."

A kiss on her lips and he had gone. She went to the window to watch him drive away, silently praying that this would be his break. He deserved that much at least. He had sent out so many applications for jobs, but every day that passed he became more and more dejected. She suddenly realised that she had absolutely no idea what job the interview was for. Well whatever it was it would mean an income.

She was so lucky to have a husband like Jack. But would she still have him if he ever found out about the mess she was in? She tried not to look at the hands of the clock but failed. He had been gone for at least an hour and a half. Surely that had to be a good sign. She gave up trying to be busy and sat by the window and waited.

At last his car crawled to a halt outside their house. She ran to the front door and opened it. Shifting from foot to foot she watched Eric, their neighbour, intercept Jack and try to engage him in conversation. Jack eventually managed to get away from him and hurried up the path.

She quickly closed the door as soon as Jack stepped in to prevent Eric from starting a conversation with her too. "So how did it go?"

"Good, it seemed to go well. I've got my fingers crossed anyway."

"I forgot to ask you what the job is." She followed him into the kitchen.

He turned and tapped the side of his nose. "Let's not tempt fate by talking about it. I'll tell you when I hear some news."

It was good to see Jack so up-beat and yet there was something niggling her that she just couldn't put her finger on.

74

Amanda

He had called her beautiful. Her. Amanda. She wasn't beautiful of course, but that didn't matter. He had called her beautiful. She looked at the pale skinny woman that stared back.

"You should eat more." Her mother stared at the reflection too. "It's good to have a bit of padding. Not too much. Not like your Aunt Beatrice, God rest her soul, she had enough padding to upholster a cinema."

Peering closely into the glass Amanda examined her features. She didn't have the classic Jewish nose, but she had inherited her mother's almond shaped eyes. She supposed they could be called pretty, just missing out on being exotic, but still a little above ordinary she thought.

"You need some colour in your cheeks. I don't know why you don't put a little blusher on. Make yourself pretty." Her mother's head tilted to one side as she studied her. "Maybe you should wear a fringe. It would make your forehead look smaller and shorten your face."

"Thanks." She didn't need enemies when she had her mother.

"I'm just trying to help. So what am I supposed to do? I'm only your mother."

She had to admit her mother was right. She had a face that wasn't ugly. And a figure that could be flattered by the right clothes. Her musings were interrupted by the slamming of the front door. She stepped away from the mirror in guilty confusion over her rare vanity.

"Amanda... Amanda come down I've got a surprise for you." David's voice sounded cheerful, almost too cheerful.

She slowly went down stairs. Without realising it, her fingers were in her mouth and she was chewing at the flesh around her nails. By the time she entered the kitchen he was sitting at the table, brightly coloured brochures spread across its wooden surface. He looked up then patted the seat next to him. "We're moving."

"Moving?" She remained in the doorway.

"Yes, moving. Come and sit down and I'll show you the properties I've chosen."

"But why do we need to move?" She didn't want to get any closer to him, and she certainly didn't want to look at the slick brochures that were fanned out in his hand.

"It's a deal I've been working on for a while. I've persuaded the company to open an office in Aberdeenshire. And I'm going to be running it." He smiled triumphantly. "They want me to do a recce first and then it's all systems go. We'll rent initially whilst we have a look round." He waved his hand across the photographs of pretty cottages and dry walled fields.

"But what about everything we have here?" Her world was being snatched away from her. The menacing vision of a life in a remote cottage with just her and David was suffocating. She took gulps of air before slipping into the chair at the furthest end of the table.

"What do you mean 'everything we have here'? We don't have anything to keep us here." David stared at her.

"My job. My friends."

He laughed. It was a cruel and cold sound. "What friends are they then my lonely Amanda? Are they real or as imaginary as your dead mother?"

She felt her face flush. Her need to talk to her dead mother was none of his business. As for her friends..."Well I do have friends, real friends!"

"You don't need them, you've got me." His tone was sharp. Patience clearly exhausted. "You'd better give notice that you'll be leaving your sad little job. I want to be able to move within the next few weeks." He gathered up the property catalogues, walked round the table and dropped the pile in front of her. They landed with a smack and she jumped. "I'm sure you'll find something that suits." He reached the door and looked over his shoulder. "And don't worry those friends of yours will soon forget you."

The sad thing was that he was right. She laid her head on the glossy paper. She could smell the ink. She closed her eyes shutting out the bright interiors and pretty gardens.

75

Jane

"Hellooo." Her mother's sing song voice accompanied her as she swept into the office. Jane's father followed. Hormones played with her emotions like puppeteers, and the tears that were never far away welled in her eyes as she exchanged hugs and kisses with her parents. Her mother stepped back holding Jane at arm's length as she stared at her daughter. She stiffened under her mother's scrutiny.

"How is everyone?" Jane tried to keep her tone bright and breezy as she broke away from her mother.

"We're fine darling. Your father's still trying to play golf. I've given up on baking cakes for the church fund. I'm quite sure most don't even get to the cake sale. All I can say is the Vicar's getting fatter and fatter. But enough about us, how are you?" Translation: have you got a boyfriend yet? "And how was your weekend away?" Translation: tell me if there were any potential boyfriends there.

She had forgotten that she'd told them that she was going away with the girls, her chest tightened with panic.

"Your girly weekend darling, how was it?" Translation: I really need to know if you received any romantic advances.

"Oh it was lovely. We had such a great time. You know lots of giggles, shopping and wine... That kind of thing." Lying made her feel sick – as so many things did these days.

"We can't wait to hear all about it. Did you see lots of interesting places?" Translation: I want details of any flirting that took place. Her mother settled herself into the chair and waited with a look of expectancy on her face. Her father meanwhile was studying the certificates which decorated Jane's wall. His hands clasped behind his back as he slowly moved along the wall.

She loved her parents so much. They had given her everything. She hoped that she would be just as good a parent. A wave of emotion crashed down on her and she gulped back the tears. Just as her mother reached out to her, concern written all over her face, there was a knock at the door. Jane snatched at the distraction. "Come in."

Hayley and Marianne almost fell into the room like a pair of Siamese twins.

"Oh sorry Jane, we didn't know you were busy." Hayley started backing out forcing Marianne to reverse too.

"Don't be silly girls, come on in." She waved them in. "Mum, these are my two friends Hayley and Marianne."

"How wonderful to meet you both." Jane's mum got to her feet and shook first Hayley's hand then Marianne's. "And were you two on Jane's girly weekend away?"

Jane's eyes widened. She opened her mouth but couldn't think of anything to say.

There was a hush in the room. She watched Hayley glance in her direction. Hayley must have received the silent message as she nodded vigorously. "Yes, yes we were and it was really... great wasn't it Marianne?"

"Er...yes... it was fabulous actually, and we can't wait to do it all over again." Marianne smiled at Jane's mum.

Jane mouthed thank you at the girls whilst her mother settled herself once again in the chair. Her father returned to reading the wall. She wasn't ready to tell her parents that she had just spent a dirty weekend with the married father of her unborn child. She wasn't sure she would ever be ready for that.

76

Hayley

She had waited for Neil to come home, sitting at the kitchen table with her eyes trained on the window. His head eventually bobbed past. Opening the kitchen door, he made an exaggerated stride to the piece of newspaper like it was an island surrounded by shark infested waters. After balancing on one leg and then the other to remove his boots he smiled apologetically at her. "Sorry I'm late I got carried away tying up the sweet peas."

She arranged a smile on her face. "Well I'm sure it's easy to lose track of time when you're so busy tying things up. How's the allotment coming on? I really should go down there sometime." Her smile was even sweeter.

"Yes, everything's super, coming on a treat. You don't need to come down though because I'll be able to start bringing produce home soon enough."

"I can't wait to see the results of your labour of love." 'Ask him Hayley, ask him,' that Hayley urged, but she couldn't, not yet.

The weekend held thoughts about her battle with this unknown interloper within her marriage, and they didn't disappear when she got back into work. She had never thought she would have to fight for her own husband. The past few weeks had been full of things she would never have thought she would be doing. Paying for a leather pencil skirt and sheer blouse was something else she never thought she would be doing but here she was doing just that. She hurriedly took her purchases down to the staff room. She opened the bag and inhaled the rich scent of leather before tucking it underneath her coat. She blamed that Hayley for this. All night her head had been filled with suggestions of seduction and guile. Now she had to push these thoughts aside and try to concentrate on work. With a determined effort she went in search of Marianne.

Kneeling on the floor emptying boxes Marianne seemed to be in her own world.

"Are you ready to go and see Jane?" Hayley called from the stock room door.

"Yes I'll just tidy these up then I'll be with you."

She watched Marianne finally close the last box. "Right let's go then."

Hayley wasn't sure how she was going to approach the subject of using Jane's office without telling Jane exactly what she wanted to use it for. She didn't think Jane was a prude, but whether she was broad-minded enough to consider her suggestion was a different matter.

They clattered up the staff stair-well. For once it was Hayley making the small talk. Marianne was unusually quiet. As they turned into the plush corridor leading to Jane's office, Hayley's determination wobbled. 'Come on Hayley,' she admonished herself and with shoulders back she marched to the office door. She knocked and without allowing herself another hesitation, strode straight in with Marianne right behind.

She hadn't met Jane's parents before, but she recognised them from the photograph on the desk. Embarrassment quelled anything that she may have been planning to say as she apologised and tried to make a hasty retreat.

She hadn't expected to be quizzed about a girly weekend by Jane's mum, and it was obvious from the look of horror on Jane's face that she hadn't been expecting that either. One look at Jane and she knew she had to lie. She would have helped Jane anyway, but the favour would add weight to her own request, when the opportunity arose to make it.

She thought that she and Marianne had made a great double act. They recounted tales of the wonderful weekend they'd had and intricate details of the food they'd eaten and the sights they'd visited. By the time they left Jane and her parents, she had almost convinced herself that she had just got back from Barcelona. Perhaps, she wondered, the double act was something they could work on for the chat line?

The working day came to an end and she guarded her precious shopping bags on the crowded bus home. She put the elegant carrier bags with rope handles in the cupboard under the stairs next to less elegant bags sporting hopping bunny rabbits and fluffy chicks. She closed the door on the bizarre contrast of treasures and went into the kitchen.

She wasn't sure she was ready to confront Neil about his so-called visits to the allotment, mainly because she was too afraid of what he might say. He could, and not unjustly, say well what did you expect me to do, whilst you're drooling over babies and pining for a cradle to rock? 'Get your marriage back on track. You know how.' The voice inside her head was calm but firm, 'let me handle him.'

77

Marianne

"Morning Charlie." The weather was getting warmer and her mood was optimistic. Jack's confidence seemed to have been boosted following his interview and she was managing to make the reduced payments set by the debt collector. In fact he would be calling to see her later today to pick up her next instalment. Perhaps things were turning a corner at last.

"Charlie, a gentleman will be calling to see me this afternoon. Please could you send him up to lingerie?"

"Exotic Friend." Charlie's head was buried in his paper.

"No, not really. He's just an acquaintance, and quite ordinary actually."

Charlie looked up. "No, Exotic Friend, nine to two at Lingfield."

"Right yes, Exotic Friend, nine to two at Lingfield. I'll make a mental note."

"You do that Miss." Charlie nodded at her as she went through the double doors.

Was it her imagination, or was Charlie looking so much better these days? His hands didn't appear quite so gnarled, and his movements seemed a little easier.

Guilt slithered through her body. She would take all the overtime she could get and pay back the store. Continuing the lower instalments to pay back the debt wouldn't be too bad, especially if Jack got a new job. She might not even have to go back to the chat line at all. With a slightly lighter heart she went about the sales routine and waited for Joseph Spanker to collect his money. She didn't have to wait too long. At two minutes past one, with his trademark trench coat, he emerged from the lift and raised his hand to Marianne, a gesture halfway between a salute and a wave.

They went to their usual seat and like two spies exchanging secrets, she handed over an envelope. He slipped it into his pocket. His normally clean shaven face was shadowed with stubble and his eyes didn't make contact with hers.

"Mr Spanker is everything alright? I am making the payments that you told me to."

Joe shook his head. "I'm afraid I've got some bad news Mrs Drummond. The agency didn't entirely agree with my solution to your problem and they are terminating my employment." He looked past her, as though the answer could be found on the sports bra display. "They found out about the reduced payment plan and said I had no authority to offer it to you. It's a sackable offence. They've given me two weeks' notice and have already found a replacement. I'm sorry Mrs Drummond but you'll be dealing with someone else in future and the repayments will go back to what they were."

"Oh Mr Spanker... Joe, I'm so sorry too that you've lost your job. That's terrible." Her sympathy for Joe was compounded by the horror of the insurmountable debt she was facing once again.

She watched his figure slowly disappear down the escalator as though he was in sinking sand, taking any hope she had with him.

78

Amanda

She lay on the edge of the bed, always on the edge. Clinging to the cord trim of the mattress was so much second nature to her that she did it in her sleep. She slowly opened her eyes. Daylight had prized its way through a chink in the curtains. It illuminated a slice of the bedroom and the side of David's face as he knelt on the floor by her side. Inwardly her whole being recoiled, but her tightening grip on the mattress was the only outward reaction.

The half of his face she could see was smiling indulgently at her. The other half was veiled by darkness.

"Good morning my love, did you sleep well?"

It was a question which would have been normal had it been asked over the breakfast table. He cocked his head to one side as he waited for her to answer.

"Yes...thank you." She kept her voice as steady as she could whilst looking into the eyes of insanity.

"That's good, very good indeed." He leant in towards her. She forced herself to remain still as he curled a stray strand of hair round her ear, his fingers lightly brushing her cheek.

"I think we should spend the day together. I'll call the store for you. I'm sure it won't be a problem. I can spend all day looking after my Mandy."

"No, no I can't take time..."

His finger pressed against her lips silencing her. "Everything will be fine, you'll see."

Humming quietly he left the room.

She swallowed a sob before it bubbled to the surface. Sam would be calling in to see her today and she had so little time left with him as it was. Now she would have to wait for her next chance to see him.

She could hear David on the phone, explaining his wife's absence. She could imagine the secretary on the other end of the line marvelling at this charming man and his obvious devotion to his ailing wife. Curling into a ball she waited for him to return to 'look after her'.

79

Jane

Jane had spent the rest of the day avoiding her mother's probing looks and the weekend dodging any questions relating to her social activities.

Was there a right or a wrong order in which to tell someone they were going to be a parent or grandparent? Was there a certain protocol that she should follow? On balance, she thought Tony should be told first – why break with tradition?

In the morning she left a message on his voice mail asking to see him. She had been tempted to leave a message explaining she was pregnant too but decided that really wasn't acceptable. Barcelona seemed a lifetime ago, and the silly girl who went there with ideas of romance and love had suddenly grown up. She had glimpsed a Tony that was selfish and arrogant and she now knew that his reaction to the baby was highly unlikely to be one of delight and unrestrained joy.

She didn't have to wait for long.

"Hello Janey, have you been missing me?" His head appeared round the door.

"Desperately." She hadn't meant to sound so sarcastic. It appeared that the sarcasm was wasted on him anyway as his confident strut into the office told her that he truly believed she had missed him desperately.

"Do you want to play out with Tony?" He perched on the edge of her desk.

She was tired of the childish way he always asked questions. How had she not been irritated before by his wheedling?

"No I don't want to play out with you. I have something very important to discuss." She sat back in her chair creating a space between them.

"Ooh, that does sound serious. Is Janey going to tell Tony off?" His bottom lip curled down in a mock pout.

Weeks ago she would have laughed at his boyish behaviour, and found it endearing. Not today. Today she wanted to slap him and tell him to grow up.

"You're going to be a father." That was the slap. There had really been no other way to put it.

"I'm going to be a what now?" He was frowning as he swayed slightly on his perch.

"A father. You know a daddy to a baby." What little patience she had was beginning to fade.

He almost fell off the desk and stumbled into the chair opposite. He was staring at her. His mouth was moving like a fish gasping for air. She waited. She checked her watch. She waited some more. Remembering that she, at least, had had some time to get used to the idea, she refrained from tapping the desk with her finger nails. She felt curiously calm as she waited.

Suddenly, as though the news had finally filtered through his maze of thoughts, his head snapped up. "How do you know I'm the father?"

So no flirting now, she thought wryly. "Because Tony you are the only man I have slept with. Unless you count a three week romance back at university, but that would make it an incredibly long gestation."

"How do I know you've not been sleeping around with anything in trousers?" His face looked pale and clammy.

"I haven't and you're the father." It was a simple statement of fact, not a hysterical finger pointing accusation.

"You'll have it aborted, of course."

"And why would I do that?" At no point had she ever considered an abortion. Perhaps she shouldn't have been shocked at his knee jerk reaction, but instinctively her hands flew to her stomach forming a protective barrier.

"Because it's not wanted." His face twisted as he spat the words out of his mouth.

"You are so wrong. This baby is wanted more than anything else in the world." She tightened her hold, as though he might just rip the baby right out of her.

He jumped out of his seat. "You're not going to pin this one on me. I know what you want. You've always wanted to trap me. You're just desperate and pathetic. Women like you, you're all the same. Picking on vulnerable men, making them pay for it for the rest of their lives. Well you can't trap me. You slag you've probably been putting it about all over the place. Sitting there all prim and proper like butter wouldn't melt, yeah and the rest!" He was panting now, and his cheeks were infused with colour.

She pressed herself as far back into the chair as she could. "Tony we need..."

"No we don't need to do anything. I don't need to do anything because it's not mine." Kicking the chair out of the way he stormed out of the office.

She sat still, cradling the unborn child in her belly. "It's just me and you then."

80

Hayley

They had become almost strangers. Polite, courteous but detached. The crevice had opened up silently and it grew day by day. She would go to work and come home. Neil would go to work and then pretend to go to the allotment. Sometimes she was in bed by the time he arrived home. Any intimacy they had shared had waned to nothing. She couldn't even remember when she had last seen him undress or get dressed in front of her, so distant had their relationship become. She accepted that she had initiated the wedge by becoming so obsessed about having a baby. But the subject had not been raised for a long time and yet the rift continued to grow. It was as though neither one of them knew how to bridge it.

Finding the solution was like trying to find the end of a roll of sticky tape. It didn't matter how many times you turned the reel, the end never materialised. Before she had even reached the staff door it was swung open by Charlie. He held the door with one hand and waved her through with the other. A smile fixed to his face.

"Welcome Miss Hayley." He stepped smartly back to his chair.

Hayley's eyebrows shot up.

"Charlie you're bright and breezy this morning." She looked at the elderly gentleman who somehow didn't appear that elderly at all today.

"It's Ada's cooking. It's marvellous. She said it would do me good, and by God it has. She brought me breakfast this morning and now I feel as though I could climb a mountain." He breathed in deeply the scent of the carnation in his lapel. "Miracle Cure."

"It certainly looks as though it is." Hayley nodded at him.

"No, Miracle Cure, ten to one at Leopardstown."

"Of course, I should have known." Hayley left Charlie once again studying the form.

She tried to sweep her worries about her marriage aside as she began to plan her approach to Jane. Somehow she had to persuade Jane to agree to her using the office for her somewhat intimate lunchtime telephone conversations. Although the current state of her relationship did call into question whether IVF with Neil was even going to be an option. Pushing these thoughts aside she rehearsed her speech, much as she had before her appraisal. Tuesday afternoon and she once again found herself outside Jane's door. This time she waited for permission to enter.

Jane looked pale and tired, but she smiled as Hayley stepped into the room.

"I just wanted to say thank you Hayley for the other day, you know with my parents and the Barcelona thing? You were very good. I almost believed that I had been on a girly weekend away with you. Perhaps you should consider amateur dramatics?" As Jane spoke she waved to the chair opposite her, inviting Hayley to sit.

It was déjà vu, as Hayley's well-rehearsed speech was thrown out of the metaphorical window.

"Well it's funny you should say that because I have a little role playing side line that I'd really like to discuss with you."

Jane leant forward. She could see a spark of interest in Jane's otherwise weary eyes. "Go on."

"You know when Marianne and I were in the toilets the day that you found out you were pregnant?"

"Yes."

"And Marianne's phone kept ringing?"

"Vaguely, I was in a bit of a state at the time." Jane frowned as she tried to recall.

"Yes, yes of course. Well to be truthful with you, we were trying to run an adult chat line. I know it probably

213

sounds bizarre but that's what we were doing." She rushed on before Jane could interrupt. "For the money you see, but Marianne was a little uncomfortable with it. So that's when I stepped in, and although I say it myself, I'm not bad at... you know... chatting, so to speak. Anyway it's the toilet traffic that's the problem."

Jane held up her hand. "So let me just get this straight. You and Marianne..."

"Mainly me."

"... alright mainly you, have been trying to run a sex chat line from the first floor staff toilets during your lunch break, and it's the toilet traffic that you find disturbing?"

Hayley looked down at her hands. The eczema that had been dormant since the arrival of 'that Hayley' began to itch. She shouldn't have mentioned it. Out in the open it did sound ridiculous.

Jane shook her head slowly "I really don't know what to say. Why are you telling me this Hayley?"

"I wondered if I could use your office at lunchtimes, instead of the Ladies. Only when you don't need to be here... if you don't need to be here, I mean..." her voice trailed off as she continued to stare at her hands.

"I can't believe what you're asking me Hayley. Is that why you jumped in to help me with the story about Barcelona? Is it payback time?"

"No, not at all, please Jane don't think that!"

Jane rubbed her forehead. "Well I really don't know what to think. It's morally wrong and completely unprofessional – using Peltham's premises for a sordid chat line!"

Hayley saw a flash of Neil's face as he spoke about natural selection and what would be would be. "You don't understand!" Hayley jumped to her feet "I need the money to have a baby. I can't have a baby, not like you." She waved her hand in the direction of Jane's abdomen. "I can't get pregnant, not without help. And help costs five thousand pounds." Sinking back onto the chair she covered her face with her hands. They were all against her. Maybe Neil was right and it was never meant to be.

"What do you mean, help costs five thousand pounds?"

Hayley raised her head. "IVF that's what I'm talking about. I am one of the five percent who can't have a child." A tight smile crept onto her face. Neil would be proud that she'd used statistics at least.

Jane skirted round the desk and laid her hand on Hayley's arm. "I'm so sorry I didn't know. And there I was – devastated because I am pregnant. But you didn't say or do anything but be really sweet."

"It doesn't matter now. I was probably stupid to think I could earn enough doing that anyway." Hayley stood up and Jane's hand fell away. "I've taken up enough of your time. I'll leave you to get on." She turned towards the door.

"So it would be a kind of time share arrangement?"

Hayley slowly turned back. "Excuse me?"

"A time share arrangement. I go out, you come in, and so on?"

"Yes that's exactly it!"

"Naturally I wouldn't know what you were doing in my office, because you have only told me that you are merely polishing your public relations and communications skills." Jane's stare didn't flinch.

"Yes just polishing my public relations and communications skills," Hayley repeated.

"I have to admit Hayley I wasn't expecting to have this conversation with you."

"Two weeks ago neither was I."

Jane remained silent for several minutes before clearing her throat. "Okay, I'll let you use my office for your telephone calls, but please be discreet Hayley."

"I will, thank you so much Jane. I just can't give up on it."

"I can see that."

Hayley left Jane's office. Relief swept through her. No more perching on the toilet seat trying to sound like a rampant sex goddess. As she went down to the sales floor her thoughts drifted back to her own, non-existent sex life. Something had to be done, and it had to be done soon.

81

Marianne

Mr Spanker's shock announcement had thrown her back into the financial quagmire. How was she ever going to get her hands on the money that she needed? Absorbed in the financial tangle that faced her she jumped when she felt something caress her backside. Anthony Pickard was grinning, his hands outstretched. "I couldn't help myself."

The urge to slap him was so strong she had to clench her hands by her sides. "Please don't ever touch me again." Her voice was low, but she pronounced every word slowly.

"Oh come on." He shrugged and stepped towards her. "You shouldn't be so irresistible then should you?" His voice was just as low as hers but silky smooth.

The smell of his aftershave was overpowering. Not like Jack's sensual and musky, Pickard's was spiced and sharp. Her eyes began to water.

"Now don't get upset. I know you ladies enjoy playing hard to get, and I don't mind playing along... for a while." With his hand on the small of her back he guided her towards the staff room. As they reached the door he leant across the door frame blocking her way.

"I was chatting to young Sharon the other day. She had quite a lot to say about you." He raised his eyebrows. "I would be interested to hear your views on her comments. Perhaps we could talk about it later... over a drink?"

She froze. Everything seemed to fade out of focus apart from his face that loomed over hers. What had Sharon said? Before she could respond she heard Jane's voice calling down the corridor. "Marianne, could I see you for a moment?"

Anthony sprang away from the door frame and Marianne.

"Yes, of course Jane." She didn't care if the relief was all too evident in her voice.

"Right, I'll leave you to it." He slowly began to turn away, but not before giving Jane a look of such loathing it stunned Marianne to the core. His footsteps echoed down the stairwell as Marianne felt herself being ushered into the staffroom.

"Is something going on between the two of you?" The question from Jane was a gentle one. Filled more with concern than criticism.

"No, absolutely not. To be honest he makes me feel sick."

"Me too," Jane massaged her stomach, "in more ways than one."

Her gaze followed Jane's hands. "Oh I see... so he's..."

"Yes, lucky old me, he's the father."

From the look she had seen on Anthony's face when he saw Jane, he obviously wasn't happy about his impending fatherhood. She wasn't sure how to react to this piece of news. Her gut instinct was to offer her commiserations but she opted for something banal instead. "Well there you go then, fancy that."

"Yes quite, fancy that. Anyway, I wanted to thank you for helping me out the other day in front of my mother, and I want to talk to you about your overtime request. It seems that we do have a few hours that I can give you."

"Oh that would be fantastic. Thank you so much. You see I've got myself into a bit of a pickle and I really need to earn some extra money."

"Happy to help, I should have offered it to you earlier. I'm sorry about that. I'll send the rota down to you. If you can choose which hours you can do and give the form back to Mr Pickard. I'm going away for a couple of days."

"No, no I can't do that." Panic swept through her body at the thought of asking Pickard for anything.

"What's the matter?" Jane's eyes narrowed. "What's he done?"

"Nothing... yet." She looked down at the floor.

"You can talk to me. I know I haven't given you that impression in the past, but I'm beginning to realise how wrong I've been... about so many things."

When she raised her head she saw the sincerity in Jane's face and she felt crushed by the weight of guilt. She couldn't tell Jane what she had done, even though it amounted to very little in terms of money. It was still theft. Who was she kidding with writing 'I owe you's'? "It's okay everything's fine."

Jane didn't look convinced but repeated her offer of a listening ear before leaving Marianne to collect her coat and go home.

"Your young man's in a good mood." Eric was chopping at the hedge which divided the two gardens. His shirt was open to reveal a mat of grey hairs. She tried to look away but the fragments of leaves caught up in those wiry hairs mesmerised her. "I could hear him singing and whistling all afternoon." He nodded vigorously as though she might question the validity of his statement. "Ever since the postman came this morning. If you ask me you're in for a good night tonight." The grin showed his crooked teeth and she had to bite back the urge to tell him that she would never ask him anything. And from the look on his face she could see he was already imagining what a good time they would be having tonight. Her skin crawled as she dragged her eyes away from his sweaty chest which was now rising rapidly as he panted.

She had to get inside. Surely her day had to improve?

"I've got it!" Jack scooped her up as soon as she walked through the door and spun her round. His smile of delight was hard not to return.

"The letter came today. I was going to phone you but then I thought it would be so much better if I could see your face." He did a little jig as he waved a letter in his hand. "And now I'm going to pour you a lovely glass of bubbly. Not real champagne but we can have that when I get my first pay packet."

He skipped into the kitchen. She could hear glasses chink as he lifted them out of the cupboard. She took her coat off and hung it up. At least they would have another salary coming into the house at last. That surely must give her time to clear some of the debts, if not all of them, before Jack found out. She mentally tried to bolster her mood, so that Jack would see how pleased she was for him. "I'm so proud of you darling. I knew they wouldn't be able to resist you. Who can?"

He was still grinning as he passed her a champagne flute. She tried to raise her own spirits as she watched the bubbles rise to the top.

"To us!" Clinking his glass to hers he then tipped the bubbles into his mouth.

"To us." Her response was a little more subdued.

"I've bought a new shirt and tie. Hang on a minute and I'll show you." He ran out of the room like a schoolboy at playtime. They would be alright. They had to be. She went over to the bottle of wine and topped up each glass before straightening the letter Jack had left on the worktop. 'Cloons and Dunnit Debt Solutions are delighted to offer you the position...'

82

Amanda

She let the hot water sting her body, trying to purge herself from the outside in. The memory of his hands sliding over her body lingered. She had watched from the top right hand corner of the room. Her observation was dispassionate, totally removed from what was taking place below. Finally he had lain beside her stroking her thigh. He hadn't noticed the tears that dampened her cheeks. Or that her eyes remained open staring beyond his pounding body.

"I'll look after you Mandy," he softly chanted, over and over again as he stroked.

Eventually he stirred. "I'll make us something to eat whilst you shower." After kissing her forehead he left the room. Mechanically she got up and went into the bathroom.

It didn't matter how hard she scrubbed, the essence of the creature downstairs had seeped into her pores. Watery jets drummed against the glass shower screen but they couldn't drown out the sound of his footsteps on the stairs. She moved further into the corner of the cubicle, shivering despite the hot water.

"How long are you going to wait Amanda?" Her mother perched on the edge of the bath. "A spider will slowly cocoon a fly in soft silk threads. Keeping it alive until it's ready. You are the fly Amanda, so use those wings. The web's already started."

She half closed her eyes and reached out towards the memory of her mother as wisps of pale blue disappeared behind swirls of steam. But her mother's perfume remained. The smell flooded her nostrils and her eyes snapped open.

"There's an outfit on the bed I'd like you to wear when you come down for dinner."

His instruction from the other side of the door was firm and uncompromising and in no way resembled a request. She had learnt that hard lesson from experience.

Forcing her body out from behind her glass shield she wrapped a towel around her. She was glad the mirror showed nothing but a white shroud. She didn't want to look into the wide eyes of the trapped animal that would be staring back at her.

"I'm waiting Amanda, don't be long." The sing song voice drifted insidiously up the stair well.

She stepped into the bedroom. Her silk wedding dress lay on the bed. Beside it an intricately woven veil. The web was closing in.

83

Jane

She had decided to travel back with her parents. Telling them on their own territory might make it easier for them to accept. Taking a few days leave could be just the thing she needed. She hurled comfortable pyjamas and cosy socks into her case. A very different assortment of clothes from the last time she had packed.

Her mother had been delighted at having her daughter all to herself. Jane wondered just how long this delight would last when she discovered that she would be sharing her with an illegitimate grandchild. She stared at the passing fields and trees as the train sped through the countryside. 'Illegitimate' sounded such an old fashioned word. Having a child 'out of wedlock', another archaic phrase. She almost felt as if she had been transported into the pages of a Catherine Cookson novel. Her mother chatted away through the remaining eleven stations and four level crossings whilst she imagined herself being sent to a home for unmarried mothers where she would be forced to secretly give her child away.

Theirs was a small red brick house and, whereas it didn't have roses around the door, it certainly had a healthy wisteria wrapping itself round the wooden window frames. She dropped her bag in the hallway and slowly went from room to room, reacquainting herself with the worn furniture, and pretty floral cushions. Her mother bustled in behind her with her father in tow, as usual.

"Whenever you're ready to talk Jane, I'm ready to listen." Her mother was spooning loose tea into a big brown tea pot. She didn't look up. Translation: tell me... now.

Her father seemed to sense the onset of 'women's talk' and made a hasty retreat.

"You know I'm not one to pry." Translation: I need to know exactly what's going on, in as much detail as possible. "I do understand if you would rather not talk right now it's just that your wellbeing is my only concern." Translation: not telling me is not an option.

The moment had come. Jane sat down at the oak dining table. She had made papier-măchè models on this table. Crayoned hundreds of pictures for the fridge door. Poured over times tables and spelling lists, then poured over glossy magazines before hiding them under text books.

She couldn't be as blunt as she had with Tony. "You know how you've always wanted me to settle down?"

Her mother made a dive for the nearest chair and plonked herself down. "You've found a man haven't you?" Her eyes shone and she leaned closer towards Jane. "You've fallen in love and he's asked you to marry him hasn't he? George, George get in here. Great news darling!"

She heard her father's slippers shuffling along the hall. "No, no Mum, please that's not it." But her mother wasn't listening.

"Jane's found a man and they're going to be married. Tell us all about him." Her mother's chin rested on her clasped hands. Her father hovered uncertainly by his wife's side.

"I'm pregnant." So much for not being blunt.

Two sharp intakes of breath as her parents digested this information.

"Well that's jumping the gun a bit sweetie, but it's still wonderful news." Her mother left her seat as quickly as she had taken it and rushed over to Jane, kissing her cheeks. She swept a stray hair from Jane's forehead. "We can still have the wedding. Nothing's impossible my love so don't you worry."

The contrast in Tony's reaction and that of her mother was stark. She looked at her father over her mother's shoulder. She could see by the look on his face that he knew something wasn't right.

"I think the fact that he's married to someone else might make it a tiny bit impossible. Oh and the fact that he doesn't want anything to do with the child or me."

Her father said nothing as he gently pulled her to her feet and held her in his arms. The floodgates opened and the dam holding all her emotions and fears emptied all over his tweed jacket. She could smell faint traces of moth balls mixed with pipe tobacco as she cried into her father's shoulder. She wondered if his jacket held a map of her emotional journey through life as she had grown from a small child crying into his lap and travelling up to his collar as a woman.

"I'm sorry Mum. I know this isn't what you wanted to hear, but I'm happy that I'm going to have a baby, even if I am alone." Did she detect a hollow note in her own voice? She cleared her throat. "We'll be fine, I know we will. And we'll have you two. What more could we need?"

84

Hayley

"Marianne, are you sure you don't mind helping me?" She had felt shy asking for Marianne's help, but she didn't dare trust herself to do it alone. Using Jane's office had made Hayley's second job so much easier. She was more relaxed and even more playful with her clients. But this injection of confidence still wasn't enough to carry out the task in hand by herself.

"Are you joking? Of course I don't mind. This is my idea of heaven." Marianne expertly flicked through the rack of flimsy lingerie. Hayley watched with self-conscious fascination. Finally, Marianne found what she had been looking for and triumphantly held up a black lace basque.

"Oh no, I'm not sure about that!" She was confused. Uncertainty flirted with excitement as Hayley reached out to touch the exquisite lattice of lace.

"It's perfect." Marianne quashed any opportunity she had of backtracking as she marched off to the curtained cubicles. Pulling the curtain aside she handed Hayley the underwear. "Try it on whilst I find you some shoes. It may be bedroom wear but that is never an excuse not to wear heels." She yanked the curtain shut and left Hayley staring at the exotic piece.

She climbed out of her own mismatched underclothes and carefully wrapped the black lace bodice around her. With trembling fingers she managed to fasten the hooks and eyes which ran down the front. The boned sections cinched in her waist giving her an hour glass figure she couldn't quite believe.

"Stockings." A hand thrust a pair of black silk stockings through the crack of the curtain. "Shoes." A pair of black patent shoes with five inch heels and red soles followed.

With the outfit complete she timidly pulled the curtain open.

"Bloody hell!" Marianne stepped back.

"It's too tarty isn't it? I knew it wouldn't suit me. I just can't pull this kind of thing off." Hayley looked down at legs that didn't appear to belong to her, and feet that screamed vixen in the killer heels.

"You won't have to pull anything off. I think when Neil sees you he'll be the one pulling it off! You look amazing Hayley, absolutely bloody incredible!"

Marianne shoved her back into the changing room and both women looked at the image of 'that Hayley' who stared back.

"God help him, that's all I can say." Marianne shook her head as she looked over Hayley's shoulder. "You are one hot babe in that outfit."

Hayley glanced at the pile of brown and beige clothes dumped on the chair. They reminded her of the skin shed from a snake, and then back to the woman in the mirror. God help them both she thought.

"Anyway you had better get used to showing off that body with the Fashion show coming up."

Hayley still couldn't believe that she had been persuaded to take part.

"It'll be a hoot, don't worry so much. And you definitely owe it to yourself to buy that lingerie. I won't let you leave without it."

It had been bought, wrapped and surreptitiously slipped into her locker. Hayley returned to the sales floor.

"You know sometimes I think he's just using me."

"Yeah I know what you mean, but Shaz, and I'm not being funny right, but you don't make it difficult for him do yer?"

The voices floated through the open stock room door as Hayley moved the sparse spring stock to the front of the display racks.

"What are you trying to say? That I'm easy?" the pitch was rising.

"Well yeah."

The pitch rose yet another level. "I'm not easy! I'm just very affectionate. It's in my nature – everybody says so!"

"That's not what I've eard..."

The rest was mumbled and Hayley couldn't quite catch it. Maybe Shaz had the other girl by the throat and she couldn't finish the rest of her sentence. She wondered whether she should go in there to save them from killing each other, but she held back.

"Anyways he said he really likes me, and he's gonna give me something nice."

"A bit like what he gave the stuck up bitch."

"What do you mean?"

Hayley held her breath.

"The bloody Ice Queen's up the duff in't she. And he's been sniffing round that Marianne tart. Looks like you're last in line Shaz love."

'Shaz' stormed out of the room knocking Hayley out of the way as she went. Her scrawny friend hurried after her. "I'm not even joking right but he's rank anyway Shaz...Shaz..."

Shaz stopped and turned a seething face towards her friend. "I'll teach him to mess with other women whilst he's having relations with me." Her head bobbed up and down as she chewed maniacally on her chewing gum. "I bet Mrs Tony Pickard doesn't know what her lovely husband's been up to." Her eyes narrowed. "What a shame if a little bird was to whisper in her ear." She turned on her heel and marched away. Her friend scurried after her but not before Hayley saw a look of evil delight cross her face.

Alone, Hayley was stunned at the speed gossip flew around the store and she pondered what the fallout from Shaz's revelation would be for Jane. Should she try to get in touch with her to warn her or should she stay out of it? Her basic instinct was to warn her, but how? She didn't know where Jane's parents lived or what Jane's mobile number was. She would just have to make sure that she got to Jane first.

Charlie's lap was covered in crumbs as he popped the remainder of a muffin into his mouth. She smiled as he stood to greet her sending the crumbs scattering over the lobby floor. "I don't know Charlie, eating on the job whatever next?" She saw him blush and immediately felt guilty about teasing him. "I'm only kidding. You need building up anyway." She gently pressed him down into his seat.

"I can't help myself Miss. It's these cakes that Ada's been making. I just can't get enough of them." His eyes gleamed and momentarily Hayley saw a glimpse of a much younger and very handsome Charlie.

"They certainly seem to be doing you some good. I could do with getting the recipe." She ran her fingers through her wiry hair as she thought of the reason for her visit. "I need to get in touch with Jane, Charlie, and I just wondered if you knew where I could find her number." She looked over her shoulder before leaning in towards him. "I don't really want to bother personnel you see."

Charlie looked over his own shoulder before he too leant closer to Hayley. "She's staying at her parents. Everything's alright though isn't it?"

The look of alarm that descended over his features touched her. She squeezed his shoulder. "Yes, of course, I just need to have a quick word with her that's all."

Charlie appeared to be reassured and took an old leather book from his breast pocket. His hand trembled slightly as he slid each page open. "Ah, here we are. I'll give you both numbers." Ripping a corner of The Racing Post he scribbled down the numbers. He gently placed it in her palm and closed her fingers around it with his own. "You look after her Miss. She's a good girl."

"I will Charlie, I will." Now she just had to speak to her before Tony or, worse still, his wife did.

85

Marianne

She had no option but to try again with the adult chat line. It seemed to her that just as Hayley's confidence with her sexuality was now over-spilling into real life, Marianne's self-belief was disappearing rapidly. She smiled at the memory of Hayley trying on lingerie earlier, her sweet naivety in sharp contrast to the persona of Madame Estate Agent.

Marianne knew that she probably only had two weeks whilst Jack did his induction training, before he would be released into the world of debt collection – her world. She would have to work every break and evenings after work to make even a small amount.

She found Hayley leaning against the wall in the corridor, her phone gripped to her ear. Marianne waited, not wanting to intrude on Hayley's conversation. The silence however indicated that it was either a very one sided conversation or there was actually no-one on the other end. She cleared her throat and Hayley spun round. "There's no-one answering. It's just ringing out. I must have tried a hundred times." Hayley stared at the object of her frustration.

"Who are you trying to call?"

She sensed a slight hesitation before Hayley replied.

"Jane. I was trying to call Jane. Sharon might tell Pickard's wife about Jane's baby. I thought I ought to warn her."

"God yes you're absolutely right." She could just imagine the reaction to that little piece of news.

"Sharon will probably mention you too." Hayley's voice was barely a whisper.

"What do you mean mention me? What has Tony Pickard got to do with me?" Fear squeezed her vocal chords turning her words into a squeal.

"I think you're next on his shopping list and Sharon doesn't like it." Hayley was now looking at the floor.

"Next on his shopping list... I'll give him next on his shopping list!" She was furious. The very idea that she would ever be unfaithful to Jack at all, let alone with a low life like Tony Pickard was beyond ridiculous. "You didn't think that I would ever... with that horrible man did you?" Suddenly Hayley's opinion was very important to her.

"No, of course I didn't, but then again I couldn't understand why Jane actually did."

Grudgingly she had to accept that on the surface Tony appeared to be the debonair, charming man about town. Whereas in reality he was a snake of a man, but a very manipulative one. He had obviously completely fooled Jane. She shuddered at the very thought of being close to him.

"He calls me a lesbian." Hayley said brightly. She was smiling and Marianne detected more than a hint of mischief. "But he hasn't met 'that Hayley' yet has he?"

She burst into laughter as she recalled Hayley in sexy lingerie and impossibly high shoes. "I don't think he'd call you a lesbian if he saw you in your 'bedroom attire'. Not to mention if he listened to you as Madame Estate Agent. Talking of which I'm going to try to be your assistant estate agent if that's okay?"

"Fantastic! We'll make a brilliant team." Hayley's enthusiasm seemed genuine and she felt a trickle of confidence in her ability to learn the art of telephone seduction.

Hayley prodded the key pad before grinding the phone to her ear. Meanwhile Marianne decided she couldn't tell Jack about the extent of the overtime she was planning to do. He would be bound to question her urgent need for money, especially in the light of his new employment. She would just invent a busy social calendar. What could go wrong?

86

Amanda

Her cream satin shoes had been placed neatly at the end of the bed. All that was missing was a bridal bouquet. She stared at the garments and shook her head. The cloying scent of insanity wafted around her as she stepped into the dress.

The evening had been surreal. But not to him.

"Now here's my lovely bride!" He clapped his hands steadily, receiving his wife, whilst she took her seat. He dropped a small jewellery box onto the table in front of her. "Go on, open it up."

The slender fingers that untied the ribbon and opened the wrapping seemed to belong to someone else. Not to her. Pearl earrings nestled in velvet folds.

"I'll help you." He leapt up and within two strides was by her side. She could feel his quickening breath on her skin. Her hands dropped to her lap and she stared straight ahead whilst he inserted the silver threads through her lobes. He stepped back. "Just finishes the outfit off beautifully!"

Appearing to be satisfied he attacked his meal with gusto. He made no comment when she didn't touch her food. He made no comment when he scraped the entire contents of her plate into the bin. He made no comment when he left his 'bride' sitting at the table with her hands still folded in her lap. The television went on in the front room and still she stared straight ahead.

"Pearls, for a marriage full of tears." Her mother was standing by the back door. "Your Aunt Beatrice, God rest her soul, wore opals like leaves on a tree. It wasn't the bad luck of the actual stones that killed your Uncle Max. No, she just bled him dry to buy them."

Amanda was sitting at the kitchen table in her wedding dress, talking to her dead mother about precious stones. Perhaps that was his idea, to make her believe she was going mad.

It was working.

87

Jane

She was physically and emotionally exhausted and wanted to sleep. Without getting undressed she lay on her small bed. Lemon daisies danced on the walls and the matching eiderdown was a yellow meadow beneath her. Her breathing slowed and she felt herself drift off to sleep. For once her phone and the outside world had been silenced for the sleep she so desperately needed.

"I didn't want to wake you darling but a young girl from the store's been on the phone. She said it was quite important that you call her." Her mother gently shook her shoulder. She handed Jane a pretty notelet. Tiny pink rose buds surrounded Hayley's name and number which was neatly written in the middle.

Confused and still fuzzy from her deep sleep Jane reached for her mobile. "What time is it?" She flicked the display on. 12:07 it said. Even though she had slept on and off for hours she felt a weariness descend over her, dragging her back to the depths of slumber. But she knew she couldn't succumb to it. Her mother hovered by the bedroom door. "Shall I make you a nice cup of tea?" That was her mother's answer to most difficult situations.

"Yes that would be lovely. Thanks Mum."

She heard her mother go down the narrow stairs which were flanked by watercolours of local beauty spots. Jane's teddy bears, as always, arranged in order of size sat on her dressing table. This whole house was a comfort to her. Her safety net. A place where she was not just loved but cherished, and now the outside world was intruding on her sanctuary. She looked back at her phone, seven missed calls and a text message from Tony.

She read the text message first. 'Launch in less than a week. Get back here. You can't walk away from everything just because you're an easy lay."

What had she seen in him? Stupid Jane!

She dialled the number on the notelet. After two rings she heard Hayley's voice. "Hello?"

"Hayley it's Jane. You've been trying to contact me?" She couldn't think why Hayley would want to speak to her so urgently.

Hayley's words came in a torrent. Details of the overheard conversation between Sharon and her friend and the subsequent veiled threat to tell all to Tony's wife slid down the zip wire of space and into Jane's head. She thanked Hayley for the warning before finishing the call, just as her mother came in carrying a tray with a china tea cup and saucer and a plate hot buttered toast. She placed the tray on Jane's lap and settled herself on the edge of the bed. "Is everything alright?" She nodded at the phone still in Jane's hand. "No problems at work I hope?" Translation: I know that everything isn't alright by the urgent message and I would really like to know exactly what problems there clearly are.

"Yes Mum everything's alright, just a minor glitch at work that's all." She looked at the thickly buttered toast and resisted the urge to push the plate away.

"Well as long as everything's alright dear. I'll leave you to your breakfast and see you downstairs in a little while." Translation: I don't believe a word of it but I'll let it go for now – but only for now. She patted Jane's knee and left.

She had stayed in bed all day. Her wallowing had only been punctuated by her mother bobbing in and out with various tit bits of food to try to entice her to eat. Her mood swung from self-pity to self-loathing, neither were good. She didn't bother turning the pretty bedside lamp on with its china base covered in more painted daisies. What was there to see? The light from the hallway that shone under her door was suddenly interrupted by a shadow. Then came a gentle knocking.

"Jane, can I come in?" Her father's voice sounded tired and full of worry. She immediately felt a rush of remorse at putting them through this.

"Yes Daddy, come in." She was six years old again and she had broken her mother's favourite vase. Her mother had been very upset and although she had never raised her voice she had seen tears in her eyes that were far worse than any scolding. Her father had come to her bedroom. His big frame perched on the side of the bed. He had held her hands and moved his head to her ear. "I've always hated that vase," he had whispered and a chuckle rose from deep within his chest. And she had giggled with him like two conspirators.

Somehow he always made things right. He perched his now stooped frame on the edge of the bed and held her hands. "You know Jane, you're a good person and you're a strong woman. You will make an amazing mother, of that I have no doubt. The world will throw many things at you. This won't be the last, but I know in here," he punched his chest, "that you will do the right thing, for you and for your child, and that you will do it brilliantly."

She buried her face in his chest and he rocked her to and fro, just as he had when she was a child. Strength and determination filtered through her like osmosis.

She could do it by herself. It wouldn't be easy being a single parent, but with a new resolve she was sure that somehow she could do it. She didn't know how she was going to manage financially. She certainly couldn't expect any help from Tony. That had been made very clear. But this child was not going to suffer because of it. This child would want for nothing.

She would go back and face the music with head held high. In her head she glossed over such minor details as the hysterical father to her unborn child, and the likelihood that his wife was equally as hysterical. Recalling Tony's text, even though she hated to admit it,

Tony was right she had to go back and try to secure the store's future.

88

Hayley

All through the evening she had worried whether she would be able to reach Jane before anyone else. Even Neil's late return from his fantasy visit to the allotment hadn't dislodged the anxiety. He was just something else to worry about. Finally she had managed to leave a message with Jane's mother, asking her to call her as soon as she could. She just hoped that would be enough.

After a fitful night she was back at the store. Marianne was chatting to a tall, imposing looking man. He didn't look like the average mid-morning customer. Maybe he was a forgetful husband who had just realised it was his wife's birthday or anniversary. They did get a few of those in, but usually either first thing in the morning or dashing in last thing at night. Marianne was pointing in the direction of the lifts from where Mr Pickard was emerging.

Hayley glared at Tony as he passed, unable to hide the distaste she felt. He, in turn, barely even glanced in her direction, which she supposed was par for the course in her world.

"Morning Mr Pickard....sir." Sharon was leaning casually against the sales counter. Her low cut blouse offering a generous amount of cleavage

"Yes, morning." Tony's attention hadn't wavered from the man who was now approaching him.

Just as the two men disappeared up the escalator Marianne reached Hayley's side.

"Hi Hayley, are you ready to fire up the phone line? I've not got very long because I've got to sort out clothes for the models to wear."

"Sure we'll go up to Jane's office. Let's just give Pickard a chance to get to his own office first. I can do without bumping into him."

"I know what you mean."

She could see her own distaste reflected in Marianne's expression.

Once safely inside Jane's office, she logged onto the phone line and almost immediately it shrilled into action. She handed the phone to Marianne and nodded encouragement for her to answer it.

Marianne hesitated for a moment then haltingly breathed into the mouthpiece "Hello Estate Agent extraordinaire, how may I help you today?"

She watched Marianne's eyes widen when she heard how the caller thought she may be able to help him. Marianne slowly began to shake her head. "I see and Chewbacca likes that too does he, whilst Princess Leia looks on? ...mmm yes I can imagine that you would need a wet room for that kind of activity..."

She tried to suppress a giggle as she listened to Marianne's brave attempt at seduction with a light sabre. Finally Marianne ended the call. She held the phone out to Hayley as though it had just been rescued from the bowl of a filthy toilet.

"I take it that was our very own Luke Skywalker?" She laughed at Marianne's look of horror.

"You mean you have him regularly?"

"Oh yes he's one of my most frequent clients." Hayley nodded.

"He's my neighbour."

Hayley's mouth dropped open. "Oh my God, you're joking!"

"I hear him and Princess Leia every Saturday night and twice on a Thursday."

It was Hayley's turn to shake her head. Poor Marianne, her second attempt at the chat line hadn't been a raving success.

"I'm sorry Hayley, this just isn't for me." Marianne slumped down in Jane's chair and buried her head in her hands.

89

Marianne

She wished it was winter and she could scurry into the house under the cover of darkness. Even though she had worked late, Eric, aka Luke Skywalker, would still be out in his garden catching the dying rays of sunshine. He would be lying in wait with his ridiculous comb-over and string vest. As she neared her house she saw him sitting on a fold out deck chair. It was worse than she had feared. He was naked from the waist up. His chest glistened with sun tan oil which he appeared to still be rubbing in. The circular motion of his hands over his torso seemed to quicken as she got closer.

"Hello gorgeous." His tongue flicked out as he licked his lips.

"Eric." She nodded curtly and hurried up the path, cursing that she hadn't already got the keys out of her bag.

"Makes you want to take all your clothes off this weather don't it." His fingers had moved to his nipples.

She found the sight both repulsive and hypnotic. Dragging her eyes away she rummaged around in her bag and snatched at the cold metal loop of keys.

"Hubby's been back a while. He's been out a couple of times, looking up the road for you. Reckon he's been missing you petal." His hands slithered down to rest on his groin area.

She shoved the door open and slammed it shut behind her. Leaning heavily against it she tried to dismiss the image of Eric and his light sabre. It was all just too much.

"You're late." It wasn't a complaint. It was more a hurt reproach

"I know, I'm sorry I got chatting to the girls, and one coffee led to another. You know how we girls are when we get chatting." She went over to him and wrapped her arms around his firm body. He ran his fingers round his collar, pulling the stiff material away from his neck. Undoing his top button she kissed his throat. Slowly she began to undo the remaining buttons and slid her hands down his body. She felt him relax under her touch. He lifted her in his arms and carried her to the bed. Their love making was tender but with an intensity that made them speechless. Lying in Jack's arms she prayed that everything would be alright. But time was running out.

90

Amanda

She had stuffed the wedding dress in a bin bag and buried it at the back of her wardrobe. If she could have she would have sold it on Ebay. But who knew when David might want to play weddings again. With no fresh bruises to worry about she chose a dress which made her feel a little more feminine than usual. Hope that she might see Sam fizzed at the bottom of her stomach like an Alka Seltzer.

In the staff room she checked the tiny buttons on the bodice and pinched her cheeks to give some colour.

"You should dress up more often." Her mother's arms were folded neatly in front of her. "Your Aunt Beatrice, God rest her soul, was always dressing up. She'd have seen your Uncle Max in rags so long as she could dress in her finery. Mind you they weren't so much dresses, more like tents. That woman needed so much material to cover her flesh it wouldn't have looked out of place at a circus. I said to your Uncle Max, Max I said, you can dress a dog's dinner up all you like, but underneath it's still a dog's dinner."

She looked at her mother, immaculate in her blue suit, and smiled. She must have given both Beatrice and Max such a hard time she thought. Even in death she wouldn't let it go.

"There's nothing wrong with dressing up Mum."

"Did I say there was anything wrong with dressing up? You just don't do it enough."

Amanda looked down at the delicate fabric that covered her slim frame. "What do I need to get dressed up for? I come here, I go home. That's my life. That really is all..."

"Oops sorry to interrupt." Hayley's head popped round the door jam. She looked around the room then back at Amanda. "Oh I thought you were with someone."

"No, I'm all alone." Amanda sank onto the bench. How true that was.

"It's just that I could have sworn I heard voices." Hayley's voice was soft. "I didn't want to interrupt." Her eyes swept the room again.

Amanda was overwhelmed by a desperate loneliness. "I talk to my dead mother." She waited for Hayley's reaction. Expecting ridicule and contempt, she braced herself.

"That's alright I talk to myself all the time. I'm always giving myself advice that I never take and instructions that I never follow. Because I think, sorry used to think I was invisible myself, I used to have an imaginary friend called Leon. I even had a row with him and we fell out!" Hayley's eyes were full of sincerity. No judgement or derision lurked there. Hayley sat down next to her. "Does she answer you?"

"In her own way she does. It's not always useful. In fact, most of the time, her responses are eccentric to say the least. I'm not sure what that says about me."

"You know, if people were more honest you would find that most talk to themselves, to invisible others, or even worse to inanimate objects." Hayley's nod defied contradiction.

"But I sometimes think that I'm going insane." Amanda pictured herself at the kitchen table wearing her wedding dress.

"So what can you do? Sanity is so overrated!"

Amanda looked up sharply expecting to see her mother again, but it had been Hayley's words. "My God you sound just like my Mother." She spluttered. "You're not related to the Davis's are you?"

Hayley smiled. "No, I'm not, but Mrs Davis sounds like a lovely mother who just wants to look after her daughter, and there's nothing wrong with that. My mother doesn't even know who I am most of the time."

"Oh I'm sorry, that's awful."

"It's alright, you get used to it. Anyway I have a message for you from someone called Sam?"

All thoughts of her mother disappeared.

"He called in to say he'll be around about twelve if you had a spare minute."

Hayley rose and went to the door. "And next time, don't forget to say hello to Mrs Davis from me."

"I won't." The door closed and Amanda's thoughts flew to Sam's visit. She didn't have to wait for long.

"Well fancy bumping into you!" His smile was wide and warm.

"I know, we must stop meeting like this." Amanda felt her smile was even wider than his.

"Must we?"

His response threw her and suddenly his smile had gone. She didn't know how to answer him and cursed herself for being so tongue tied and somehow inadequate for a situation such as this.

"Listen Amanda, I'm leaving for America soon and I'd really like to spend some time with you." His eyes were earnest as he reached out and held her hand. "I know it's difficult for you, but even if we could just snatch a couple of hours talking. That's all I'm asking for."

She looked at their fingers entwined. 'That's all he was asking for.' He might as well have asked her for a million dollars' worth of gold bullion. She just couldn't see how she could get away with meeting him even for an hour.

"Look, I'll tell you what. How about if I happen to be at the wine bar at eight o'clock next Friday? And you just happen to be passing at that time, maybe meeting up with Marianne or something for a drink. We might accidentally bump into each other then. What do you think?"

She wanted to say yes so desperately but the price she would have to pay was huge.

Letting go of her hand he said "Well, I will be there so if you can make it, great. If not don't worry, at least I won't have far to go to drown my sorrows." He brushed her cheek with his lips, slowly turned and walked away.

Terror danced with hope in the ballroom of her mind as she watched him go.

"Amanda... Amanda" A voice cut into her thoughts. "Management want to see you straight away in Mr Pickard's office."

"They want to see me?" Could it be that the position she was hoping to secure had been finalised? Murmuring her thanks she rushed up to the top floor. Her feet making no sound on the deep pile as she raced up the corridor. She knocked on the door and waited.

"Come," came the curt response.

Her heart pounding with illicit optimism, she pushed open the door. The two men turned to look at her. Mr Pickard in his sharp pin striped suit and David her husband.

"I believe a farewell is in order." Tony Pickard stood and offered his hand to shake. David was smiling benignly.

Ignoring the outstretched hand she looked from one man to the other. Her skin moments earlier had been flushed with excitement but now felt cold and clammy. David was in the store, her store. Had he seen her with Sam? "What's the matter? What are you doing here?" She fixed her stare on David. How she hated him.

"Amanda darling, I was just explaining to Mr Pickard here that you'll be leaving Pelthams'. I thought you might have already mentioned it but it appears not."

Once again he had trapped her.

Tony had put his redundant hand into his pocket and returned to his seat. "So I understand that you'll be going to pastures new in a couple of weeks? Ordinarily we would ask for a month's notice, but you've been with us a considerable length of time and, as your husband has explained, you're keen to make a fresh start. I certainly won't stand in your way. You've been a very loyal and conscientious member of staff and I wish you much happiness in the future."

"That's very kind of you Mr Pickard. Isn't it darling?"

Without waiting for a reply the two men rose from their chairs and shook hands. The deal had been done. Sold to the man on the left. Any protestations stayed firmly lodged by the lump in her throat as David propelled her out of the office.

"You see that wasn't so bad was it?" His grip, to any passer-by would be seen as no more than a guiding hand, pressing relentlessly into her skin. She bit her lip to stop a yelp from escaping as they moved silently through the corridor. She had two weeks left. Two weeks before she had to say goodbye to Pelthams' and two weeks before she had to say goodbye to Sam.

91

Jane

The catwalk had been assembled in the main fashion hall. Shards of light bounced off the glassware in the champagne bar. And overhead the newly polished chandelier glittered, reminiscent of the store's heyday. But Jane's eyes were drawn to the fluttering bunting which festooned the makeshift stage from where the elite group of visitors would watch the show.

This was make or break for Pelthams'. Hiding her tension was becoming increasingly hard. She wasn't supposed to know about the possible takeover, and so she pasted a confident smile on her face and orchestrated the press gallery. "Yes Valerie, I know you're from a national but we have to be fair to everyone, if you wouldn't mind sitting in the second row? No John, please take the camera round to the other side, otherwise the girls will be falling over the tripod."

"Where do you want me?" The words were accompanied by the popping of bubble gum.

Jane turned to see Sharon wearing a very pink and very tight fitting Chanel style suit which barely contained her ample bosom. The hat was so wide its brim virtually covered her face. She resembled a cerise mushroom. "We've almost two hours before the show begins Sharon. Don't you think it's a bit early to be getting changed?"

"I've been wearing it since twelve." She sniffed each armpit in turn. "But don't worry I've stuffed tissues under me pits and worn extra deodorant." She tipped her head back so Jane could see the smile on her face under the shadow of the hat. "I wanted to make sure I didn't let you down Miss."

After being warned – by Hayley – about Sharon's threat to speak to Tony's wife, she had been waiting for the fallout – but nothing, yet. "Thank you for your diligence Sharon. It's very much appreciated." She tried to mask the wariness in her voice and busied herself with setting out name cards. Sharon clattered away in shoes that overflowed with flesh.

Tony had been kept occupied by entertaining the Americans at head office. Sycophancy was definitely his forte, whilst Jane had been juggling caterers and press for the past three days. She wasn't sure which were the most dramatic. The caterers: "Vol-au-vents are so passé darling and the show simply can't go on without asparagus wrapped in Parma ham!" Or the press: "I'm not sitting next to The Advertiser, not a journalist of my calibre!"

Jane was exhausted but with or without Parma ham the show must indeed go on. Racks of clothes had been pressed and were ready for the models to slip into before strutting down the catwalk. Jane had already spoken to Marianne and Hayley about the parts they were to play. Hayley had tried to back out several times but both Jane and Marianne had coaxed her with promises of make-up artists and hair stylists.

Uniformed bar tenders filled buckets of ice, and bottles of Pimms were being poured into crystal jugs decorated with lush sprigs of mint. She would have loved to have been able to sink into one of the seats, slip off her shoes and drink a delicious cocktail, but time was disappearing. The Americans were on their way.

92

Hayley

It was one thing to convince someone over the phone that you were a stunning seductress who positively oozed sex appeal. It was quite another to convince a live audience that you were a glamorous model oozing confidence. Where was 'that Hayley' when you needed her? She thought as she scratched at the dry skin on her hand.

"These are your out-fits, lovey." The stock control clerk handed her four coat hangers laden with a selection of sumptuous silks and floral chiffon. "Your accessories are just over there." She waved to a display counter buried beneath a dazzling array of hats, pashminas, and gloves. There were sequinned clutch bags and velvet pouches. How on earth did anyone fit anything into those tiny pockets she wondered?

"We're using the stock room for changing, lovey."

Hayley, carefully carrying the clothes, reversed through the stock room door. Marianne was already there.

"Look at this!" squealed Marianne as she held up a peach dress. The intricate lace was jewelled with tiny pearls. It was breathtaking. "And the shoes!" Marianne pointed a peach satin clad foot in Hayley's direction, turning it this way and that. "Aren't they just divine?"

Hayley could see that Marianne was almost delirious. Bright pink spots illuminated her cheeks and her eyes shone.

"Let's see what you've got then." Marianne scooped the hangers from Hayley's arms and expertly swung them onto the rail. She gasped as she gripped the last hanger. "This is the show stopper of all time!" She held out a deep emerald dress. "The colour is perfect for you. Just a second." She disappeared leaving Hayley staring at the contours of the dress. Surely she would never fit into that? She was convinced her body didn't curve that way.

"Here we are!" Marianne held a pair of emerald stilettos in one hand and a beautiful pillbox hat in the other. "You'll look amazing!" Hayley wished she held the same unwavering belief, but at that moment it was all she could do not to run away.

Soon the stock room filled up with more amateur models. The air was sweet with perfume and hairspray as the stylists worked their magic. The only person who was quieter than Hayley was Amanda. A few minutes earlier Hayley had seen her slip into the room clutching a raw silk gown of oyster and chocolate brown. Hayley watched as one of the make-up artists swept Amanda along to an empty chair where she was lost under brushes and powder. Following their conversation the day before, Hayley knew that Amanda's mother would be proud of her.

Would anyone be proud of Hayley she wondered? She had mentioned the Launch to Neil that morning but he seemed distracted and said that he would have to work late. In her heart she knew he was lying, and she would have to confront him about it very soon.

93

Marianne

Surrounded by stunning dresses and shoes she could only dream of buying, Marianne could briefly push aside her worries about debt. She flitted around the room handing out advice and accessories, feeling as though she had an enormous dressing up box at her disposal. She was five years old again and the only worry on her horizon was whether her mother would let her stay up late to play out. It was Sharon who dragged her back from her quantum leap.

"You know that them clothes are only borrowed right? They're not for taking home, if you know what I mean." The words floated out from under the brim of her huge hat.

"I know that Sharon. I don't know what you're trying to infer but I wish you would drop it." Marianne moved away as quickly as she could. Accusations and finger pointing would be the end of her career and probably her marriage. She found herself standing next to Amanda who was being systematically transformed. Gone were the dark circles. Warmth had been brushed onto her skin and her eyes looked magnificent, framed by caramel hues and long black lashes.

Seeing Amanda like this Marianne could understand her husband's desire to cosset and protect her. Only yesterday he had come into the store asking for directions to the manager. For a horrible moment Marianne thought he was going to make a complaint about her verbal explosion at Amanda.

"Well it would really depend on the nature of your enquiry as to who should deal with it. If it was concerning a complaint then it would be Miss Farrell, but if it was for something else...?"

He had smiled that charming smile. "No, no it's not a complaint." He lowered his voice and leant towards her. "I have some rather wonderful news." He checked over his left shoulder before continuing. "You see Amanda's leaving – we're trying for a family, and I want her to be stress free and get as much rest as possible. I know Amanda won't speak up, but I wanted to ask if she could give shorter notice than would be normal. The sooner I can move her to that beautiful cottage in the country the better." She noticed his eyes had misted over with tears, and her heart tightened.

"Then it's Mr Pickard you need to speak to. He's just over there." She waved in the direction of the lifts. "I hope it goes well – she's a very lucky woman!"

"Thank you and thank you yet again for your help, you really are an angel." He turned and walked towards Mr Pickard.

As she thought about the charming husband of this incredibly exotic creature now in front of her, it seemed so unfair that her brother had insisted on coming to the Launch to see Amanda.

"You look very glamorous Amanda." Marianne felt she had to say something.

Suddenly Amanda reached out and touched Marianne's hand. "Do you think this looks okay? It doesn't look over the top?"

Was she fishing for yet more compliments? "No, it looks... fine." She deliberately hesitated just to be sure that Amanda would feel an element of doubt.

"Thanks Marianne."

"Marianne it's your turn to strut your stuff." The call came from the other side of the curtains.

"Be right with you." Turning away from Amanda, she could feel Sharon's eyes boring into her back but she refused to show her that she was intimidated. She stepped towards the curtains. Just as she reached them Tony yanked them open. "Hello ladies." He tottered forward as though it was he in the five inch heels.

"Good evening Mr Pickard." Marianne and Amanda responded woodenly.

"Hello Tony... I mean Mr Pickard." Marianne would never have associated Sharon with being coquettish but that was exactly how she sounded. Tony ignored Sharon completely. "And don't you look the little fire cracker." He tilted Marianne's chin with his finger. "I think I'm going to have to escort you out there. I don't want anyone else to light your fuse." He chortled at his own joke and gripped her waist. As she was swept into the waiting spotlights she caught a glimpse of Sharon's thunderous face.

94

Amanda

She sat under intense make up lights and tried not to sneeze through the mist of scent laden air. Could he really force her to move away? He had forced her to do many things over the years, but could he actually do this? The voice in her head was barely a whisper, 'Only if you let him.'

When she had returned home after David's surprise visit his mood was almost jovial. He clearly felt that he was back in control. He had reined her in good and proper. She was still uncertain whether he had seen her with Sam. She ran through their meeting again in her head. Yes, he had held her hands, and it would be very difficult to dismiss that with the notion that he was just a happy customer. But had he seen? David often hid his anger beneath a mask of amiability, false affection and fake smiles. But she knew his anger would still be there – waiting. Waiting for the opportunity to pounce like a cat toying with an injured bird.

"Amanda, you've not shown any interest in the property brochures I brought for you to look at." The brochures were still on the window sill exactly where they had been left a week before. There was just a hint of reproach in his voice as he lifted the pile to the kitchen table. "Not to worry, I'm going up there next week to do a spot of scouting so I'll sort it all out myself." Humming he flicked through the pages, appearing to be completely absorbed in the glossy pictures. She stepped towards the door to the hallway.

"Where are you going my love?" His head was still bent over the magazines and his fingers continued to turn the pages.

"I thought I'd go and get changed." Her hand dropped away from the door knob.

"Why don't you sit down and tell me all about your day? I want to hear all about what you've been doing and who you've been seeing." He slowly raised his head and looked at her.

She edged back into the room. "It was just the usual kind of day, serving customers, stacking shelves, you know that kind of thing, until you came in." She fought to keep her voice level and confident.

"Yes, of course, that kind of thing..." He stared off into the distance.

Every nerve in her body tightened like steel wires. Even if it was the end of the conversation for the moment, she knew it wouldn't be the end of the conversation completely. She reached for the door knob once again.

"Amanda..."

"Yes?" She didn't turn from the door.

"... it doesn't matter. It will keep."

She took a quick look over her shoulder. His head was down again but he was now clawing through the pages seemingly unaware of the torn paper beneath his fingers.

The sight of him froze her soul and her base instincts told her that if ever danger could be measured the needle would be in the red zone. With her knees hunched up to her chest she sat on the bed and stared at the top right hand corner of the room. Where are you now Mum? For once her mother was silent and she had never felt more lost.

95

Jane

Chivvying the girls into position, she wished she could tell them how important this evening was. Instead she raced between preening divas and the petulant press, whilst Tony indulged himself and the visitors in champagne cocktails and canapés. He hadn't bothered to introduce her to the group of business men whose approval was vital to the store. She knew a couple from head office but the rest were complete strangers.

The audience were noisily filling up the rows of chairs. Programmes rustled before being made into paper fans. Charlie gently guided Ada to a seat and swept imaginary dust from it before allowing her to sit down. Then Jane caught Joe's eye who was following behind. She smiled, she wasn't sure why, but she was delighted to see him. He warmly returned her smile before taking his place beside Ada.

Sporadic coughing punctuated the announcement that the show was about to begin, and the magnificent chandelier dimmed. One after another the models began their journey along the raised pathway. Glorious summer cocktail dresses accompanied by jaunty top hat and tails. Hayley was one of the first to appear. As she walked past the men on the stage she stopped. Jane prayed that it was just nerves and mentally willed her to continue. Hayley seemed to stare at one of the men before straightening her shoulders and stepping purposefully out onto the walkway. Shiny red coils of hair bounced below the pillbox hat. Even the netting couldn't mask the green of her eyes. Emerald clung to every curve of her body. The audience silenced in reverence before roaring their appreciation.   The evening sparkled with glitz and laughter. Even Sharon's pink mushroom ensemble was met with applause. Jane surveyed the scene. Things were at last going well, and perhaps the store's future would be safe.

96

Hayley

She wasn't expecting the reaction she received from the audience. As she stepped out a hush fell over the room followed by spontaneous applause. The only thing that could have shocked her more was the sight of her brother, Adam sitting amongst the honoured guests on stage. Her eyes locked with his and she could see that he was just as stupefied as she was.

Mentally she kick-started her body and propelled herself through the cheering throng. How had he ended up here? The last time she had seen him was at the reading of her father's will and that had been a cold and formal affair. He hadn't managed to attend the funeral but he had miraculously been able to hear what he was going to gain from his father's death.

Through the myriad of blurred faces she returned to the temporary dressing room. 'H..H..Hayley the j..j..jack hammer, H..H..Hayley the j..j..jack hammer!' she could hear his voice.

"Hayley, is that really you?" It was the same voice. He had followed her into the changing room.

"Adam..."

"Excuse me Hayley, but there's been a phone call. The care home has been trying to get hold of you." One of the administration staff held out a note.

'Call Mrs Westland as soon as possible.' Her hands were shaking as she read the note. What had happened now?

She lunged for her bag and scrabbled around for the phone.

"Hello Mrs Westland?"

"Mrs Townsend, we've been calling you for over an hour. We couldn't get anyone on the home number either." Hayley picked up an edge of panic in Mrs Westland's voice.

"Mrs Westland what's wrong, is Mum okay?" Her heart was hammering in her chest.

"I don't suppose Sheila's with you is she?"

"What do you mean with me? Why would she be with me?" Alarm ripped through her.

"Well the thing is erm... I'm really not sure how to tell you this but erm... it would appear that we've lost her." The Mrs Westland that she had last spoken to had been cold and officious. This one sounded terrified.

"What do you mean you've lost her? How can you lose my mother?" She was well aware that she was shouting down the phone but could do little to stop herself.

"She was here at afternoon tea, but... well... since then nobody's seen her. And something else..." She heard her take a deep breath "She's taken her suitcase and money."

"Oh my God! She's a frail, old woman for God's sake. In your care and you've lost her! Have you called the police?"

"No, not yet, we thought she may have just popped round to yours." Mrs Westland's voice trailed off.

"She's been with you for five years. Let me just ask you this. How many times in those five years have you known her to 'just pop round to mine'? She doesn't know who I am most of the time."

"Well... never." The voice was even lower.

"Call the police. I'll be with you in ten minutes."

"I'll come with you." Adam reached over and touched her shoulder.

Without responding she dialled Neil's number. It rang out. She dialled it again, then again. No answer. They were in the taxi by the time Neil called her back. He sounded breathless and she could only imagine what he'd been doing, but now wasn't the time to raise the issue. "Just get yourself to the care home now Neil. I'm not interested in what you're doing. Just stop whatever it is and meet me as soon as you can. My mother's gone missing." Before he could reply she terminated the call and stared out of the window. How had they ended up like this?

"I couldn't believe it was you."

Adam's voice startled her. As the doubts about the future of her marriage, and the safety of her mother swirled around her head she had forgotten that her brother had followed her in to the taxi. "Well it wasn't exactly what I expected either." It was difficult to hide the pain from the years of being second best to him in her mother's eyes and being inconsequential in her brother's eyes. Was this where her fixation with being invisible stemmed from?

She glared at him as he shifted uncomfortably in his seat. "Tell me Adam, were you going to bother to come to see Mum, or me for that matter, or would you have been much too busy and important?"

"Woah, Hayley that's a bit unfair isn't it?" He looked genuinely shocked.

"You're quite right. What a ridiculous accusation to make. After all you have been the perfect brother and son, haven't you? By the way when was the last time you spoke to mum?"

"Okay, okay so maybe I haven't been in touch as regularly as I should but it doesn't mean I don't think about you both." He leant forward his elbows resting on his knees as he stared at her.

She thought about listing all the things he hadn't done 'as regularly as he should'. Like seeing his father when he was dying, helping them with the funeral arrangements, supporting his mother in her grief. She didn't say any of those things. She leant her head against the cold glass window and hoped that her mother was alright. That was going to have to be her priority now. She had very little else left.

97

Marianne

Cameras flashed as Marianne stepped out into the throng. Tony's hands still firmly gripped her waist as he guided her onto the platform. At that moment she was glad that Jack hadn't come tonight to see this slimy individual pawing her. Marianne could see Jane's head bobbing up and down at the back of the crowd as she tried to get a better view. Marianne brushed Tony's hands away and strode forwards, leaving him to stumble in her wake before resuming his seat with the American dignitaries.

Her skin tingled under the spotlights. Every sense seemed heightened. She belonged here, wearing beautiful clothes, playing to the audience. Perhaps when this financial nightmare was behind her she could look into this kind of career. And with Jane guaranteeing her as much overtime as she could, then that day might be sooner rather than later. There was row upon row of smart suits, fine gowns and a tartan shopping trolley. Ada was sitting between Charlie and Joe Spanker. She was waving at the girls as they paraded up and down. Charlie's eyes darted between Ada and the catwalk, but always returned to Ada. As Marianne approached, Charlie stood up and held out the red rose bud that had been nestling in his lapel. She took it from him and mouthed 'thank you'. Once again a lump rose to her throat. She would repay the store and then deal with the rest.

As Marianne returned to the stage area, Amanda stepped out from between the curtains, a delicate column of shimmering silk. Opal threads melted into each other creating soft translucent waves around her body. It was as though the dress had no real substance, just a ghost of a garment draped over an ephemeral frame. Marianne watched her float through the awed onlookers. There was an air of raw fragility about Amanda that Marianne had never noticed before. The thought that she could have been wrong about her made her feel uncomfortable and so, she did what she always did, and pushed unwanted notions to one side.

98

Amanda

Whenever Jane had mentioned her search for volunteer models for the Launch, Amanda had managed to side-step the issue. That was until two days before the event.

"Amanda, I know this is short notice, but is there any chance we could use you for the show?" Jane had smiled sweetly before throwing in her trump card. "It would look very good on any application you made, you know, a willingness to go that extra mile?"

Jane must have known that Amanda wouldn't allow anything to jeopardise her chance of securing the new role on offer. "If you're desperate then what can I say?"

"Wonderful, thanks Amanda. I knew I could depend on you."

And so here she was with an arm full of silk and a hairdresser nipping at her heels. She was used to blending in. She had never been forced into the limelight. Even on her wedding day she had chosen a demure gown, and low heels. Her mother had worn orange organza with a spray of daylilies pinned to her lapel. Amanda could see her now sitting in the front pew. Even though the synagogue was full it was her mother who stood out. It was her mother who had shouted 'Mazel Tov' the loudest and it was her mother who had cheered first when David crushed the glass beneath his foot. Little knowing that this was going to be the first of many destructive acts in their marriage.

As the make-up girl laboured on her canvas, Amanda recognised the person in front of her less and less. Amanda forced herself to gather the few shreds of self-confidence she had and step into the folds of raw silk.

The oyster silk shimmered and rich caramel and chestnut tones warmed her pale skin. When she looked at her reflection, for the first time in her life, she almost believed that she was beautiful. She waited in the wings to be called out. The Americans were on the right of the stage offering the first and best view of the parade. She looked down at her ragged nails. Her hand was halfway to her mouth when she saw a whisper of blue linen.

"Amanda you are my angel, my butterfly. In all my days I have never seen you look more beautiful. Thank God you take after me, not your father. The only thing your father had that was pleasing to the eye was his bank balance. Your Aunt Beatrice, God rest her soul, didn't even have that!" Her mother was peering at the audience through a gap in the curtains. "You go out there with your head held high and slightly turned to the left, reduces the profile of your nose."

Amanda couldn't stop smiling as she walked out onto the temporary runway. Trying to stare straight in front of her, but with her head slightly turned to the left, she saw Sam. When he saw her he half stood, before sitting back down and apologising to the person behind. A person whose hair was never an inch out of place and whose fists would be clenched in his lap. But Sam's was the only face she saw.

99

Jane

As the show drew to a close, handsome bartenders entertained giggling middle aged women by juggling liquor bottles and hurling cocktail shakers in the air. Jane watched as photographers and journalists mingled with the crowd.

One woman in particular appeared to be the centre of attention. Wearing an elegant black shift dress adorned with giant pearls at the throat stood Mrs Pickard. She was laughing at something a young journalist was saying, her head close to his. As Jane watched, Mrs Pickard stepped back and a flash of pink split the conversation. At first Tony's wife's expression remained passive but then the facade crumbled and shocked anger settled there instead. The flash of pink disappeared in the ebb and flow of the crowd. But it was the white gleam of pearls that Jane locked onto. She followed Mrs Pickard's progress to the stage and then on up the wooden steps. Tony was leaning back in his chair clearly relaxed in his role of grand host when she slapped him.

It was as though someone had pressed pause. No-one on the stage moved. Even Tony didn't move. The only stirring was the rise and fall of his wife's chest as she stood over him. "Who is she?" Her scream shattered the spell and Tony shot to his feet. His head swung between the business men and his wife like a loose gate in the wind. Her hands were now gripping his lapels as she spat in his face. "Don't try to protect her. Tell me you bastard."

The crowd had moved closer, hypnotised by the scene unravelling before them. Jane noticed some journalists' heads were bent as they scribbled in their note pads. She couldn't get through the mass of bodies. She watched helplessly as Tony bundled his wife off the stage leaving onlookers astonished and bewildered. Tearing her eyes away from the frozen tableaux of American business men she buried her head in her hands and sank onto a nearby seat. This was hardly the slick, professional finale she had been depending on.

100

Hayley

Mrs Westland and a police officer met Hayley at the entrance to the care home. She could barely look at the care home manager let alone speak to her. Mary, the plump care assistant, stood behind wringing her hands and chewing on her bottom lip.

"So, what do we do? How are we going to find her?" The question was directed to the police officer.

"We've had a cursory look over her bedroom, but there are no obvious clues as to her whereabouts. Our officers have been given a description, and as we speak I have cars patrolling the area searching for her."

She had to see for herself. Half walking and half running, as much as her high heels would allow, she went to her mother's room, Adam hurried after her. She could smell her mother's rose water scent. Opening drawers and wardrobe doors she searched. Her eye caught the book on the bedside table. She flicked through it. A piece of paper fell out and wafted to the floor. Even before she picked it up she knew what it was. It was a train timetable for a journey that she had never believed her mother would make.

Officer, I think my mother's gone to Washington."

"Washington, America?" The officer pushed his hat further back on his head.

"No Officer, Washington, Tyne and Wear." She held up the timetable. "I think she got a little confused."

She handed over the timetable to the officer just as Neil walked through the door. He stopped suddenly causing Mary who was following to stumble against him. He mumbled an apology but his eyes never left Hayley.

He was wearing Lycra shorts and a t-shirt that was damp with fresh perspiration. He seemed to shake himself back into action. Crossing the polished floor his trainers squeaked until he reached Hayley's side. She had never seen him dress this way. She hadn't noticed how broad his shoulders were and how defined his muscles had become which could be seen even through the material of his t-shirt. Adam coughed from the corner of the room. She had completely forgotten he was there.

"I'll go with the officer. See if there's anything I can do." Adam and the officer disappeared and Mrs Westland followed. Hayley was left standing next to a man that she didn't know at all.

He fumbled for her hand. "It'll be alright Hayley. They'll find her."

He sounded like her husband. His hand in hers felt familiar. She looked into his face. His eyes were the same. But gone were the sprouting hairs from his nostrils. His fine hair was closely cropped to his head. Not wispy like it used to be. There was a firmness that was evident from the set of his jaw right through his well-toned torso to his sculpted thighs. This was Neil. Her Neil, or did he belong to someone else now?

"You look amazing. I know this probably isn't the time, but Hayley I hardly recognized you in those clothes. You're incredible!"

His words reflected exactly the way she was feeling about him. How had she not seen him change?

They stood together in an awkward silence. Moments seemed to her like hours as they waited.

Mary's footsteps rippled the smooth quiet as she bustled in with a tray of tea and a plate of biscuits. "Here we are." She placed the tea and biscuits down on the bedside table. The dimpled flesh on her upper arms wobbled as she set about stirring sugar into the tea that neither one had asked for. Appearing to be satisfied that she, at least, had made the best of a bad situation, she handed a steaming mug to each and left them once more alone.

"I have a confession to make." His voice was low and his eyes remained fixed on the murky liquid.

Here we go, she thought. This is where he tells me he's met someone else. Probably a younger model with blond hair and blue eyes. Not a wiry redhead with dirty green eyes. He's going to confess how he's fallen head over heels and that he's very sorry that it didn't work out but it's probably for the best. Mentally she steeled herself for the loss of her husband. In one day she had lost her mother and her husband – way to go Hayley!

"I've not been going to the allotment."

"I know." She had no energy to run away. "Who is she Neil?"

"What... what do you mean who is she?" His head jerked up and tea slopped over the side of the cup.

"It's alright. I know there's never a good time but if I'm at rock bottom now then at least there's only one way to go." She put the untouched tea back on the tray. She would have dearly liked to curl up on her mother's bed but she knew the restrictions of the gown she was wearing wouldn't allow it, so she stood and waited for the axe to fall.

"There is no 'she'. There's a 'he' called Jonathan who is my personal trainer at the gym. And I don't mean a significant 'he' or anything like that." His face was pink.

"The gym? What gym and why? I don't understand." She searched his face for a clue.

Again his head went down. "I thought you were falling out of love with me. I thought I wasn't enough of a man for you because I can't give you a baby. So I decided that if I built myself up, you know, get fit and toned, that you might see me in a different light. So I lied about the allotment. I've been going to the gym for months. I just wanted to be good enough for you. I don't want to lose you Hayley. I love you."

She went to sink down onto the bed before her emerald wrappings forced her to straighten. The door opened and the police officer walked into the room, his radio still chattering in his hand. "They've found her and she's fine. Got as far as York, mind you."

"Oh thank God, thank you so much officer!" Once again her knees weakened but Neil held her up.

"She said she'd always wanted to go to Washington apparently. She wanted to visit her son," the officer continued. "She said she was a bit tired and was ready to come home for her tea."

She couldn't hold back the tears of relief that she had lost neither her mother nor her husband. Neil wrapped her in his arms and held her tightly to him.

The officer cleared his throat. "Right then, well I'll be getting along and leave you folks to it." His footsteps retreated into the hall.

Neil tilted her face up to his. "I love you Mrs Townsend. Please say you love me too."

She felt his hard body pressing against hers and a wave of desire swept over her. "I love you Mr Townsend," She kissed his mouth. "And tonight I'm going to show you how much," 'that Hayley' said.

101

Marianne

Marianne had been buzzing all weekend after her modelling debut, but it was Monday and time to knuckle down to work and earn that extra cash. "I'll be a bit late tonight honey." Marianne hurried down the stairs just as Jack emerged from the kitchen carrying the local newspaper. "The girls want to have a quick drink after work." She stood on tiptoe to kiss his cheek. He didn't lean forward as he normally would to accept her kiss. His body was rigid.

"You seem to be very much in demand lately." He studied her face. "With the girls." His eyes travelled over her body, then returned to her face. His expression was blank.

"It's only a little get together, that's all. I'll try not to be too late. Bye darling have a good day." Her tone was artificially bright.

"You too." His was flat and dull.

Her walk to work was plagued with the confessions that she should have made to Jack. But it was impossible. She was in too deep to expect him to forgive her.

Charlie's kind eyes didn't waver from her face when she walked into the lobby. "Well that's a troubled soul."

"Is that a horse Charlie?" She smiled at his quirky habits.

"No, why would you think that? It's you, that's what it is - a troubled soul." He nodded affirmation to himself.

She rolled her eyes. The only time she thought she was one step ahead of him with his racing tips and she was wrong. "I'm not a troubled soul Charlie, I'm just a little bit lost that's all." But not for long she hoped. Today she could replace the money in the till. Of course it would throw the opening balance out but at least her conscience would be clear.

All the glitter and frivolity of the Summer Launch had been buffed and polished away by the army of cleaners over the weekend and the store was back to normal. Normal except for the whispers and sniggers as tills spewed receipts and staff spewed gossip about Mrs Pickard's attack on her husband. Marianne was not going to be dragged in to feed the growing hunger for sordid details. Instead she avoided the huddles of gleeful scandalmongers and ignored the sulky looks Sharon kept throwing in her direction. Marianne couldn't start worrying about her as well, so she carried on with her business as pleasantly as she could. The last of the customers were trailing out of the shop and she felt as though she could sleep for a week. Waiting until she was alone on the sales floor, she slipped the cash into the till drawer. The maintenance crew seamlessly swapped places with the sales staff and the machine rolled on.

Her shift including overtime eventually came to an end. Her footsteps echoed in the stairwell and a few seconds later she became aware of others joining hers. She half turned to say goodnight when the words froze in her throat. Tony Pickard jumped two steps at once and landed next to her.

"Fancy a little drinky?" His breath smelled as though he had already had more than a little drinky.

She backed away, catching her foot on the edge of the stair. Trying to regain her balance she grabbed at the handrail but he had already wrapped his arms around her pulling her back against his body.

"Thank you but I'm alright." She tried to push him away.

"But I've just saved your life. You should be grateful." His bottom lip curled into a pout and his arms tightened around her.

"Right, well I've said thank you, now please let me go."

His face came down to hers and the fumes threatened to engulf her. They were rocking dangerously close to the edge. His body weight pressing into her.

"Stop it!" With all her strength she pushed him away and stumbled down the rest of the stairs.

"Now that's not very nice is it?" His words were slurred as he lurched forwards. "That's not very nice at all. You don't sound very grateful to me. I think you should show me how grateful you are."

A figure appeared at the top of the stairs. Marianne didn't want to wait to find out who it was. She just wanted to get out.

"Stay away from me!" She made a dive for the door at the same time as he lunged towards her. They both fell out into the night air locked in what felt to her like a bizarre waltz.

"Marianne!" A voice that she knew and loved. Jack stepped out of the shadows. "So what's going on Marianne?"

Tony still had his arms around her and was leaning heavily against her. "We're just going for a little drinky, and she's going to show me how grateful she is. Anyway what's it got to do with you?"

"Marianne?" The hurt was raw.

She opened her mouth to protest when someone stepped out from the door behind them.

"Marianne?" Jack's eyes searched her face for an explanation. "What are you doing?"

"I'll tell you what she's doing shall I?" Sharon's thick set legs shuffled forwards.

Marianne knew that Sharon hated her. She suspected it was because she was jealous of the attention Tony had given her recently, but Sharon must have known that it hadn't been reciprocated or wanted. She stared at Sharon, silently begging her to tell the truth. She had to have seen what had happened.

The women's eyes locked.

"Yes I'll tell you what she was doing." Sharon squared her shoulders and turned to look at Tony. Marianne held her breath.

"She was trying to get away from this creep. That's what she was doing. He was trying to force himself on her. He's done it to all of us."

Tony's mouth dropped open but before he had time to speak Jack's fist made flesh splitting contact with Tony's nose. His arms flew back releasing Marianne and he sprawled backwards into a heap.

A tight smile played about Sharon's lips as she stepped over him.

"Thank you," Marianne whispered as she passed her. A bubble popped out of Sharon's mouth in response as she walked away.

"I'll bleedin sue I will." The words were muffled through Tony's hands as he nursed his nose.

"Come on let's get you home." Jack guided her round Tony's slumped body. "I just thought something was going on. And then when I saw the photograph in the paper..." He looked wretched and she reached up with a kiss to silence him.

"I would never do that to you Jack. I love you and have always loved you."

He nodded and he held her closer. "The thought that you might be deceiving me just ate me up. I'm sorry Marianne."

"So am I," she said into the dark. "So am I."

102

Amanda

She had basked in Sam's unwavering attention, feeling his eyes watching her every move. But by the time she had shed the temporary facade of 'beautiful Amanda' Sam had gone. His seat was empty, a discarded programme the only evidence that anyone had been there. The carnival spirit pulsing its way through the crowd only served to make her disappointment sharper. Excusing herself she passed an elegant looking woman engrossed in a conversation with one of the young shop assistants and disappeared into the night.

The weekend passed almost wordlessly. David had withdrawn into himself, and she had tiptoed round him, trying not to wake the creature within. She knew that something was brewing and by Sunday evening her body twitched with nerves raw and exposed. She lay in bed listening to the constant drone of the television below. Finally the sound stopped and he slipped into bed beside her. Her body was rigid until his breathing became slow and even. Allowing her muscles to relax just a little she closed her eyes, but sleep wouldn't come. Just before dawn she felt herself slip into the spiral of unconsciousness. His hands were clawing, not at the pages of a glossy brochure but at her flesh. Her screams made no sound inside the vacuum of her dream. She jolted awake. A film of cold sweat covered her body. She tentatively put a hand out to feel the bed beside her. It was empty and cold.

Pushing tangled hair away from her face she slipped a dressing gown on and tiptoed to the window. Please God let his car be gone. There was a dry patch on the tarmac indicating where his car had recently been parked. She held on to the curtains a little longer to steady herself before turning back to the empty room.

Sam would be leaving soon. And he wanted to meet her before he left. She couldn't meet him could she? David said he would be away searching for a home for them to move to. She could arrange her own leaving do and meet Sam under that pretext. Perhaps she could go just for a little while. Just to say good bye to Sam and please take me with you. Fool! Why would he want you? You're nothing but damaged goods, damaged being the operative word.

Her mother leant against the dressing table, her arms folded across her blue suit. "You think you're worth so little? I thought I'd brought you up to be a princess. The hands on a clock can be cruel Amanda but the hands on a man can be worse. You have both working against you so you need to do something now. If you listen to me only this once, do as I say. Take the leap of faith. You have nothing to lose but so much to gain."

Her mother made no mention of Aunt Beatrice, Uncle Max or unusual hobbies. And her tone had an edge that she had never noticed before. Was her mother telling her to go ahead and meet Sam, or was she just telling her to run away?

Perhaps she could take Jane to one side and explain that she didn't want to leave. Could she somehow persuade her to fast track the job offer so that she could make her escape? One way or another she was going to get away, or she was going to die trying.

103

Jane

After the fashion show, the Americans' departure had been an awkward one. Tony's departure with his seething wife was probably even more awkward, Jane surmised as she tried to plan how she was going to gloss over this domestic drama. How much damage had it done? She knew that they had been impressed by the prime location that the store occupied. They had visibly drooled over its aristocratic opulence. And having given strict instructions as to which less impressive areas of the shop must remain out of sight Jane had guided them away from many of the negative features.

She was almost convinced that it wouldn't be a question of whether they would take on the business. It was more a question of who they employ to run it. Would it be the Americans themselves, new staff that they selected or the original members of the team? The latter was looking less and less likely.

Management would be the first to be scrutinised, then attention would filter through the ranks. Her own position may already be regarded as tenuous just by being pregnant and relationships between members of staff were always actively discouraged. Stupid Jane. Her career was hanging by a thread for a man who had just used her, and now couldn't stand the sight of her.

Throughout the night her fears leapt between her own future and that of the staff that worked so hard. Marianne could lose her overtime and possibly her job. Hayley's temporary contract could be terminated at any moment and would they honour the role Jane had enthusiastically outlined to Amanda? Finally the image of stalwart Charlie sprang to mind. What would happen to him? Would they just put him out to grass like one of his beloved horses?

For all that she disliked Tony, perhaps the only answer was to put on a united front and face them together. Surely they were adult enough to do that?

104

Hayley

They had lain in each other's arms, neither speaking. Making love had never been like that before. One moment tender and gentle the next, almost savage in its animal passion. She stared at his profile as her fingers traced the outline of his jaw. He turned to look at her, his breath on her cheek.

"I was wrong Hayley about the IVF." He shifted onto his elbow and stroked her hair away from her face. "Part of me thought that having IVF treatment would be an admission of failure, for me I mean, not you. That somehow it would be a declaration to the world that I wasn't man enough." She went to speak but he gently shook his head. "When I was training at the gym, all I could think about was losing you. You will be an amazing mother and I was so wrong to try to deprive you of that. So I worked out that if we saved our wages we could probably try IVF in less than three years. Well actually, it would take thirty-two months."

She smiled, that was Neil the accountant speaking. Only he would come up with the exact time scale for saving. If she asked him, she thought, he would probably be able to tell her precisely how many weeks and days it would take.

"So, what do you think? Shall we save to become a mummy and daddy?" His voice cracked with emotion.

She flung her arms round his neck and pulled him down to kiss him. That seemed to be all the answer he needed before tenderly making love to her again. Saturday and Sunday were filled with passion and promises.

When she woke on Monday morning the bed beside her was empty. Stricken she sat up. Surely she hadn't dreamt the whole thing? But then she saw a stocking strewn over the lamp shade and another hanging on the bed post. Swinging her legs out of bed she padded to the bedroom door and opened it a crack to listen. She heard water splashing into the shower tray and Neil quietly singing to himself. Going back into the bedroom she caught the tousled image of herself in the mirror. She stepped back and studied her red hair that was wildly curly. She fluffed it out even more, shaking it into a lion's mane. Throughout most of her adult life she had tried to tame the curls and cover up the fiery tones. This morning she was proud of them.

"Good morning darling." Neil emerged from his shower wearing a towel wrapped around his waist and he blew her a kiss.

Once again she was struck by his amazing physique. She looked over at the tempting sight of the empty bed. "Do you think it would be really bad if I was a little late today?" She sat back down on the bed and playfully patted the sheets beside her.

"I don't think so," he said as he joined her. "It's not as though you're going to get sacked is it?"

105

Marianne

Jack had apologised all the way home for getting it wrong. Each apology ripped into her heart. Wretchedly Jack had told her about the photograph he had seen in the local press of Marianne on the catwalk. Her boss was grabbing her round the waist and how he couldn't bear the thought of losing her. Yes, he had got that bit wrong but what about the rest of her misdemeanours?

She had less than two weeks to clear the debt so that it wouldn't appear on his collection sheets. Jack had helpfully explained the process for recovering money so she knew exactly when the information would be passed over to him.

"I've a good mind to go to the police." Jack was standing at the back door, staring out into their small garden. "He can't be allowed to get away with that... that abuse!" He said to the fence.

"Jack, please calm down. Let's just let it go. I really don't want any more fuss." She could tell from the set of his shoulders that he was still angry from the night before. But the last thing she wanted was another showdown between her husband and her boss. She still wasn't sure whether Tony had any inkling about her brief criminal career. "And anyway I'm not sure the police are a good idea, particularly after you punching him." As she stroked his back trying to ease some of his tension she saw Eric step out of his back door and shuffle along the path towards his shed.

"Well someone should teach him a lesson because he's really got it coming to him. Who does he think he is, strutting around like he owns the universe?" Jack shouted as he waved his arms encompassing all that he could see.

Eric's head swivelled towards Jack. "Not the whole universe." He mumbled before shooting into his shed. Marianne heard the bolt rapidly being drawn across the door and she quickly suppressed a smile.

Jack frowned. "What was that all about?"

"You really don't want to know. You really, really don't want to know." She gently led him back into the kitchen hoping that she had done enough to persuade him not to take out a personal vendetta against Tony Pickard.

On the shop floor Sharon had nodded in her direction and Marianne had returned the gesture. It was an unspoken acknowledgement of their acceptance of one another. The morning rolled into afternoon. The sales floor hummed with conversation broken by the ringing of a bell to summon staff to their tills. She was just about to take her afternoon break when there was an enormous crashing sound from the other side of the department. Both she and Sharon dashed over to where the commotion was coming from.

Ada was holding one end of an empty cutlery box. Tony was holding the other. They appeared to be in the middle of a tug of war when the contents of the box had spilled all over the floor.

"You can't just take things. You have to pay." Tony's face was purple and spittle flew from his mouth as he shouted into Ada's face.

Marianne swooped to Ada's side. "She never really takes anything." She slipped her arm round Ada's frail shoulder protectively. It was the first time she had seen him that day and the horror of his behaviour from the night before was fresh in her mind. "She just gets confused."

"I'll give you bloody confused. I'm calling the police. Come on." He roughly grabbed Ada's elbow. "Let's get you to my office and then we can see exactly what you were planning to steal."

Ada's eyes were wide with fear and Marianne's heart went out to her. "This isn't really necessary. We'll just put everything back and let her go." She nearly added 'that's what we usually do.'

"Oh she might look like a weak old woman, but it's people like this that close our stores. Well she's not closing my store!" He began leading Ada away.

Ada looked over her shoulder pleadingly at Marianne.

"Well I'll come too as a erm... witness." Marianne hurried after them but not before whispering instructions to Sharon to alert Charlie of what had happened.

Tony silently marched on with Ada struggling to keep up.

Once in Tony's office Ada's trembling hands rested on the top of her tartan trolley. Tony stood in front of her with his arms folded across his chest. "Empty your trolley."

Ada looked from Tony to Marianne and back to Tony.

"Are you going deaf? I said empty your trolley," he barked.

Ada flinched and slowly began taking items from the depths of tartan and placed them on the desk. There was a knock at the door and Sharon popped her head round.

"Yes? What do you want?" Tony didn't take his eyes off Ada.

"I've just got a message from Charlie." Sharon walked over to the desk which was now cluttered with kitchen utensils. Between chews she told Tony that Charlie was talking to the police. The message ended with the pop of a bubble.

"That's it. That's everything." Ada closed the lid of the bag.

"Are you sure that's everything?" Tony reached over and flung the lid open. He leant into the bag and ran his hands round the dark interior. "And what's this?" Triumphantly he held up a small see-through bag containing, what looked to Marianne, like burnt grass.

"Come on then, tell us all what it is." He threw the bag onto the table. It landed next to a cheese grater. All eyes were on Ada.

Then more tapping on the door. Tony strode over and opened it with a flourish. But instead of police waiting to come in Marianne could see Joe and Charlie standing there. Her mind was working overtime trying to think how she could help Ada. Out of the corner of her eye she saw Sharon take the packet and slip it into the desk drawer.

"Where are the police? I asked you to call the police."

Ignoring Tony's question Joe walked straight past him to Ada's side. "Mum, what have you been doing now?" His voice was gentle and his eyes full of worry. Marianne remembered that look from when he had tried to collect her debt. So this was Ada's son.

"She's been shoplifting and..." Tony went to the desk. Lifting up the cheese grater he looked underneath. Then he began pushing the other utensils around the desk, his movements getting more and more frantic. "Where is it?" He stared at everyone's faces one by one. He lifted the cheese grater once again and put it down. "Where's it gone?"

"Where's what gone?" Sharon's voice was pure innocence.

"You know what. You all know what!"

"Do you know what he's talking about Marianne?" Sharon turned to her with raised eyebrows.

"No, no I really don't." She shook her head, hoping that she looked as mystified as Sharon had sounded.

"Have you been shoplifting Mum?" Joe's question brought the group's attention back to Ada.

"No Joe, I just like to put things in my trolley. I always fill it up too full and then the girls help me to unload it."

Joe squeezed his mum's hand.

Marianne ducked out of the way as Tony waved his pointed finger at Ada.

"She's a thief!"

Charlie spoke from where he had been standing in the doorway. "I think you'll find, sir, that the definition of theft is the intention to permanently deprive and clearly that wasn't Ada's intention at all."

There were murmurs of agreement from around the room. Only Tony remained silent.

"Shall we get these things back on the shelves where they belong?" Marianne started reloading Ada's trolley and Sharon joined her.

"Come on Mum, let's go home." Joe put his arm round his mother and guided her to the door.

"Can I have my hish hash back now? I'm going to be doing some baking for Charlie later." Joe quickly ushered her out of the room. Marianne and Sharon stifled their giggles as they and Charlie hurried behind, closing the door on a man who looked about to explode.

"Come on, we'd better get back to the sales floor." Marianne nudged Sharon.

"Yes we had. We don't want to go upsetting the management now do we?" Sharon linked her arm as they made their way down to their department.

106

Amanda

Since seeing Sam at the Launch on Friday she had been consumed with thoughts of meeting up with him, as he'd asked. But how could she get away with it? The only excuse she had come up with was her leaving do – she could say that the girls had arranged a farewell meal at the local wine bar. It just happened to be on Friday. That all sounded perfectly acceptable to her in her head. But she wasn't David and who knew what went on in his head. She would have to actually mention it to the girls so that it would provide the cover she needed.

Working in different departments she hadn't seen Marianne or Hayley, and so she had left notes in their lockers inviting them to the wine bar before leaving. As she neared home she saw David's car parked outside the house. She looked up at the bedroom window. His silhouette dominated the bay. He had been waiting for her. She forced her legs to keep moving forward.

"I'm home!" she called up the stairs. As if he didn't know, she thought.

"Come on up, you can give me a hand." His voice gave nothing away.

She didn't want to go upstairs. She didn't want to go anywhere near him. But still her legs carried her up each step, relentlessly on. She tried pushing the bedroom door open but it would only open a few inches.

"Oh, just a second, sorry let me just... there!" The door was suddenly freed and David stepped out from behind it. She looked beyond his tall frame and gasped. The room looked as though it had been ransacked. Clothes and shoes were scattered everywhere. Her eyes immediately flew to the wardrobe where her metal box was kept. The doors were open revealing empty hangers where they had been stripped. Some hangers were twisted so savage was the attack. On the top shelf the hat box appeared to be untouched which meant that, hopefully, so was the metal container.

"Just doing a bit of packing. Don't want to leave it until the last minute, do we?" He grinned and handed her an empty suitcase. Turning away from her he began hurling clothes into an already overfilled case. Pressing the clothes down he forced the lid shut. Sleeves and socks were still hanging out of the sides but he didn't seem to notice. "Come on, I'm not doing it all by myself." He nudged her, still grinning widely.

He's gone totally mad she thought as she put the empty case onto the bed. She eyed the clothes strewn over the floor. Item by item she picked them up and slowly placed them in the case whilst David watched. "I'll need some clothes David. I have to wear something over the next few days." She kept her back to him as she spoke. Just looking at his face terrified her.

"You won't need much. It's not as if you're going anywhere is it?"

This was her opportunity to tell him about the 'leaving do'. She took a deep breath.

"You're not going anywhere are you Amanda?"

She exhaled. "No, I'm not going anywhere apart from work." She put two pairs of shoes, a skirt and blouse back into the wardrobe. He hadn't touched her underwear drawer yet so the key was still safe. She watched him scoop up a pile of jumpers and throw them into the case. Whilst his back was turned she pulled a turquoise dress from the tangled pile of fabric at the bottom of the wardrobe and draped it over a hanger before taking the rest of the pile over to the bed.

"That's a good girl! See nearly done." His eyes darted over the room.

She lingered by the chest of drawers trying to shield it from his gaze. "I think that's enough for now, don't you?

We can sort the rest out later." She stretched her lips into a smile. "Come on darling I'll make you some dinner and pour you a glass of wine." She reached out and touched his arm. Briefly, very briefly she saw a flash of the old David, the one she had fallen in love with.

"Yes okay we'll sort it out later."

As he left the room she closed the closet doors on her hat box and the metal container holding her future.

107

Jane

Monday's business was to limit the damage done on the Friday before. Head office was re-assured that the incident was borne of a wildly insecure wife who was suffering from depression. As outrageous as the lie was, she had no choice but to calm any jittery nerves before the meeting on Wednesday which was when a final decision would be announced.

It was Tuesday and she had just one day before D-day. She had to be strong, their jobs depended on it. Dispensing with the formality of knocking she went straight in to Tony's office. He had been leaning back in his chair. Eyes closed and his hand loosely cupping a glass filled with amber liquid. She watched him jerk forwards at her entrance, spilling the liquid over his trousers.

"What the hell...? You don't even knock now?"

"I thought with us knowing each other so intimately there was no need to knock. What's the matter Tony? Caught you at a bad time?" Her eyes wide with innocence.

He scrubbed at the stain on his trousers. "As if you haven't caused me enough trouble." He spat the words out as he continued to scrub. "I hope you haven't come here to 'talk' about your little problem. I've told you I'm having nothing to do with it or you."

"It isn't 'my little problem' as you so delicately put it. It's a baby – our baby. Anyway I'm not here to discuss that. I'm here to discuss our future, not yours and mine, God forbid, but our future as management of the store. I think, as much as it galls me to say it, we have to stick together on this one, and try to persuade them that we are worth keeping." She leant across the desk so that her face was level with his. "This is bigger than you and me, so for once try and think about the people we have working here and think about how we can save their jobs too."

"I don't have to think about them or about you for that matter. In my view a clean sweep is exactly what this store needs. Get rid of those sluts and lesbians is what I say. Some fresh new blood is exactly what the doctor ordered. And as for me, well apart from Friday's little performance, which I'm sure I can smooth over, I am pretty sure my position is safe." He relaxed back in his chair. "Oh don't look so horrified. I know that you all gossip about me behind my back. You all want a piece of me, that's what it is. Every one of you is gagging for it."

He winked slowly. "I can read the signs. But I've had enough of your little gang of bitches. They're all up to no good and I'm going to personally make sure they're out of the door first. I'll leave you until last so that you can watch." He reached over to the filing cabinet. Had he got a secret dossier on all of them? Maybe he had discovered Hayley and Marianne using her office. Her mind went into overtime trying to think of an excuse for them.

He pulled out a bottle of whisky. She silently sent up a prayer of thanks.

"One of your little friends is leaving of her own accord. I didn't have to do anything there other than tell her husband that I would waive the usual notice period. Nice man that, a very nice man." He was concentrating on refilling his glass and didn't see her frown.

"Your other little friend has no-one to blame but herself – thieving cow she is. Well I know all about her sticky fingers, and I'll make sure that the management do too." A smug smile played about his lips as he ran a finger round the rim of the glass. "And the lesbian, she's only on a temporary contract – very precarious these days, what with the way the world is." He shook his head in mock despair. "You know, cut backs and the like."

He took a sip from the glass and licked his lips. "I've called a meeting with the managers from head office for tomorrow. You might like to warn Marianne that she'll be expected to attend. And I think you should attend too. After all she was under your direct supervision."

Suddenly the fight had gone out of her. What was he talking about? She had to see the girls and fast. Without uttering another word she turned to leave the room.

"Bye Jane, have a good day now!" Just as she closed the door she heard him pick up the handset by his side. "Yes send up Hayley Townsend would you?"

108

Hayley

Ordinarily she hated being late. She would become stressed at the mere thought of being seconds late. But that hour had been worth it. She couldn't stop smiling and it seemed to be infectious as both customers and staff returned her smiles. She had also been invited out for a meal with the girls on Friday. She was no longer invisible.

Monday's euphoria spread into Tuesday. Delicious butterflies danced in her stomach as she thought of going home to Neil. Nothing, she thought, could dampen her mood.

"Hayley!" One of the administration girls called over. "Mr Pickard wants to see you in his office as soon as."

Butterfly wings stilled. "Are you sure he wants to see me?"

"That's what he said. Send Hayley Townsend up." The girl shrugged and walked away.

She had never been late before. Surely he wasn't going to reprimand her for that? She couldn't think of any other reason for his request. For the first time in two days her smile faded from her lips. She rehearsed her apology for being late the day before and searched for an appropriate excuse as she made her way to his office.

"Sit down Mrs Townsend." He waved at the chair in front of him.

She sat. Her hands clasped in her lap. The smell of alcohol wafted over the desk.

"I regret having to call this meeting Mrs Townsend, but I'm afraid it is something that I can no longer avoid." He rocked back in his seat.

"I..I...I can explain Mr Pickard, you see what happened was... I was on my way to w..w..work when I got a call from my mother's care home, and w..w..well you see, they thought they had lost her and anyway they found her again, so everything was alright except that it all made me late for work."

"Well I'm sure that's all very interesting but..."

"I..I..I'll work late. I'll put in extra hours. I've never been late before Mr Pickard." She felt a familiar itching begin between her thumb and forefinger.

He held his hands up to halt her flow. "I'm sorry Mrs Townsend but it's not about you being late, although that doesn't help matters. The problem is we're having to look at areas that we can economise in. I'm sure you'll appreciate that in the current financial climate things are very difficult for every business and this one is no exception."

"D..d..do you mean you want me to go part time?" Neil would seriously have to make some recalculations she thought.

"No, not part time. No time. I'm letting you go." He laid his hands flat on the desk and studied her for a few minutes. "And don't go thinking that it's anything personal, you know about you, or your... leanings."

"You're letting me go? You mean you're sacking me?"

"Not so much sacking you, as releasing you."

"And what do you mean 'my leanings'?" She flushed as it dawned on her what he had meant. "I'm not a lesbian. Not that it would matter if I was. It's nothing to do with you!"

"No, of course not. Now then I think you'll find that a week's notice is required. But I'll throw in an extra couple of days, how's that?" He smiled as though he had bestowed a wonderful gift on her. "That makes your last day next Friday. If you can make sure your locker is cleared and any company property is returned by then."

She stood up shakily. She knew he wanted her to leave but she was rooted to the spot. "Is there anything that could change your mind?" She couldn't lose her job.

He lazily eyed her up and down, his stare lingering on her thighs. "No, I don't think so."

She hadn't meant it like that. Humiliated and with tears stinging her eyes she left the office. Neil might as well put his calculator away altogether.

109

Marianne

It had been a long day. It had also been a surprising one. Not only because of Ada's shoplifting antics but Marianne had found an invitation stuffed in her locker. Amanda wanted her to go for a meal at the wine bar on Friday – now that was a turn up for the books. Maybe she wants a tearful farewell party before she goes off to her perfect little cottage in the country. She carefully re-read the invitation. She felt sure that Sam had asked Amanda to meet him there too. Suddenly it all became very clear. Amanda was going to use it as a cover for having a little fling. How devious, that poor husband of hers, and Sam should really know better.

She silently fumed about Amanda's casual treatment of her marriage as she helped Sharon put Ada's shopping back on the displays. The tills were about to be closed when Jane came rushing across the sales floor.

"Marianne I need to talk to you." Jane pulled her to one side. "Alone." She glanced at Sharon who merely shrugged and walked away.

"Oh? Is it about Amanda's invitation for a meal at the wine bar? Because I'm not sure I want to go."

Jane looked blank. "No it's not about that."

"What's the matter? Are you feeling alright?"

Jane still gripped her arm and hissed. "It's him." She jerked her head back and flicked her eyes towards the upper floors. "He reckons he's got something on you. He called you a thief. He's mistaken isn't he Marianne?"

She went cold, staring in silence at Jane.

"Marianne, he's wrong isn't he? Tell me he's wrong Marianne!" Jane's fingers were pinching her skin.

She bowed her head. Shame made her recoil inside. "No he isn't wrong." The floor became blurred as tears filled her eyes.

"No Marianne! He has to be wrong! You wouldn't do that. Surely you couldn't do that." Jane dropped Marianne's arm and took a step back from her.

Marianne dragged her eyes away from the ground and looked at Jane.

"I am so sorry, I made a mistake. I was really, really stupid."

Jane slowly shook her head. "What did you do?" The question was asked softly.

"I was desperate Jane. I only did it once, and I did put it back. And I did write an 'I owe you'." Marianne looked back down at the floor. She couldn't bear to see Jane's disappointment any longer.

"Oh Marianne, I knew you were struggling, but I didn't know you were so desperate."

To her surprise, instead of marching away in disgust Jane reached out and took hold of her hands in her own. "Why didn't you tell me? I might have been able to do something."

"There's nothing anybody can do. I'm in too deep.

"We're just going to have to do some more damage limitation, that's the only thing for it. Now you say you put the money back?"

She nodded.

"How much are we talking about?"

"Thirty-eight pounds," she mumbled. "You see I wasn't even very good at that."

There was a hint of a smile on Jane's face. "No you weren't were you? Well, we've got until tomorrow to think of something we can say in your defence." Jane let go of her hands. "We'll think of something." She patted her arm and began to walk away. Suddenly she stopped. "Really? Thirty-eight pounds?"

"Yes. I know."

Jane shook her head again and left the department.

So when I go home and Jack asks me how my day was, I can just explain that I protected a known shoplifter, conspired to hide her drugs. Tomorrow I will probably lose my job and be arrested for theft myself. On the whole a pretty quiet day really.

110

Amanda

He had loaded the car with cases bursting with clothes. Amanda watched him from the front door. He had said very little after his frantic packing session. If she didn't know better she would have described him as docile, but she did know better. And she had never felt so sure that this was just the preamble to total derangement.

"I'll be back on Saturday," he had told her, as he tucked his immaculate shirt into his immaculate trousers. "I'll find us the perfect place, then I can look after you properly. Just me and you." The craziness was still there, barely lurking below the surface.

She waved goodbye and quickly closed the door. She had a reprieve for a few days at least.

Her mother sat on the stairs. "How far do you think you'll get from him? So you think he won't find you?" She plucked a piece of lint from her skirt. "He'll never give up. You will have to stop him. It's the only way, I tell you."

"How can I stop him?"

"You have to be strong. You have to think about what you need, what is right for you. Holding onto your dream is the only thing that will release you from this nightmare. And don't forget Amanda - the leap of faith. That will be the most important thing."

She knew deep down that he would always find her. She didn't even have a passport so it wouldn't be difficult. She would apply for a passport then she would have an escape route. She wanted to add 'to Sam' but she had been trying not to think about him. Friday was only a few days away and David wouldn't even be here so it would be possible to see Sam.

She went upstairs and opened her depleted wardrobe. A Turquoise dress, a pair of black shoes, two blouses and a skirt hung forlornly on the rail. Who was she kidding? She couldn't go and meet Sam dressed in any of those things. She was well and truly trapped. Her mother's words echoed round her head, "You have to be strong." Okay, she thought, even if I look like a boring secretary or a relic from a seventies cocktail party I will go on Friday. With the decision made she resolved to make a trip to the post office to pick up a passport application form.

111

Jane

After the initial shock of Marianne's confession, Jane had felt nothing but sheer anger towards Tony. He mustn't be allowed to win. And what had he meant about his job being safe? She wasn't sure how she could save Hayley when she was on a temporary contract but somehow she had to protect Marianne. She found herself back in her office staring at a computer screen full of figures. Scrolling through the daily logs she found the till roll showing an amount of thirty eight pounds up on Marianne's till. But as she studied the previous figures there was no record of the money being taken out. So unless Tony had a witness the only accusation he could make was that Marianne had put extra money into the till.

Satisfied that she had some sort of argument to fight Marianne's corner, she eventually went home. Her apartment was clinical in comparison to her parents' home. She longed for the well-worn clutter and the constant crackling music from the radio in the kitchen. She would scrimp and save to buy a little house for her and the baby. And decorate it with soft rugs and cosy armchairs like her own childhood home.

By the morning, in her head, she had furnished a whole house, planted a magical garden with a tree house and fish pond. Now, back in reality, she stood in front of Tony's office. She checked her watch. It was only a few hours before she would find out whether anyone had a job.

Smoothing down her skirt and straightening her shoulders she tapped on the door.

"Yes?"

She opened the door and stepped in. Two men who she recognised from head office flanked Tony and a very pale Marianne sat in front of them.

112

Hayley

Neil was at home waiting for her. Bluebells filled a vase on the kitchen table.

"They were the only things growing at the allotment apart from weeds." He smiled apologetically. "Maybe we could work on the allotment together. What do you think?"

She looked at his face. It shone with enthusiasm and love. "Sit down Neil I have something to tell you."

"It's not your mum is it? She's not gone missing again?" He pulled out a chair and sat down.

"No, it's not Mum. There's no easy way to tell you this but I've been... how shall I put it?... 'let go'."

"Let go? What do you mean?"

"I mean sacked, dismissed, 'released'," she said through gritted teeth.

She described her meeting with Tony Pickard, leaving out his lewd innuendo. "And so by the end of next week, I won't have a job."

"What about Adam, can't you ask him to pull some strings? You've done so much for your family when he's not even lifted a finger to help. Surely he owes you something?"

"I've never asked him for anything, and I'm not about to start now. Give him yet another opportunity to poke fun at me? No I can't go to Adam. I'm sorry I've let you down."

"You haven't let me down. You could never let me down." He stood up, knocking the chair over and went to her side. "You'll get another job. There must be hundreds of things you'd be good at."

"Well there is one thing I've found that I'm pretty good at." She looked into his pale eyes framed by his national health glasses. Was he ready to hear about Hayley the estate agent? There was only one way to find out. "Come upstairs and I'll tell you all about it."

Gently tugging at his tie she led him into the bedroom. "Now this sir is bedroom number one. As you can see it has dual aspect windows, and a rather generous king-size bed with matching head and foot boards." She trailed her fingers over the post, caressing the wooden bulb on the top. "Which, I like to feel, gives an air of stateliness as well as being ideal for manacles." She glanced quickly at Neil's confused face before continuing. "The en-suite shower room is perfect for those really filthy moments when nothing but hot steam will do. I'll demonstrate."

She stepped into the shower and flicked the switch. Water shot out of the shower head drenching her blouse. The flimsy material barely concealed the curve of her breasts as she beckoned him to join her. With glasses rapidly steaming up Neil stumbled into the cubicle and into the arms of Madame Estate Agent.

It might have been 'that Hayley' who enticed him into the shower but it was Hayley Townsend who made love to him. It was Hayley Townsend who had teased him a second and third time before seducing him yet again. It was Hayley Townsend who had been in control.

"I think I've shown you all of the original features, unless there are any other areas that you feel might require a second viewing?" She kissed his neck.

"I believe I'm going to have to carry out a full survey. I need to examine every nook and cranny."

Wrapping her arms round her husband, she pressed her body into his and silently said goodbye to 'that Hayley'. Her work here was done and now she had to let her go.

113

Marianne

She hadn't told Jack. She couldn't bring herself to do it. It was just one more deceit to add to the Jenga pile of deceits that made up her life. Which one would be pulled out first? She wondered.

She waited in the corridor to be called in. She could hear men's voices but she couldn't pick out specific words. That was probably a good thing, she surmised.

"Mrs Drummond would you come in?" Mr Pickard held the door open for her.

"Do sit down," he said as he too took his seat between two smartly dressed men.

"If you don't mind I won't make any introductions until Miss Farrell arrives."

The three men sat facing her in stony silence.

Finally there was a tap on the door.

"Yes?" Mr Pickard's voice was sharp.

"Good morning gentlemen." Jane swept into the room "Good morning Marianne." She smiled confidently at Marianne who tried to return the smile.

"Well now that we're all here I'll make the introductions." Whilst Mr Pickard introduced the staff from head office she concentrated on twisting her wedding ring round her finger.

"The situation is this." He held his hands out palms up as if offering a present. "I am aware that Mrs Drummond here has been stealing money from the store and whereas I don't think she can do anything but offer an apology before we decide what action to take, we have to give her an opportunity to speak." He turned to her, but before she could utter a word Jane stood up.

"Just a moment, that certainly isn't the correct procedure to follow at all. You have accused a member of staff of theft. That's a very serious accusation, Mr Pickard and I sincerely hope you have substantial evidence to support your claim. Well, have you?" There was a core of steel to Jane's voice.

"Evidence?" He was on his feet. Leaning on his desk with his chin thrust out towards Jane, he hissed, "Oh I've got evidence! I've got a witness!"

Heat spread through Marianne's body. She thought she was going to faint.

"Ask Sharon to come in." He spoke into the telephone handset. Moments later the door opened and Marianne watched as Sharon strutted in. Her face showed no emotion.

"Go on, tell them what you saw. Tell them about her stealing." Waving his hand in Marianne's direction, his voice had risen several pitches. He seemed almost giddy with excitement.

All eyes were on Sharon as she slowly chewed her gum.

"I'm not right sure what you mean Mr Pickard. I've not seen her do nothin." A bubble popped as she stood there staring back at the three men.

Mr Pickard's eyes bulged from his head. His mouth twitched.

It was Jane who spoke. "I seriously have to question your judgement Mr Pickard." She moved across the office to the filing cabinet. "I wasn't going to bring this up today, but perhaps under the circumstances it would be appropriate to do so." Marianne saw her reach into the cabinet and lift out a half empty bottle of Scotch. Holding it between forefinger and thumb she stared at Tony Pickard. "You see Mr Pickard, I don't think it's acceptable for you to be under the influence of alcohol whilst trying to carry out your duties. I can only think that it's the alcohol which causes you to make wild accusations which are clearly unfounded."

A bubble popped again. "That and the drugs." Heads swung towards Sharon. "Them drugs don't help, I've told you Mr Pickard." She shook her head sadly and reached across the desk. Her pendulous breasts swinging dangerously close to one of the men's faces as she slid open the drawer. "I think this is all the gear he's got at the minute." She tossed a snap bag onto the desk.

Mr Pickard's mouth dropped open.

The man to Marianne's left stood up. "I think we've found ourselves involved in a whole new situation. Mrs Drummond, in the light of these events I think we owe you an apology and I would ask that everybody..." He placed a restraining hand on Mr Pickard's arm, "except you Tony, leave us to discuss how we should proceed."

In a daze Marianne stood and left the office with Jane and Sharon close behind.

Once in the corridor they could hear angry voices from the other side of the door. Quite a difference from the muted tones of earlier Marianne thought.

"Just shows yer, yer can't trust no-one." Sharon smiled then pulled out a string of gum from between her teeth before snapping it back in again. "See you's later."

Marianne and Jane watched her hips swaying down the corridor.

"See you later and thanks again Sharon." Marianne called after her.

Without turning Sharon held up a heavily jewelled hand in acknowledgement and carried on her way.

Well that deceit hadn't toppled her Jenga tower. Which one would be next? She thought.

114

Amanda

The electric strip lights hummed and flickered over the heads of those standing in line. Obediently they shuffled forward as one when a cashier became free. With her passport application form safely in her bag Amanda scanned the room. The photo booth was tucked into the far corner next to a rack displaying leaflets offering various services.

She slid onto the swivel stool and pulled the grey curtain shut. Staring into the dark depths of the shutter she waited. The machine flashed and whirred before asking her whether she wanted to accept the image of the fragile woman that stared back at her. Grudgingly she accepted this sallow picture and stepped outside to wait for the photographs to be dispensed.

Although only minutes had passed, to Amanda it could have been hours. With clammy hands she snatched the glossy paper out of the slot as soon as it appeared. Checking over her shoulder she carefully slipped the strip into her bag alongside the form. To the ordinary people queuing for their pensions and stamps her actions would be no more than mundane. But to her, it was an act of such treachery and betrayal she felt dizzy just thinking about it.

Jane's promise of a new job would be her first break for freedom, but a passport would mean distance, real distance. She only had a few days before David's return so she knew she would have to complete the form quickly and get it into the post. There would be no second chances.

115

Jane

Jane had been asked to rejoin the men from head office an hour later.

"I can't tell you Miss Farrell how disappointed we are about Mr Pickard's behaviour. Regrettably he has also pointed a finger at you. He claims that you and he had some sort of...er...relationship going on, and that you are now pregnant, and all of this." He waved a hand round the room, "was all just a scheme to get your revenge for his rejection. A woman scorned and so forth..." His voice trailed off and he ran his finger round his tight collar.

Indignation welled up from Jane's stomach. "I am most certainly not 'a woman scorned' as you put it. I made the decision that I was going to bring up this child alone. I didn't give him a chance to reject me." She began to tremble.

Uneasy glances were exchanged between the two men. "Now Miss Farrell don't upset yourself, not in your condition."

"And do you honestly think I would be able, even if I had wanted to, to persuade those members of staff to conspire with me for revenge?" She glared at them "Well do you?"

"Now calm down Miss Farrell. We just have to explore all the possibilities. Mr Pickard has been with us for some considerable time and particularly recently has been quite an asset to the company. His knowledge of market trends and proposed forecasts has impressed not just us but indeed the whole American conglomerate."

Jane couldn't believe what she was hearing. "You mean the flow charts and graphs? The historical and projected statistics?"

"Well yes – they were all very insightful and contributed to the formation of a very favourable contract."

"The graphs and plans that I drew up? The predicted market trends and proposed reactions to those trends that I spent days collating and refining?" She wanted to pummel her fists against the desk.

This time it was an alarmed look which passed between the two men.

"That you drew up? That you collated? Can you prove that?"

Without uttering another word she left the office, returning minutes later with her files overflowing with all the statistics and charts she had worked tirelessly on. She dropped the pile of papers onto the desk. All of a sudden she was exhausted. The fact that Tony, her erstwhile lover, and she had thought future partner, had taken all the credit for her work was the final insult.

Both men leant in and started flicking through Jane's neatly hand written notes. "Well Miss Farrell that does shed a rather different light on Mr Pickard's future, but I'm afraid it will make little difference to the future of the store. The American's have already commenced the selection process for their own team, and it's unlikely that all but a skeleton of current staff will remain at Peltham's. We will, of course, confirm the finer details within the next few days. An announcement will also be made to the staff then."

She walked back to her office in a daze. Everything was collapsing around her. Nobody's job was safe and she had to warn them.

Hayley, Marianne and Amanda sat in front of her. Concern stretched across their features.

"I'm afraid that you may have to prepare yourselves for some bad news. Nothing's definite yet, but I have a feeling that the outcome is inevitable." Jane paused. She wasn't sure how she should break it to them. Concern had been replaced by apprehension. "The store is going to be taken over by an American company, and I think they are going to bring in their own people. Very few of us will remain working here."

Marianne's mouth dropped open. Amanda slowly shook her head. Colour flushed Hayley's cheeks. The room was silent.

116

Hayley

Her shock wasn't so great. Her own job had already been taken away from her, but to see the others' despair broke her heart. Each one had so much more to lose. Amanda with her bruised wrists and look of a hunted animal. Marianne's desperate pleas on the phone for more time to pay. And her naive but brave attempts on the chatline. Finally, Jane who was going to have to bring up her baby alone.

It was no good she would have to speak to Adam. Not for herself but for them. If nothing else he owed it to her to listen. She dialled his number and waited.

Their childhood relationship had been a rocky one. Adam was three years her senior. From the very first day she could remember she felt that her presence had been nothing more than an inconvenience. Her mother had blithely told her that she hadn't been planned. In fact, she had told her, that she had been more than happy to devote her life to only child Adam. But then Hayley had arrived.

Hayley remembered quite vividly her mother standing at the kitchen sink, her eyes trained on Adam playing in the back garden. "Look at him – he's such a handsome boy." Even though Hayley couldn't see her mother's face she knew she was smiling.

"Am I pretty mummy?" Her six-year-old younger self asked.

Her mother's vigorous scrubbing stopped. She didn't turn. "You've got lots of qualities Hayley, we can't all be blessed with good looks."

At six Hayley didn't want to know about lots of other qualities. She just wanted to know if she was pretty. Her mother slowly went back to scrubbing and Hayley went back to being invisible.

At last he answered. "Hi Hayley, I'm sorry it's not a good time for me to talk right now. I'm in an important meeting. Can I call you back?"

"No, you can't. I need to speak to you now. Later is no good for me." Her voice was firm and level. She didn't stammer once.

She heard a muffled excuse and a door close. "What is it Hayley? Is it mum again?"

She was furious at the note of irritation in his voice. How dare he feel aggrieved. "No it isn't mum... again, not that you've ever bothered about her before. I don't need to tell you how totally useless you've been. And I'm quite sure your colleagues aren't aware of your total neglect of your own mother and father." Before allowing him to protest she ploughed on. "It's about what you're going to do for me." Without stumbling over words, and with complete authority she explained what had happened and the recommendations she wanted him to put forward. "...and that's Amanda Freedman, Jane Farrell and Marianne Drummond, oh and Charlie. If you do this for me I will never ask you for anything again, and I will never expect anything from you." It was eerily quiet. "Hello? Adam are you still there?"

"Yes I'm still here. I..I..I'll do my best."

Curiously satisfied she ended the call. Who was stammering now?

117

Marianne

This was it. This was the end of the road. She would tell Jack tonight. Then she would pack her things and move back to her parents. It wouldn't be fair to expect Jack to live with her after all her deception and lies.

"Nothing is forever." Charlie nodded at her as she walked through reception.

"I think you're probably right Charlie, nothing is forever, good or bad."

"No, Nothing Is Forever, six to one at Wincanton."

She stopped and blinked. Slowly she turned back to Charlie. "What did you say?"

"Nothing Is Forever, six to one at Wincanton, it's a dead cert that one is. I'd bet my life on it."

"Charlie," She looked into the old man's eyes, "do you think you could come up with a tip for us, I mean the girls? A big winner?" Her heart was pounding.

He gazed back at her, then a smile swathed his face. "Pippa's Pride, thirty to one at Chester next Thursday."

"Are you sure Charlie?" She held her breath.

"I couldn't be more sure Miss Marianne."

She hugged him fiercely then retraced her steps up to the staff room.

Hayley, Amanda and Jane were gathering their bags and coats. The room was silent as Marianne flung the door open. "You might think that this is complete madness but it could be worth a go." Three pairs of listless eyes looked at her as she relayed Charlie's guaranteed tip. Gradually she could see sparks of interest slowly begin to flicker in each. "So what do you think? I've not got much to use as a stake but I'm willing to do it. Are you?"

It was Amanda who spoke first. "I'll do it." Marianne hadn't expected Amanda to be remotely interested. Surely she had everything that she wanted. Perhaps she needed some pocket money for any extramarital activities she had in mind. Marianne shrugged and turned to Jane and Hayley.

"Count me in too." Hayley was scratching the skin on her left hand.

"I've got some money I was saving for a rainy day. I could use that." Jane stroked the tiny bump of her belly. "Yes, I'll do it too."

"What do you think Mrs Davis would say to this wager?" Hayley grinned at Amanda.

"She would probably say that it was about time I did something crazy."

"Who on earth is Mrs Davis?" Jane asked.

"Well that's the thing, she's not on earth." Hayley jumped in with the story of Amanda and her mother's conversations which death hadn't been able to interrupt.

Marianne couldn't decide if they were trying to make a fool of her, but she wasn't going to let it spoil the moment.

The pact was made.

Hayley seemed to glow with excitement. "We can make all the arrangements on Friday in the wine bar. Everyone's coming aren't they?"

Caught up in the moment, and temporarily forgetting her intention to avoid the event, Marianne agreed.

"So Friday it is then, can't wait." Amanda's usually pale cheeks were rosy, Marianne noted. Clearly she was getting quite brazen about her little rendezvous.

Marianne was curious as to whether Amanda would be honest about her scheme to meet up with Sam. "I'll walk home with you if you like?" She could use the walk home to do a bit of digging.

"Sorry Marianne, I've got to drop something off at the synagogue, so I'm not going straight home."

That sounded rich. She was happy to flaunt an affair and still have the gall to drop in at a house of God. But, Marianne reasoned, there was nothing she could do about it. She had her own problems to deal with. And she would have left it at that, had she not seen Amanda's husband huddled in the driver's seat of his car outside the staff entrance.

118

Amanda

So there would be no job taking her all over the country. A bet on a horse and a passport were her only escape now. She was the last to leave. After checking that the application form and photographs were still tucked in her bag she skirted round the outside of the building. She didn't notice her husband's car parked a short distance from the staff entrance.

Creeping into the dark hallway of the synagogue she could smell the mustiness of ancient scriptures. Wood panelled walls stretched from floor to ceiling. The place always reminded her of her mother. Amanda would stand here for hours waiting for her to stop chatting to all the women as they emerged after the prayer service. The men, including her father would leave the building separately giving her mother a full social reign.

"Look at Edna Sher, if she wore any more jewellery she wouldn't be able to lift her arms." These kinds of asides would be whispered in Amanda's ear as the subject approached. Her mother would then throw her arms wide in a warm embrace.

"Amanda is that you?"

Amanda spun round. "Rabbi Silverman!" She held out her hand.

"How are you my dear?" He clasped her hand in both of his. "I think of your mother often. I miss her."

"So do I. More than you'll ever know." Her throat constricted.

"She's still with us though Amanda, just remember that." He patted her hand.

"I don't need reminding, believe me." Smiling into his wise face she reached into her handbag and pulled out a folded piece of paper. "Rabbi Silverman, please would you sign this for me?"

He studied the passport application through his thick lenses. "Are you going away Amanda?" His voice was gentle.

"I have to." She had no energy left to pretend it was for a jolly holiday or some such diversion. Would he tell David? She didn't know.

"I will sign it and post it for you if it helps."

"Thank you so much. The sooner it's processed the better."

He shuffled into his office and a few moments later returned. "Take good care Amanda, take good care."

She thanked him and left the dark building for the evening sunshine. She was one step closer.

119

Jane

She had enough money to pay the rent on her apartment for three months. After that she would have to move back home. As much as she loved her parents the thought stifled her. It wasn't at all the way she had envisaged her life.

The store was practically empty. She wandered through the perfume hall, marvelling as she always did at the magnificent arches and ornate cornices. Charlie waited patiently by the staff doors.

"Evening Miss Jane."

"Evening Charlie, Marianne told us about your tip, so we're going to follow your recommendation. If anyone can pick a winner it's you Charlie. You didn't let Ada get away did you?"

"I certainly didn't ma'am, she's the best prize I've ever won. And that son of hers, Joe he's another recommendation of mine." He studied her face. "Mark my words Miss." His eyes held hers before he cleared his throat. "Well you have a good night and always remember – the only thing that matters in racing is the result. The rest is just a story."

Jane wasn't entirely sure what Charlie was trying to say to her, but she was pretty sure it wasn't all about turf. Her mind drifted to Joe. She had liked him instantly, she had to admit. Had Charlie seen that too? Where would they all be without Charlie's necessities and recommendations she wondered.

120

Amanda

Rabbi Silverman had promised to post the form straight away. That had been two days ago. Tonight Amanda was preparing for the farewell meal. Perhaps if she undid the top button of her blouse she wouldn't look so dowdy? No, that didn't work. It just made her look desperate and dowdy. The doorbell chimed. She froze. David hadn't come back early and forgotten his keys, had he?

She started down the stairs bending down so she could see the silhouette through the frosted glass. The only person she knew with a halo of red hair was Hayley. She hurried down the remaining steps and opened the door. Hayley stood in the doorway with a carrier bag in her outstretched hand. "Here this is for you."

Amanda was baffled but took the bag and peeked inside. A black leather skirt was neatly folded together with layers of chiffon and lace. She looked back at Hayley.

"You wear that tonight. I've put a wide belt in there too as it may be a little loose for you. I'll see you later." She kissed Amanda's cheek and was gone as quickly as she had arrived.

Clutching the carrier bag Amanda went back upstairs. She had never worn clothes which demanded attention. Without breathing she slipped the skirt over her hips. A hint of the exotic underwear could just be seen through the sheer fabric of the blouse. As she stepped into the shoes her mother said, "Well I did tell you that you were a princess, and I wasn't wrong. Your Aunt Beatrice, God rest her soul, she could never wear an outfit like that. It would take a herd of cows to cover those hips!"

She felt almost beautiful. Not quite, but almost.

The wine bar was busy. It buzzed with happy chatter and the chink of glasses. Amanda couldn't remember the last time she had been anywhere like this. She hesitated in the doorway. The girls were nowhere to be seen but sitting at the end of the bar was Sam. His eyes had been trained on the door. He stood up and beckoned her over.

She felt so self-conscious she had to concentrate on putting one glamorous foot in front of the other without falling off the high heels. His eyes never deviated from her.

"I can't believe you're here." He opened his arms to her.

"Neither can I." she said as she stepped into them.

Marianne arrived next. "Aren't you a little overdressed for a wine bar, or are you going on somewhere else?" She studied Amanda's outfit from top to toe.

"Mari, that's not very nice. I think she looks amazing, absolutely stunning." Sam jumped to Amanda's defence.

"I'm sure you do Sam."

Amanda was stung by the sharpness of Marianne's retort, but before she could dwell on it the others arrived. To Amanda the evening was magical, even Marianne's snipes didn't detract from it. She had never felt so alive and so loved. She never wanted it to end, but as other merry revellers began to disperse she knew it wouldn't be long before she was one of them.

"Can I walk you home?" he whispered. His face so close to hers. If she had wanted to she could have just turned and kissed him. The desire to do so was so strong it frightened her.

"No, I'm sorry, but no." Going near the house with him would be insane. She couldn't trust herself to be alone with him. Fear jockeyed with desire.

"I shouldn't have asked." He looked totally dejected. She wanted nothing more than to leave with him, but not to go back to her own house. She wanted to run away with him. The wine had swept aside her doubts and had replaced them with courage and the words 'will you take me with you?' teased her lips. Suddenly he turned away from her. The moment was lost and the question would never be asked.

All the emptiness that she had felt crowded back into her heart. She couldn't breathe. "I have to go." She plucked up her handbag from the bar.

"Well if you wait just ten minutes we can all go together." Hayley waggled a half full bottle of wine at her. Sam remained silent.

"No, I need to go. I'll flag a cab down and see you on Monday." She had to get out. The thought of never seeing Sam again threatened to crush the life from her. She needed air.

121

Marianne

There they were flirting outrageously. The others may not have noticed it, but it was obvious to Marianne. When she had seen Amanda's husband in his car outside the store he told her that he'd been waiting to catch Amanda as she left work.

"I just wanted to say goodbye before I drive to Aberdeen. I've never been away from her for more than one night." His grin was boyish. "I know it sounds silly but I'm missing her already and I only left her this morning but all day at work I've been thinking about her."

"It doesn't sound silly at all. I think it's rather sweet of you."

He shrugged diffidently.

"Is she still working?" He looked over Marianne's shoulder at the staff door.

"Yes she should be out soon, but she said she was calling in at the synagogue, so she might leave by the other doors."

"Ok thanks."

"Will you be back in time for Amanda's leaving do at the wine bar on Friday?" She knew she was deliberately scuppering Amanda's liaison, but somebody had to stop it.

"Her leaving do? Oh, I wouldn't want to be in the way."

"Don't you worry about that, I'm sure she'd love to have you there."

"I might try, I'll see. Anyway, lovely talking to you, maybe I'll see you before we leave for Aberdeen?"

"I'll look forward to it." She had waved goodbye and left. And now Amanda was behaving like a love struck teenager. Marianne had kept a constant vigil on the door of the wine bar hoping to see David stride in then she could announce that Amanda's husband was joining them and stop the pair in their tracks.

When Amanda got up to leave Marianne felt a smug satisfaction that Sam didn't jump up and follow her. Maybe he had finally come to his senses.

"It's such a shame David couldn't make it tonight, don't you think?" She sucked on the straw in her cocktail.

Hayley began to choke as Sam's head swivelled in her direction. "Why would David be coming here?" His voice was dangerously low.

"Well because I told him about it." She could see Sam's face darken. His eyes narrowed to slits. She felt awkward and clammy under his gaze. "I thought it would be a nice surprise."

"A nice surprise? A NICE SURPRISE?" Hayley's voice was so shrill it was almost a screech.

Suddenly the cocktail didn't taste so sweet. Marianne's gaze flicked from one to the other. What was the matter with everyone? "He is her husband you know, or maybe it had slipped your mind Sam!"

"He might be her husband but he is also a wife beating monster!" As his voice rose, conversation in the room hushed to a lull. Marianne looked at Hayley who was nodding vigorously.

"I don't understand.... what are you saying? He's such a charming man." Sam, Hayley and Jane stared at her.

She swallowed. The polo neck jumpers, pulling her cuffs over her hands, thick foundation, that raw vulnerability at the fashion show, it all began to make sense. Sam had seen it, Hayley had seen it but she had been so wrapped up in her own world she hadn't noticed a thing. And David had told her exactly what she wanted to believe.

Hayley sounded frightened as she grasped Sam's hand. "He's probably been outside

Watching. He'll be waiting for her."

"Let's go." Sam jumped up and raced to the door. Hayley and Jane were right behind. Marianne followed. She had done this. She had sent Amanda straight into the rage of a mad man.

122

Amanda

The taxi pulled up outside her house. She climbed out and watched the tail lights disappear. The sigh that escaped her came straight from her soul. Closing the front door she double locked it and flung the keys on the hall table as she passed. She stopped suddenly. Slowly she turned her head towards the living room. He was sitting in complete darkness. His chair faced the open door.

"Did you have a lovely evening Amanda?"

Her breath caught in her throat and her knees buckled. She grabbed the door frame to steady herself. "David... I didn't know... what are you...?"

"What's that darling? What am I doing in my own home? Well I'm waiting for my beautiful wife to come home from the wine bar, that's what I'm doing." He flicked the flint of a lighter. The flame illuminated his face before he slowly lowered it to the envelope in his hand. The light danced over the words 'Passport Office'. It was then that she smelled petrol. She took a step back and then another. Her eyes remained on him.

"Where are you going my love?" His usually smooth skin was dark with stubble and his hair was standing on end as though he had been constantly raking his fingers through it.

"I....I....have to go."

"No you don't. You don't have to go anywhere. Come and sit with me."

She heard a muffled ring from the phone in her bag.

"That might be lover boy. Perhaps you should answer it."

The lighter flicking on and off became more agitated. She was running out of time.

One more step and her back grazed the edge of the hall table. She ran her fingers over the cold glass searching for her keys.

"Don't you want to come and sit with me?" He rose out of the chair still snapping the lighter on and off.

She felt the jagged edge of a key. Grasping the bunch she lunged for the front door. He was fast, too fast. He sprang forwards diving for her legs and pulled her to the floor. She screamed in pain as her leg twisted beneath her. Her shoe bounced off the skirting board and the contents of her bag scattered over the narrow hall. Even though her face was pressed into the carpet she could still smell the petrol on his skin. He gripped her arms and flipped her over. Sitting astride her legs his hands slid over her shoulders and caressed her neck. The caress hardened to a vice. His face loomed over hers.

"I told you, you're not going anywhere. We are going to stay together forever."

Her eyes were streaming. There was no escaping the pungent smell of fuel. It filled her lungs. With horror she understood how he was going to kill her. He had doused himself in petrol. This would be his last embrace before he dropped the lighter. She felt around her for anything she could use as a weapon. Her fingers closed round the smooth leather toe of her shoe. He lowered his face to hers, crushing her ribs with his weight. He was panting now. Short sharp breaths sent sprays of saliva onto her skin.

Suddenly footsteps on the path. A shadow thrown by the street light grew the length of the hallway as someone approached.

"Be strong Amanda, now!" Amanda had never heard her mother raise her voice before.

It was a perfect arc. The shoe's heel sank into his flesh. She could hear screaming, then the front door shuddered as it was rammed again and again. "Amanda,

Amanda!" It was a man's voice. She must be delirious because it sounded like Sam.

With all the strength she had she heaved David off her legs and dragged herself towards the door. David's groans got louder as he rolled over. The door splintered and Sam fell into the hallway in a shower of glass. He gathered her up in his arms and carried her out of the house whilst Hayley spoke into her phone.

Marianne was still standing by the front door. Her eyes wide with shock

"Marianne, get away from the house!" Amanda gulped at the night air. "He's going to set fire to the house."

Sam ran back and disappeared into the darkness.

"No Sam no. Don't go in there. He'll kill you."

Jane wrapped her own coat round Amanda's shoulders.

"The police will be here any minute." Hayley turned to look at the house "Who else is in there? I heard another woman's voice. Is someone still in there with David?" She took a few tentative steps towards the front door.

"No, there's no-one else in there, just him. I've hurt him but I don't know how badly. He'll come after me, Hayley. He'll find me and kill me." She was shaking violently.

Sam re-appeared with the lighter in his hand. "He can't get up, and he can't set the house on fire, but to be on the safe side let's wait over there." He slipped his arm round Amanda's waist and guided her to the pavement.

She could still see the hunched silhouette of David in the hallway. He seemed to be trying to get to his feet. Sirens wailed in the distance.

A few minutes later and blue flashing lights bounced off the dark windows along the street, uniforms swarmed past them and into the house.

"How did you know he would be waiting for me?" She held onto Sam's hand as though her life depended on it. Sam looked over at Marianne. "I didn't know for sure but I couldn't take the risk of anything happening to you."

His blond hair had fallen over his face and she couldn't read his eyes. "You see I need to ask you something." He raked back his hair and searched her face.

"What did you need to ask me?"

"Will you come away with me?"

Amanda began to cry as Police officers gently led the group over to waiting vehicles.

Race Day

Amanda

A rainbow of hats, and suits with tails paraded the walkways between marquees. Exotic plumes and grey silk ebbed and flowed around the barrier to the track.

Amanda had collected the girls' stake money during the journey. No-one spoke of the events of six nights ago. She was grateful for their silent support. Each embrace held gifts of love and tenderness.

David had been taken away in an ambulance escorted by police. From the safety of a police car she saw him being wheeled away. She had expected him to be thrashing about, trying to free himself to get to her. He lay quietly. The only movement was his fists as they clenched and unclenched.

She didn't know how long he would be kept in the hospital but the police had assured her that she would be protected. Although she doubted that anyone could protect her from such a crazed animal. But Sam's constant presence had gone some way to comforting her. None of the statements made any mention of the woman's voice telling Amanda that now was the time to be strong.

The four women skirted round the crowds and found a space at the top of the spectators' stand.

"You wait here and I'll go and place the bet." Amanda hugged her bag closer.

"Are you sure you want to do it?" Hayley anxiously reached for her friend's hand.

Amanda nodded. "I really need to do this, besides Charlie's been telling me all week how to do it. He must have been through it a hundred times." She smiled and, being careful not to strain her aching leg, she made her way to the string of book-makers that lined the course. She glanced down the row. Go to Harry Brook, Charlie had said. He'll be wearing a tweed jacket and trilby. She spotted him almost immediately. An unlit cigar was tucked into the side of his mouth. He was shouting the odds to a man behind him.

"Madeira Girl, six to four!" His cigar wobbled and looked dangerously close to toppling out from between his lips.

"Excuse me, are you Harry?"

"Certainly am young lady. What can I do for you?"

"I'd like to place a bet please."

"Well you've definitely come to the right person!"

She scanned the board. Pippa's Pride was third from the top. She was just about to speak when she saw a familiar name and slowly a smile spread across her face. She looked back at Harry's flushed cheeks. "Yes I have to place a bet."

Her heart was thumping. She dabbed sweat from her upper lip. The spectators' stand was almost full as she squeezed through the noisy groups. Her group wasn't noisy. She could feel the tension growing between the girls. Tightening her grip on the betting slip she took her place between them. She tugged Hayley's sleeve. "Hayley, I've got to tell you something..." The crowd roared as the gates sprang open drowning Amanda's voice. The pounding of the hooves got closer. As the horses neared the straight she could see the purple and white colours of Pippa's Pride. Its powerful body sliced through the other runners, until it was in the lead. Hayley strained forward and began shouting its name, Jane and Marianne followed suit. The horses thundered past. The crowd's screams were deafening but Amanda couldn't utter a sound.

Suddenly there was a shocked hush as a horse stumbled. A jockey in purple and white rolled to the side of the track. The sound of the crowd rose once more. The commentator's voice babbled with excitement as an outsider moved up the field. Amanda stared ahead. She couldn't watch.

The three women slowly sat down. Despite the noise and excitement all round them, they could hear nothing. Silence surrounded them. Each face etched with disbelief and a dawning horror at what they had lost. Amanda still stared ahead but tears flowed down her cheeks.

"We'll think of something Amanda. We'll get through this." Hayley broke the spell. She hugged her fiercely.

Amanda started to laugh. Her tears went unchecked as she waved the crumpled betting slip. "I didn't put the money on Pippa's Pride." She hiccupped as she tried to catch her breath. "I did as my mother told me."

The girls stared at her.

The PA announcement interrupted them. "First, number nine, Leap of Faith, sixty to one; second, number …"

"We won, we won sixty to one!" Amanda took off her hat and threw it in the air. "We did it!"

Puzzled expressions quickly changed to laughter and tears. Jumping up and down they held onto each other.

"This has certainly been our day, ladies!" Amanda blew her nose and wiped the tears from her face.

"To the champagne tent!" Marianne began to lead the girls out of the stand.

Amanda stooped to pick up her hat. A flutter of powder blue material caught her eye. Her mother was sitting at the end of the row.

"So today you listen to your mother!"

THE END

'The only thing that matters in racing is the result. The rest is just a story.' – Steve Letarte.

Printed in Great Britain
by Amazon